Midnight of No Return

Midnight of No Return

Midnight Blue Beach
Book Two

BY

OLIVIA JAYMES

www.OliviaJaymes.com

MIDNIGHT OF NO RETURN

Midnight of No Return

More secrets...

Willow Vaughn returns home to find out the truth about her hard drinking, womanizing late husband Alex and the secret society that he was a member of. Despite the danger hanging over her head, she needs to know the facts about his not-so-accidental death so she can move on.

More desire...

Josh Coleman will do anything to protect Willow's life, even give up his own. His feelings for the prickly widow aren't making the job any easier though. She keeps pushing him away when all he wants to do is pull her closer.

More discoveries...

With no one to depend on but each other, Willow and Josh must insinuate themselves into the mysterious Evandria, an organization shrouded in secrecy and rumors. What they find is a glittering and glamorous club for the rich and powerful but these beautiful people aren't there for the play. Evandria is deadly serious.

Chapter One

Five years earlier…

THE DOOR OF the bar opened again and the hot, sticky air of Florida in July invaded the overly air-conditioned room. Music blared from hidden speakers, and the floor and walls vibrated in time as the customers gyrated on the dance floor. The patrons ran the gamut from sober to heavily intoxicated, most on the latter end, which made this job that much easier. Their attentions were solely on their next drink and maybe the most attractive person of the opposite sex in their orbit. Everyone was looking to have a good time.

Certainly Alex Vaughn was.

The handsome billionaire had been pounding whiskey shots for the last hour and a half and the only reason he was standing upright was the alcohol tolerance he'd built up over the last several hard drinking years. He had the stamina of an elephant and could drink and snort most anyone under the table. Alex didn't discriminate among intoxicants. Pharmaceuticals were just as good as booze as far as he was concerned. Maybe even better when he needed to dull the pain. Not that he'd told friends or family, but surely a person who abused chemicals in this manner had to be in a world of pain and agony, emotional or physical.

Alex's inebriated state and the distractions of the other people made this job almost too simple. A drink on the bar left unattended for only a moment as the bartender's attention was pulled elsewhere allowed plenty of time to drop in the small tablet.

Already beyond drunk, Alex wouldn't notice or taste it. Only later, when he was driving home – like he always did – well over the legal limit for a DUI, would he feel the effects. Would it be enough? Hopefully so. It was July twenty-first, the designated day. The date had been emphasized. Important. Failure not an option.

Watching closely as Alex tossed back the shot, it was now a waiting game as the drunken reveler danced and flirted with every pretty girl he came into contact with. Sadly, he had a lovely wife at home who by all accounts was in love with him. Finally about an hour later, flushed and sweating, Alex staggered to the door where a few of the patrons tried to convince him not to drive. Stubbornly, Alex shook his head and palmed his car keys. This was the usual dance at the end of an evening. His friends begged him to call a cab and he pretended to consider it before refusing.

Tonight was no different.

Except that it was.

The local news had the headline the next morning.

Local wealthy businessman killed in accident. Alcohol and drugs suspected.

Chapter Two

Present day...

JOSH COLEMAN FLICKED on the coffee pot in Willow Vaughn's gourmet kitchen, a room he was sure she rarely visited unless it was for a popsicle or a bag of chips. A giant stack of takeout menus were strategically placed by the phone and they looked well-worn.

Yawning, he stretched his arms over his head and scratched his belly, trying to shake off a restless night. He hadn't slept well. Not because he wasn't tired but because Willow couldn't sleep. With everything she'd been through in the last few weeks it wasn't surprising. Secrets, revelations, a friend's near fatal injury, and then finally the news her own life might be in danger. She'd contemplated taking something to help her slumber but had ultimately decided against it, knowing she'd be groggy in the morning when she needed to be alert.

Currently she was sitting on the back patio next to the pool, a cell phone pressed to her ear, receiving an update on her friend Peyton's condition. The other woman was in a coma in a hospital in Williamsburg but the doctors were saying she should make a full recovery.

He stuck his head out of the French doors and she looked up from her call, brows raised.

"Is everything okay?" she asked.

"Just wondered if you wanted me to start breakfast?"

She had a housekeeper but Josh had proposed she give the woman some time off. If Willow was in danger then anyone close to her might also be. With that suggestion, she'd given her entire household staff including the gardeners who only came intermittently three weeks off with pay. She didn't tell them why, simply saying she wanted her staff to enjoy themselves and relax a little.

"Whatever you cook, I'll eat."

She wasn't a picky eater, which was a good thing considering she couldn't boil water. She'd tried to help him in the kitchen last night and it had gone downhill from there. He had new strict rules – no knives, no hot stoves or ovens, no kidding.

Following him back into the kitchen, she settled at the large granite island still chatting to her friend Bailey Scott while Josh cut up veggies and ham for an omelet. Her tone sounded upbeat so things must be looking positive for a change.

"If she wakes up, you'll tell her I'm thinking about her, right?" A pause. "I'm trying to get the president of Evandria to meet with us but all they ever say is that he'll return my call, which of course he never does. We're considering a more drastic approach." Another pause. "Nothing illegal. I'm going to try and get invited to somewhere he will be, that's all. Nothing nefarious. We need to know what he knows about our husbands. He might be a really nice guy and will just hand over any information they have about them. Stranger things have happened to us quite recently. Yes, I know, I sound like Peyton now. An optimist. Is there any news about Stephen Baxter's condition?" Willow listened for a few minutes. Whatever was going on with Baxter wasn't straightforward. "I hope he wakes up. He might have more information than he let on."

Briefly, she pulled the phone away from her ear. "Bailey, hold on. Someone is beeping in." She pressed a button. "Hello? Yes, this is Willow Vaughn."

Her eyes went wide and she hopped up from the barstool, practically jumping up and down in bare feet. She swung around the island and grabbed Josh's arm that was currently wielding a sharp knife. With a sigh, he set it out of her reach and turned to see what had her peeing her pants with excitement.

"Yes, tomorrow morning at ten sounds wonderful. We'll be there. Thank you so much."

She was waving her arms around now, a huge smile on her face. She was always beautiful, but when she was jubilant like this, it put her into a league all her own.

"Are you going to tell me what's going on?" he asked now that she had hung up. "I have never seen you this happy and I must say it's an interesting turn of events."

She held up her hand. "Let me tell Bailey and then you and I can talk about it. This is so exciting." She switched ears and reached out with her other hand, snagging a cube of ham that had been destined for the omelets. "Bailey, yes, guess who that was. Archer Caldwell, the president of Evandria. He's agreed to meet with us tomorrow morning. Yes, we should have a call this afternoon and discuss what questions I should ask. Yes, yes, we'll be here. Okay, bye."

Tossing her phone down on the island, she launched herself into Josh's arms. This was nice. He could easily get used to it. "So I guess we have something to celebrate? What did he say?"

She stepped back, her cheeks pink with excitement. "First he apologized for taking so long to return my call. He said he was out of the country, which I think is pure bullshit. But anyway, he said he had a spot in his schedule for tomorrow at ten." Her smile fell. "Only one bad thing about it. We meet at his home, not the headquarters."

"I'm sure that's by design." Josh poured the eggs into the hot skillet. "We're getting to talk to him and that's the important thing. I'm assuming he knows you're Alex's widow."

Willow waggled her eyebrows. "If what Guy Eckley says is true, they know everything."

Sprinkling in the ham and veggies, Josh played along. "I don't know what you're going to ask him but I want to know if Oswald acted alone and if the moon landing was real. My uncle swears it was fake but then he believes his neighbors are secretly taping his phone conversations so he often speaks in code which no one but him knows so we can't understand a damn thing he's talking about. As a family, we've decided to find it charming and quirky."

Giggling, she reached into the cabinet and pulled down two coffee cups. "He sounds like a real character. I'd like to meet him sometime."

"He'd love to meet you. Fancies himself something of a ladies man. He is on his fifth wife. Nice women too. Not sure what they see in him but sadly the relationships never last long.

Surprise, surprise. Play your cards right, honey, and you could be number six."

Willow rolled her eyes and groaned. "I am not looking to get married. Been there, done that. Why would I ever do it again?"

Josh shrugged, enjoying the play by play. Willow always challenged him. "I don't know. Security, maybe?"

"I have two dogs. Try again."

"Someone to warm your feet at night."

"I have two dogs. Try again."

"Someone to tell you you're pretty."

Willow handed him his coffee cup. "I can pay someone to do that."

"Then it looks like you have no need of marital bliss. Congratulations."

He flipped the huge omelet out onto a plate. It would be more than enough to share once he made some toast.

"You made a mess," Willow scolded playfully as she retrieved plates and forks and placed them on the table. "I'll have you know that's my job. No horning in on my fun."

He had made a mess. There were veggies and ham cubes on the floor where they had escaped during the transfer from cutting board to skillet. He knelt down to scoop them up in his hand and looked up as Willow refilled her coffee cup. She really shouldn't be allowed around anything that hot. She was a menace in the kitchen.

Just about to stand, he spied something way under the lip of the granite-topped island. If Willow found out she had a spider or roach in the house she might put it on the market and move. He reached up to the counter and grabbed a paper towel, capturing the invader but his fingers immediately knew this wasn't a household pest. He was a veterinarian, not a cop, but he had a feeling that what he'd found wasn't good.

Standing, he placed the paper towel on the counter and pointed to it. Willow frowned and open her mouth to speak but he pressed his hand over her lips and shook his head. She nodded silently as if understanding but her expression was questioning. He reached for the pen and paper next to the refrigerator where the housekeeper made her grocery list and scrawled a note, setting it next to the small metal object he'd found.

I don't know much about these things but I think your home is being bugged.

THEY'D LEFT THE small metal device in the kitchen while they ate outside on the back patio, the two dogs Brodie and Scout at their feet, hoping for a dropped morsel of food. Josh had taken a few pictures of it with his phone and shot them off to Ellis, so now it was a waiting game. That didn't stop Willow from being extremely pissed off. If it was what Josh thought it was, someone was going to answer for it.

"How long do you think it's been there?" she asked, her voice trembling with anger. "I don't suppose there's any chance it's part of the Wi-Fi system and we're overreacting."

Josh shoveled a bite of omelet into his mouth before answering. That was something she'd noticed about him although she'd only met him a little over a week ago. He'd take his time thinking about what he was going to say, measuring his words carefully. Perhaps it came from being a veterinarian and all the nervous pet parents like herself. Maybe it was just how he was born.

"It could be. Like I said, I'm no expert. I've only seen them in movies so at this point it could be a lot of things. But I think one thing is certain, it's not part of the kitchen island."

Pushing food around on her plate, she ran through every recent conversation she could remember. "I don't know what they were listening for. My housekeeper's recipe for lasagna?"

"I think you need to be prepared for the very real possibility that if that is what I think it is, it's not the only one in the house. They may be scattered all over. We should check Bailey and Peyton's houses as well."

Thoughts of what they might have heard had her cheeks flushing a bright red. She might be a widow and not have a man, but dammit, she still had needs. Needs that were taken care of by certain battery operated objects she kept stashed in the nightstand drawer.

"I feel so violated. Like they know all my secrets. Thank goodness they can't see me too."

She had a habit of walking around with little on when she was the only one home.

His look had her groaning in protest. "No. Just no. Do you think they have a camera too? Son of a bitch. That must be how they know all the secrets. They're spying."

"We need to sweep the house completely, honey. Every nook and cranny. I don't know what they're doing but generally where there's smoke there's fire, if you know what I mean."

She did and now she was completely squicked out. "Maybe we should go to a hotel."

Shrugging, he pointed to her barely touched food. "You need to eat. Keep up your strength. As for a hotel, who's to say what they're watching. They could have eyes everywhere."

Her stomach lurched and she stared at her plate. There was no way she could choke down this food. Maybe the toast? She listlessly bit into the dry bread, not bothering with butter or jam. "Now I am totally creeped out. My skin is tingling and I feel eyes on me everywhere. I'm so paranoid I may need a tinfoil hat. Doesn't this bother you?"

Mr. Laidback and Mellow considered the question. "I'm not thrilled about it but I'm not going to get upset until I know what we're dealing with. Besides, I cannot imagine a more boring subject for anyone to watch than me. I'm a walking cure for insomnia."

"I bet your life isn't that boring."

He reached out a hand. "I'll take that bet. Five bucks says you'd find my life a snoozefest. Deal?"

She was enjoying Josh's company more and more. She shook his hand, his callused fingers slightly rough against her skin. "I'll take that bet. So tell me about your life and be specific."

"I wake up early and feed all the dogs and then go for a run. I shower, grab a quick breakfast, then try to make it into the clinic by seven-thirty. Then I proceed to see patients for about twelve hours, possibly taking a short break for lunch where I eat a sandwich and chips. Most evenings after work I have dinner, read, or maybe watch some television. Now and then I play poker with Ellis, Chase, and a few other friends. If I take a rare day off, I might play tennis with Chase but mostly I do maintenance around the house or take the dogs for a walk. There. That's my life."

Willow didn't say a word, instead walking into the house and digging in her purse. She came back outside and slapped a five down on the table. "You win. That's pathetic, Josh. You need to get out more and have some fun. Live a little. You only get one chance at life. Don't you ever date or maybe go dancing? Travel?"

He shoved the last bite of omelet in his mouth. "My last girl-friend was about a year ago. She liked me well enough but it turns out she had a phobia regarding large dogs. I can't change who I am or what I do so there went that. Dancing? Honey, I have no rhythm. None. You don't want to see me widely gesticulating out on some dance floor like I'm playing a bizarre game of charades." He took a sip of his coffee. "And as for travel, I do enjoy that but it's hard to get away. The other vet at my clinic doesn't like to work long hours so when I'm out of the office I tend to get texts from him asking questions and complaining constantly so it's not often worth it. It's eight-thirty in the morning and last time I checked he'd already sent me three."

Now she felt like a terrible person. "That's awful. You came here for me and he's driving you crazy. Is there anything I can do to help?"

Josh laughed and scooted her still full plate closer to him. "Do you mind?"

"Help yourself. I'm too upset to eat more than this toast."

"It's sweet that you want to help but there's nothing to be

done. He's a good guy and I like him, he just doesn't want to spend his life at the clinic. I respect that. I'm not thrilled that he feels the need to pull me into every little decision he makes but I mostly just ignore him. It's all fine."

Willow let her gaze run up and down Josh, head to toe. "Do you ever get mad?"

He paused in devouring her breakfast. "Yes, but not often. I have a long fuse but when it goes, get out of the way, honey. Nothing good can come of it."

"When was the last time you got mad?"

He put the fork down on the plate. "I think that's enough about me. Let's talk about you."

No way. He knew the bare minimum and that's all he needed to know.

"Have you heard from Ellis yet?"

Josh laughed, showing off even white teeth and a dimple in his right cheek. "Good save, honey. I barely noticed the non sequiter. I'll go check my phone. I left it inside."

He picked up their plates and headed into the kitchen, whistling a lilting tune. There was no way this man was that happy all the time. There had to be something he was hiding, and she didn't need another man in her life with secrets.

Who was she kidding? She didn't need a man. Period.

Too much trouble. Too much maintenance.

She'd stick with man's best friend.

Chapter Three

I T TOOK THE better part of the day before Ellis called them back. Willow and Josh had spent the day trolling the web for information about Evandria. It was amazing how many obscure message boards and articles there were. Many were by conspiracy theory nuts and after several hours reading their diatribes, Willow was feeling more paranoid than ever. If even half this crap was true, the world was a horrible place.

Josh placed Willow's phone on the patio table. They would only speak when they were outside the house. "Who's on with us?"

"I've got Bailey, Chase, and myself," Ellis replied. "It seemed easier to tell everyone at the same time. I, personally, have never seen a listening device so I called in a friend at the FBI who confirmed for me that's what this is. He told me how to turn it off or destroy it and I'm forwarding you those instructions in your email. He agrees that the whole home has to be swept and he's recommended a security agency that he trusts. I'm sending that information too."

"What about Bailey and Peyton's homes?" Willow asked.

"Shouldn't they be swept as well?"

"They should," Ellis answered firmly. "I'm also recommending that our houses up here are swept as well. Just in case."

"Glad I'm not the only one paranoid," Willow joked but Ellis didn't laugh.

"It's not paranoia if they're really after you. Someone wants to listen in to your conversations, Willow. It may be Evandria or it could be someone completely unrelated. Do you have an admirer that won't leave you alone?"

"You mean a stalker," Josh cut in. "Some asshole who obsesses and won't take no for an answer."

"Not that I know of but I guess anything is possible."

"Willow, are you okay coordinating our homes or should I fly down there?" Bailey queried. "It's no trouble."

Willow didn't even have to think about the answer. "You stay there with Peyton. We can handle this, no problem. Someone needs to be there for her when she wakes up."

"That should be soon," Bailey said. "The doctor is weaning her off the medication so it's up to her now."

"Keep talking to her. I hear that helps."

There was an awkward silence on the other end of the line but then Bailey resumed speaking. "We are. Books, the newspaper, fun gossip. I even gave her the recipe to my Dark Chocolate Dream Cake yesterday."

"I'd ask for it too but I'm useless in the kitchen. So I only have one more question for Ellis. Should we go stay somewhere else until the house is swept? Every time we want to speak we have to walk outside."

She could hear Ellis's laughter booming through the phone.

"I wouldn't worry about it unless you're talking about the case."

It still creeped her out.

They talked some more about questions for Archer Caldwell before they hung up. Willow promised to call them the minute the meeting was over.

"I don't think I want to stay here tonight," she pronounced as she tucked her phone back into her purse. "Just the thought that they might be listening or watching bothers me. What about you?"

Josh tapped his lips and nodded. "If it were me alone I would be fine because I probably wouldn't say anything all evening, but I see your point. Do you have any ideas as to where we could stay?"

She batted her eyelashes and gave him her best mischievous smile. Didn't he know her at all? "Of course I do. Can you imagine a scenario where I wouldn't?"

Chuckling, Josh shook his head. "No, I cannot. I'll follow wherever you lead."

Damn right, he would.

AFTER DROPPING THE dogs off at the home of her housekeeper for the night, they arrived at the hotel. Willow had reserved a penthouse suite overlooking the beach. A suite. The damn thing was bigger than his first apartment when he got out of vet school. Josh wasn't a poor man; he made an excellent living running his own practice but his resources didn't run to something like this. Marble floors. Floor to ceiling windows. Crystal chandeliers. Fine oak furnishings. He would have been happy with a motel room that had a decent bed and a television.

"Does it come with a butler named Jeeves?" he asked after the manager exited, closing the door behind him. Josh had told the man that he didn't need a bellman to carry two small overnight cases but the night manager had insisted on escorting them to their room personally up the private elevator, and then stuck around to show them all the amenities. The only one Josh cared about was the free beer in the well-stocked refrigerator. He'd declined the couples massage they'd been offered.

"Funny. It's a very nice room in a lovely hotel."

He picked up their bags and headed for the bedroom area. "Never said it wasn't. It's just a little over the top, don't you think? We're only here for one night."

There were two bedrooms on either side of the hall with a gigantic bathroom in between. Since they were identical, he dropped her bag in one and his in the other. If she had some weird thing where she had to sleep in the room on the right, he'd be happy to trade.

"We might be here for longer. It depends."

The security agency had agreed to come out to the house tomorrow morning while they were meeting with Archer Caldwell. In the afternoon, he'd sweep the other two homes. Another friend was handling the houses in Williamsburg.

"So what's the plan? We've got a lot of hours to kill before ten in the morning."

Josh was struggling with his less than pure thoughts. Willow was more than attractive and he hadn't had a girlfriend in quite a while. Now they were in a hotel suite. Yes, his brain had gone there even though she'd given him no indication that she thought of him as anything more than a pesky friend she was required to have around. To be fair, he didn't really know what they were to one another either.

They were kind of friends but not really. He was attracted to her but she probably wasn't to him. She was trying to find the truth about her husband's death so this wasn't exactly the most opportune time to start a relationship. All in all, the entire situation was ambiguous at best.

Willow looked out of the windows and smiled. "How about a walk on the beach?"

"Whatever you want to do I'm fine with."

That's how Josh found himself stripping off his shoes and socks at the bottom of a small wooden staircase to the sand below. His gaze scanned the horizon, checking for any threats to her physical well-being but there was only an older woman power walking down the beach and a mother with her two children building a sandcastle. Still he needed to be vigilant, never letting his guard down. Whoever was watching the women might just be biding their time, waiting for the right moment.

Sunset this time of year was late in the evening so the day was still quite hot and humid despite it being almost six o'clock. A warm breeze blew off of the water, tousling Willow's dark blonde hair. She looked every inch at home here, a real Florida girl, dressed in a bright blue sundress that showed off her golden skin. Digging her cherry red toes into the sand, she danced at the water's edge as the water lapped at her feet, a radiant smile on her face.

She didn't look like the wealthy, perfectly groomed woman

he knew her to be. At this moment, she looked more like a happy child playing in the sand, the pure joy of life lit from within. How she managed to be both he didn't know but it made it impossible for him to tear his gaze away from her. The slanted sun created a perfect halo around her body as if she was from another world. Which she wasn't. She was of this world and in danger. It was his job to keep her safe.

Frankly, he feared he wasn't up to the job.

"Josh, you're not having any fun."

He shook off his thoughts, bringing his attention back to reality. Back to the job he was here to do. If anything happened to Willow, he'd never forgive himself. She was too full of life and happiness.

"I most certainly am. Nothing like a walk on the beach."

She tilted her head and eyed him up and down, clearly not believing a word he said. "My bullshit detector just went off. For a relaxed guy, you're kind of tense. What gives?"

He'd found the direct approach was best when dealing with Willow.

"My job is to keep you safe. You play and I guard."

Something he couldn't identify flickered across her face. It might have been determination or anger, but the smile she'd been wearing only moments before was now gone, leaving a more serious woman in its wake.

"I brought you with me to make Bailey feel better about my coming down here. My safety is not your responsibility. It's mine. If I was truly worried I'd hire a phalanx of bodyguards that used to work for the KGB or the Secret Service. Do I *feel* safer when you're around? Yes, I do, but you're not a cop, Josh, you're a goddamn vet. You hang around with four-legged friends all day and I think that's the coolest job in the world, but make no mistake. This is not all up to you."

Her little speech should have made him feel better but instead it did the opposite.

"I made a promise to Chase and Bailey that I would protect you, and by God that's what I'm going to do whether you like it or not. I'll have you know that dogs immediately know that I'm the alpha in any pack."

Her brows went up in surprise. "I believe you. I'm not casting aspersions on your abilities, just stating that this isn't really your job. I don't expect you to jump in front of a bullet for me. I think that's asking a little too much."

Scraping his fingers through his short hair, he sighed in frustration. He was taking this more seriously than she was. "Do you think this is okay because you don't really believe you're in danger? That the whole thing with Peyton was just a fluke and the listening device was there for the house's former owners? Is that where your mind is taking you? Because you need to wake the hell up."

"I know it wasn't a fluke," she said, her voice quiet. "I know that someone is watching us. All of us. They don't want us to find the truth."

He reached out and placed his hands on her shoulders. "We can't trust anyone. We don't know what they want. We don't know what they're willing to do."

Her lips trembled and she exhaled slowly. "I've been trying to put it out of my mind but you're right. The thought of someone listening in to my conversations threw me so badly. My brain shut down any thoughts from that so I could function. If I really think about this it scares the hell out of me."

"It scares me too," he replied, running his hands down her arms in what he hoped was a comforting gesture. "I'm going to do my very best not to let anything happen to you."

She linked her arm in his. "I know you will. I meant it when I said I felt safer with you. But I also meant it when I said that I don't expect you to jump in front of a bullet or a speeding car. This isn't your fight, it's mine."

That was true, but…

"I've made it mine as well. I'm here and we're doing this as a team."

She looked up at him from under her lashes. "Can I be the captain?"

"You want to be in charge?" he laughed. "I'm secure enough in my manhood to let you. Be my guest."

He was only guessing, but he had a feeling that before this was all over, they'd both need to take the lead more than once.

Chapter Four

W ILLOW WAS FEELING guilty about her earlier conversation with Josh. She was afraid he believed she didn't think he could protect her and that wasn't the case at all. Josh was smart and always in control, two qualities desirable in a bodyguard. He also looked to keep himself in excellent shape, which didn't hurt his chances either.

The fact was keeping her safe really wasn't his job. Chase and Bailey may have guilted him into coming down here with her but she didn't expect him to be Bruce Lee.

"Dinner's here," he called from the living area. "Better hurry before I eat it all."

"You better not," she called from the bedroom, levering up from the bed where she'd been resting. There was so much going on in her life she was having trouble sleeping, which was highly unusual. "I mean it, Josh. Don't eat my dinner. I'm actually hungry."

Padding on bare feet out into the living and dining area, her eyes widened in surprise. The table in front of the window was all decked out with place settings, food, damask napkins, and three flickering tapered candles in silver holders. It looked…romantic. Cozy. She swallowed hard and moved closer to where he stood to get a better view.

"Wow. This looks great."

Josh pulled out her chair and she sat down gratefully, her knees beginning to quiver. Had Josh set this up as sort of a date? A seduction? She liked him. She was attracted to him. But she'd pretty much sworn off the male species after Alex died. They were too much trouble and she liked her life the way it was. Quiet and calm.

Well, until now. She hadn't expected to find out that Alex died on the exact same day as his two friends. That had been a shock to say the least and it had certainly shook up her previously rather boring existence.

"The waiter set it all up. He insisted and I didn't have the heart to tell him no since he seemed so keen on doing it."

Oh. No date or seduction. Was she glad or disappointed? She wasn't sure.

"It looks very nice."

Shit, now she felt awkward. To cover it up, she reached for the metal covers keeping the plates of food warm. Josh leaned in to help her and their hands brushed, sending sparks through her fingers and up her arm. She snatched her hand back as if she'd been burned.

"I think two of us is overkill. I'll just let you do it."

If he thought she was acting strangely, he didn't point it out. He uncovered all the plates and placed them safely on the other end of the table. They both helped themselves and Josh poured them each a glass of wine. Outside the windows, the sun was beginning to set, turning the sky a watercolor of orange, blue, and pink.

"I don't remember the last time I watched a sunset," she sighed.

"Me either. Too busy, I guess, but I think that's what makes it special when I do. The randomness of slowing down and simply enjoying nature's artistry."

"You have a poet's soul," she teased.

"Hardly. I'm just a meat-and-potatoes kid from the Midwest."

He was far more than that and she wanted to know more about him. But the social conventions were clear. If she asked him about his life, he could ask her. She wasn't ashamed of her life. Far from it. She felt it had shaped a great deal of who she was now. She didn't talk about it much, however, because people either felt sorry for her or they judged her.

Which would Josh be?

"So how did you and Chase come to be friends?"

A safe question and she might find out more about him along the way.

"I moved in next to him," Josh answered with a grin. "I needed a place that had some privacy because of the dogs and that house went on the market at the same time I was ready to move from my old place. Not only do the dogs have room to run but Chase and I get along great. It's a win-win. Although I have to admit that at first I thought he might be a drug dealer or something."

Willow almost spit out a mouthful of dinner. The very idea of Chase doing anything against the law was ludicrous. "Are you kidding? Why?"

Chuckling, Josh dug into his steak. "Because he always had plenty of money but he didn't seem to have any means of support. He didn't work. He left the house occasionally and I thought maybe those were his deliveries to clients. We'd known each other a couple of months before I asked him about it."

Willow slapped a hand over her mouth. "You asked him? Did he punch you in the face?"

"Actually he laughed his ass off. Then he admitted that he bought and sold stocks for a living, which if I remember correctly, he said was probably as bad as being a drug dealer. We still have a laugh about that every now and then."

"You know I'm picturing Chase in some sort of 'Miami Vice' outfit now?" Willow giggled. "A pastel t-shirt under a white jacket rolled up at the sleeves."

"So this wouldn't be a good time to tell you that Chase and I dressed up one Halloween as Crockett and Tubbs?"

Her mouth was hanging open and she couldn't stop it. "Pictures or it never happened."

"It never happened," Josh admitted with an eye roll. "But I had you going there for a minute, didn't I?"

"You did. I would have paid money to see that photo."

He gave her a wink. "Halloween's coming up in a few months. I'll see what I can do. But I don't come cheap so get your checkbook ready."

"If you dress up as Tubbs, I will be more than happy to write you a check."

Josh playfully threw up his hands. "Why would I automatically be Tubbs? I could be Crockett. I could be the star of the show. You know, I always felt sorry for Tubbs. He never got to drive the car."

Willow's ribs hurt from laughing. Josh was a serious goofball. "Of course you could be Crockett. You could be Castillo too with the cool, standoffish attitude. I can see that."

His brow arched. "Are you even old enough to have seen the show?"

"No, and you aren't either. I watched them on one of the streaming services and I bet you did too."

Grinning, Josh helped himself to more potatoes from the platter in the middle of the table. There was enough food to feed an army. "I watched re-runs with my dad when I was a kid. He was really into the show. It seemed so glamorous to someone who grew up in the middle of the country, completely land-locked. Beaches and expensive cars. They solved the case and got the girl all in one hour. I couldn't get enough of it. I think I've seen every episode at least half a dozen times." He pretended to play air drums, his arms flailing. "That's where I discovered 'In the Air Tonight'. Coolest song ever."

She'd never thought of Josh as a musician. "Do you play the drums?"

"I was in a cover band in high school. I can play piano, guitar, and drums. We thought we were going to be famous."

Willow made a sad face. "I'm sorry. Did any of you go on to be in the music business?"

Josh laughed and shook his head, his cheeks red. "Tony's a dentist and Bobby owns a sports bar. Steve came the closest though. He runs one of those companies that provide background music for elevators and when businesses put you on hold."

She wasn't sure she would call that *close*.

Hearing his life story was too much fun. She wanted to know more.

"Do you still play at all?"

Scratching his chin, Josh shook his head. "I think Chase or the dogs would kill me if I played the drums. I do have a couple guitars and I get them out every now and then when I want to feel bad about myself. I'm really not that good."

"I'd like to hear you play sometime. I've always wanted to learn to play an instrument."

"I can teach you," Josh offered. "A few lessons and you'll be playing a mean rendition of 'Puff the Magic Dragon'."

"I love that song."

"Everyone loves that song, but if you really listen to the lyrics it's quite sad."

She hadn't thought about it as a child but it was. Growing up. Moving on. Leaving friends behind.

"Will you really teach me?"

Josh gave her that look. The one he'd had on the beach when he said he'd protect her.

"Sure I will. I wouldn't offer if I wasn't serious."

She didn't bother telling him she'd had all sorts of offers from men in her youth but few had truly meant what they'd said. It was all just a ruse to get in her pants.

"I might take you up on that." She pushed her plate away and gathered a little bit of courage. His words had been niggling in the back of her mind since he'd spoken them. He'd already revealed some of himself so maybe he'd answer. "You said that it's not pretty when you get mad but that you don't do it often. When was the last time you lost your temper?"

He'd been reaching for a slice of chocolate cake when she'd asked and he froze, his hands in midair. His expression turned to stone and the smile he'd been wearing only moments ago was wiped away.

"That's a...touchy subject."

Clearly. She hadn't meant to upset him. "Forget I asked. I was just curious because I can't imagine you mad. You're so calm."

He stared out of the window, the sky now purple and the sun below the horizon. "I was home visiting my parents a few years ago."

Her fingers tightened on her glass and she didn't move or say a word, too afraid she'd break the spell that had him talking. But then remorse took over and she was sorry she'd ever asked. Nosy. She was a nosy bitch and it was none of her damn business. She'd crossed a line and he didn't owe her anything, least of all an answer to a personal as hell question.

"You don't need to answer—"

He turned back abruptly, waving her objection away. "It's okay. I don't have many secrets in my life, if any. I'm just not proud of the way I acted, that's all. I don't want you to think less of me."

"Unless you shot a man in Reno just to watch him die, I doubt that would happen. I think you're a pretty great guy. You'd have to be to put up with me."

If anything, he was too wonderful. It would be better if he wasn't quite so good looking too.

The corners of his lips quirked up. "I've never even been to Reno. I swear."

"Listen, just forget I even asked."

He shrugged, his hand patting her own. "Relax, honey. I once asked someone if he was a drug dealer. That's much worse than this."

Relaxing back into her chair, she sipped her wine. "You have a point."

"Of course I do. Now where was I? I was visiting my family. I have three sisters and two brothers plus my mother and father. I also have aunts, uncles, and cousins in the vicinity. When we all get together it's a crowd, to say the least. Anyway, I was home visiting a couple of years ago. I'll make a long story short. My baby sister showed up with a black eye and bruises all over her arms and legs. She gave me some story about falling down stairs but I could see the handprints on her skin. I hightailed it out to her house where her useless piece of skin of a husband was lying on the couch, drinking and doing drugs, and breathing in oxygen that he didn't deserve. I pulled him onto his feet and gave him some of what he'd given my sister."

Willow didn't hesitate. "Good. I'm glad."

Josh snorted and shook his head. "I don't regret a moment of it but my family was up in arms when the cops showed up at our house to arrest me. That asshole had called the police on me."

Willow had known men like that. "Let me guess. He was the innocent victim and you were the bad guy? Asshole. I hope the karma bus found him eventually."

"It did," Josh confirmed. "He didn't pay his dealer and had to work for him. A deal went bad and he ended up dead. I felt badly for Monica. There was a part of her that loved him, I guess, although I can't imagine why."

"She went back to him?" Willow asked, already knowing the answer. "After you beat him up?"

He didn't answer right away. "Yeah, she did. She said she had to because if she didn't he'd kill himself. That didn't seem like a bad thing to me but apparently, she disagreed. He had her so turned around and inside out she thought everything was her responsibility. If he got a goddamn hangnail somehow it was her fault and she'd apologize. She was mad at me for putting a hurt on him. Said that I was a bully."

"And you went to jail?"

"He dropped the charges when the cops threatened to arrest him for beating up Monica and for having drugs in his house. But I did spend a few hours in the lockup. My parents still refer to it as the time I was incarcerated. They were upset, to say the least."

The question was, were they more upset about him or Monica?

"Did they want her to go back to him?"

"No, but they weren't willing to go to prison to keep that from happening. As I said, I don't regret it but they thought there was a better way to deal with the situation. There probably was but at the time I didn't care. I just wanted to protect my little sister."

"What about your brothers and sisters?"

Josh chuckled. "My two brothers are split on the issue. One wishes I'd taken him with me and the other thinks I should have used a less violent method." His smile turned evil. "Both of my sisters think I should have ripped his dick off."

Willow agreed. "I think I'd like your sisters."

"You would," he agreed. "They're ballsy, just like you."

Sputtering into her wine, Willow coughed. "Ballsy? Is that how you see me?"

He nodded. "I do. Is that a bad thing?"

She shook her head. No, it wasn't. It was kind of nice, actually. She liked the sound of it.

"Thank you for telling me. You really didn't have to but I'm glad you did. Now I know you're a real badass, Chuck Norris-type."

"Chuck's got nothing on me," Josh bragged, his eyes alight with mischief before turning serious. "I did it to protect Monica. I'm not a guy that goes around punching people. I think the time before that one was back in high school in a locker room brawl. Seriously, I'm mild-mannered."

"I believe you." She held up her hands in surrender. "I still think you did the right thing though."

His eyes narrowed and he took a gulp of his wine. "I wasn't sure you'd feel that way. I know that your husband...well...he drank quite a bit."

That was the understatement of the year. Alex had taken alcoholism to a new level.

"He did but that doesn't mean that I don't want a wife beater to get what's coming to him."

Josh studied his hands, wrapped around the stem of the glass. "Did he ever...?"

At first, she didn't know what he meant. When she figured it out, she shook her head, her body almost coming out of the chair. She was no fucking victim. "Absolutely not. Not once. Never. He wasn't the type. He was a happy drunk and he just wanted to have fun. I wouldn't have stayed with him if he'd done something like that."

"But you did stay with him. Even though he drank and took drugs."

He wasn't asking. He was stating it as fact and it was. She'd stayed for a myriad of reasons. All of them good at the time.

"I don't want to talk about it."

She hadn't meant for it to come out so abrupt. He hadn't even asked her a question and she was already shutting him down. The simple fact was she wasn't sure why she'd stayed with Alex and thinking about it made her uncomfortable.

"Then we won't," he easily agreed. "I just kind of thought we were having a moment here. Getting to know one another. You know…revealing things about ourselves."

He didn't know what he was asking. "I want to but I'm not ready."

"Fair enough. You know I'm not going to press you for your life story, right? I wouldn't do that."

He wouldn't, which made her feel all the more guilty. "Thank you, I appreciate that. You told me your story and it's only fair that I tell you mine."

He reached for the wine bottle and refilled her glass. "Honey, that's not why I told you that story."

"Then why did you tell it?"

He leaned forward, his blue gaze looking straight into her eyes. "I protected Monica as best as I knew how and I'll protect you the same way. No one is going to get close to you while I'm here. I'll do what it takes to keep you alive. I'm a man of my word."

He might be the first one of those she'd ever met.

Chapter Five

ARCHER CALDWELL WAS a handsome man who appeared to be in his mid-fifties or so. Short dark hair just touched with silver at the temples gave him a distinguished air, along with an expensive blue suit with subtle pin striping paired with Italian shoes. Everything about him screamed money and power right down to the diamond cufflinks at his wrists.

He stood from behind the desk in his home office, hand held out. "Mrs. Vaughn. Mr. Coleman. Please do come in and have a seat. It's so nice to meet you. Would you like anything? Water, coffee, tea? A soda perhaps?"

Willow and Josh declined, sitting across from him in two butter-soft leather guest chairs. Archer also sat down again, a welcoming smile on his face.

"How is it, Mrs. Vaughn, that we have never crossed paths before? I think we have many of the same friends."

"I'm not sure I would characterize most of the citizens of Midnight Blue Beach as my friends, Mr. Caldwell. And please call me Willow."

"Then you must call me Archer." A peculiar look crossed his

face but went as quickly as it came. "As for friends, I have a feeling after this meeting you will be quite popular in our little hamlet. You'll be inundated with more invitations than you know what to do with."

Tipping his hand as to how much power he held? Willow had done her homework on this man and he definitely pulled a few strings, not only here but all over the world. He had his fingers in some interesting pies. Discreetly, of course. She'd been shocked by how few photos of him existed on the net.

"Perhaps," Willow conceded. "I want to thank you for seeing us, Archer. I've found that I knew very little about my late husband's life and death. I was hoping you could help me."

He waved away her concern. "I'm just sorry it took so long to get back to you. I've been in and out of the country on business for the last several months. I've been working with an architect to restore a palazzo in Venice and turn it into a hotel. Tedious. Lots of details but the city is fantastic. Nothing like it to get out of the rat race and relax. Have you ever been?"

As she looked into his blue-gray eyes, her fingers tightened on the arms of her chair. That Guy Eckley wasn't sounding so crazy after all. Archer Caldwell knew things. All sorts of things.

He knew about her. He knew the answer to every question he planned to ask her today.

"Alex and I went there for our honeymoon," she finally said, keeping her voice deliberately cool. He wanted to get a reaction from her and she wasn't going to give him the satisfaction. She only hoped Josh would stay his calm and collected self through this. He'd agreed to let her do most of the talking but if he thought she was upset he might intervene. "It's a beautiful city, but I prefer Rome."

"Lovely city. Now why don't you tell me specifically what I can do for you?"

Taking a breath to calm her nerves, Willow plunged in, her story carefully planned and rehearsed. "Recently I've come to find out that my husband Alex and the husbands of two of my friends all died on exactly the same day. They were also childhood friends and joined your organization together. The date of their death was also the same as Gwen Baxter's fifteen years before at Keene Hill Summer Camp in Williamsburg."

Steepling his fingers, Archer nodded, his lips pursed. "I believe Stephen Baxter, her brother, will be charged with her murder. If he survives, of course."

Was that a threat? Would Caldwell make sure Stephen didn't live? Geez, she was becoming tinfoil hat paranoid.

"If you know about Stephen, then you probably knew about Alex, Frank, and Greg."

Plus a bunch of other things she had no clue about.

His brows raised and then fell back into place. "The only reason I'm familiar with Stephen's issue is because he's a member of our organization. My board brought it to my attention yesterday. We make a point to keep up with the lives of our members."

"He was shot by one of your members – Taylor Richardson."

He nodded. "And she'll be dealt with, I can assure you."

"Isn't that up to law enforcement and the courts?" Josh asked, leaning forward in his chair.

"We'll have our own internal investigation," Archer replied smoothly, an urbane smile on his tanned face. "No matter what happens with the court system, she'll have to face the consequences of what she's done to a fellow brother in Evandria. The rules are clear."

"Just what are the rules?" Josh queried. "Is there a list?"

"There's an entire book that must be memorized. But they all boil down to one simple lesson – treat others respectfully and with kindness. I think the world could use a little more of that, don't you? Kindness seems to be in short supply these days. That's why what we do at Evandria is so important. I know it sounds simple but we strive to make this world a better place. Help those who cannot help themselves. Our charitable donations are spread worldwide and they are sorely needed in our war-torn world. I worry about the world I'm leaving my children and grandchildren."

Because you don't control it yet?

"I do indeed think we need more kindness," Willow agreed, watching Archer closely for any tell. Any sign that he was nervous or tense. "I think we need more honesty as well."

If he was surprised she'd brought that up, he didn't show it. He was good. "I have to agree, Willow. We need more honesty in our business dealings, financial transactions, and much more transparency in our elected officials. I think we've reached a critical juncture where we need to show the people of the world that those who are in power can or cannot be trusted."

"Can you?"

He shook his head, his brows pulled together. "I'm sorry. I don't follow you."

"Can you be trusted? Are you transparent?"

Caldwell didn't blink an eye. "I like to think the answer is yes."

"So when I ask you a question, you'll answer it honestly?"

"I will. We have nothing to hide here."

She didn't miss that he'd changed from "I" to "we".

"I'd like to find out more about Alex, Frank, and Greg. What were they recruited to do for Evandria? How involved were they?"

Archer sat back in his leather chair. "What I think you really want to know is if there's a connection between the three men's deaths? Is that correct?"

"It is. I think it's all a little too much of a coincidence. My friends agree."

He suddenly leaned forward, his hands on the dark oak desk, and his expression intense.

"I think you and your friends are on to something, Willow. Since I got your call, I've pulled their files plus found as much as I could about their deaths. The whole situation is disturbing to say the least and I think it's something that Evandria should look into. They were our brothers and we owe them – and you – the truth."

Was he serious? An investigation that would clear Evandria of any wrongdoing?

"Why are you suddenly so interested? Alex died five years ago and no one from your organization cared then."

"And for that I apologize, Willow. I've only been in my position for a little over a year so I wasn't familiar with the circumstances of their deaths. Now that you've brought this to my attention it's going to become a very high priority for us. If there's any connection in their untimely passings, we'll find it.

You can trust that."

Josh stiffened in the chair next to her; she could feel it even if it wasn't visible. He'd already told her they couldn't trust anyone and she agreed. The last person she'd trust was Archer Caldwell.

She glanced over at Josh and then back to Caldwell. "We'd like to be part of the investigation. Transparency and all that."

Shaking his head, Archer managed to pull off a regretful look. He'd missed his calling. He should have been an actor. "I'm afraid that's out of the question. It would expose you to our internal workings, which are a secret. However, you have my personal guarantee that we will share with you even the smallest of details that we find."

A personal guarantee, huh? Lucky me.

Willow didn't press the issue. She wasn't going to change his mind, but then neither was she going to change hers.

"There isn't anything you can tell me about Alex? I find that hard to believe."

Archer reached over to the low cabinet behind his desk and retrieved a brown folder.

"Actually there is something. Here are the member files for all three men. Normally we don't release these but I think this is a special case."

She took it from his outstretched hand and laid it in her lap. She'd look through it when she didn't have him for an audience. "Thank you. I do appreciate this."

"I want to do everything I can to help you." He tapped his temple and smiled. "Speaking of helping, I need to let you know that I've located Peyton Nelson's family and informed them of her accident. They're on my private jet as we speak heading to

Williamsburg."

Okay, this she hadn't expected. How did he know…? Right, he was Evandria. He knew everything.

She must have been silent for too long because Josh spoke up. "That's very kind of you. Peyton's recovering well and I'm sure she'll want her family there when she wakes up."

"Although you and your friends weren't Evandria members, Willow, your husbands were and that makes you one of us. We're here to help in any way possible. Just let me know what you need and we'll make it happen."

One of us. It sounded rather ominous.

"I just want the truth about their deaths."

"We're going to get that. You don't need to worry about this anymore. Just leave it to us."

In other words, back the hell off and stop sticking your nose where it doesn't belong.

"One more thing, Mr. Caldwell." It was time for Josh's part in this little farce of a meeting. Everyone knew their lines perfectly. "We found this in Willow's home. Evandria wouldn't know anything about it, would they?"

The bug, wrapped in a handkerchief, was produced from Josh's pocket and laid it out on Archer's desk. To his credit, the older man didn't even flinch, although she would swear he turned a shade paler.

"What is that?"

"It's a listening device, better known as a bug. I can't imagine who would want to listen in on Willow's conversations but here it is, so someone obviously does. Is it Evandria?"

Shaking his head, Caldwell straightened his tie. Finally…a

tell. He was nervous. Good. She wanted him to know that she wasn't buying his particular brand of bullshit.

"As I said before, Evandria is a philanthropic organization, Mr. Coleman. It's about brotherhood and friendship. Helping people in crisis and making the world a better place. It is not about spying on people. Are you even sure that's what it is? Are you a police officer?"

Archer knew exactly who Josh was. Hell, he probably knew more about him than she did. He wouldn't have let someone into his home without checking them out first.

"I'm sure," Josh said, his features neutral. At this moment she applauded his laid-back personality. "If it wasn't Evandria then it was someone else. Does it concern you that someone or several someones wants to know what Willow is talking about? Especially as she's one of you and all."

Archer stood, indicating that the meeting was over. Just as well as he wasn't going to reveal anything more anyway. "It does concern me. If you'll leave that, we can make a few inquiries."

Josh scooped the bug back up and shoved it in his pocket. "Sorry, I can't. It's evidence."

"Evidence? Has a crime been committed?"

The corners of Josh's lips turned up slightly but it wasn't much of a smile. "I'm guessing there have been quite a few."

With that Willow and Josh also stood, her shoes sinking into the thick carpeting. She hadn't learned anything about Alex at this meeting but she'd learned about Caldwell and Evandria. Guy Eckley was probably telling the truth. The vibe from this man was off the charts – strange and creepy. She could absolutely see him plotting the takeover of the world.

Had Alex believed in this organization at some point? Was he killed because he stopped?

"Thank you for meeting with us." She held up the folder. "I appreciate this as well."

Archer came around the desk to shake their hands again. "Let your friends know that you and they will be receiving some long-overdue gifts soon."

"Gifts?"

"A simple plaque of service," Archer dismissed. "A few other things to show our gratitude for their years of dedication to the organization."

"Thank you, that's very kind."

"Alex gave of himself and it's the least we can do." Archer led them to the door of his study. "I'm not sure what you're doing this Saturday night but we're having a little party at The Retreat that evening. Black tie. Lots of members will be there and some of them may have known Alex, Frank, and Greg. You could come Friday night and make it a weekend. Lots of things to do. I think if you saw what we're all about, Willow, you might consider joining. You'd make an excellent addition to Evandria. We should have done this years ago. What do you say? You're welcome too, Dr. Coleman, as Willow's guest."

The Retreat? An actual invitation? Now this was completely unexpected.

"I wouldn't miss it. Thank you. We'll be there."

With bells on.

JOSH DROVE DOWN the long driveway and onto the road before speaking. After that meeting, he was as paranoid as Willow. Sign him up for a tinfoil hat. Maybe a scarf too.

"You know you can't trust anything that guy has to say, right? He reminded me of something out of *The Stepford Wives*. He was just a little too perfect and smooth."

Willow laughed, clapping her hand over her mouth. "Do you think they're planning to kidnap and kill us, replacing ourselves with incredibly lifelike cooking and cleaning robots?"

"I think that with this creepy organization that it is entirely possible."

Her brow furrowed. "You know, I never bought into that movie. It wasn't realistic."

"*The Stepford Wives*? I don't think it was supposed to be realistic, honey."

Snorting, she began to count on her fingers. "But it's supposed to be plausible. One. It was like the town of Stepford was completely isolated. Didn't their friends and family notice anything different and ask questions? Two. Not every man was a member of the Men's Association. So what if one of those wives was in a terrible car accident or something? Wouldn't the EMTs see the wires and crap? That's kind of a dead giveaway that they're not real. Three. And this is the big one. Where were they hiding all of these bodies? I mean, get real. Dozens and dozens of women replaced and they don't have a storage issue?"

The more he was with Willow the more she enchanted him. And worried him.

"You've been thinking about this a long time," he observed. "I assumed you were going with the battery angle. How did they keep them powered up? Or maybe the sex angle. Were they that lifelike that the men enjoyed the sex? I always wondered about that. They could have made a fortune in sex toys instead of turning evil."

This conversation had taken a weird turn.

"Eww, I never even thought about that. The hygiene factor is a question right there. As for batteries, maybe they plugged them in at night."

Josh shrugged. "You'd think people might notice that no one ever had any more kids after they…what's the word…changed. That would be a giveaway as well. As for the bodies, I'm guessing they cremated them. That's what I would do."

Josh had to laugh at the side-eye he was getting from Willow. "You kind of scare me a little. You've thought it through enough to know how you'd dispose of a body. That's kind of disturbing. I've heard it's the quiet ones you have to worry about. I'll sleep with one eye open tonight."

That's how he'd slept every night since agreeing to guard Willow.

"Getting back to Archer Caldwell, you know that this weekend is going to be one big performance. We won't learn anything."

"I know. He wants us to stop investigating and he wants to keep an eye on us. He thinks if we're there that we aren't nosing around. But I intend to ask lots of questions this weekend. Someone there had to have known Alex."

Josh turned down the street that led to Willow's house. They needed to check on the bug sweeper's progress. "But will they admit it? I have a feeling Caldwell has a tight grip on his members."

"One thing I learned early in life. There's always a loose can-
non. Someone who can't wait to talk and tell everyone their life
story. We just have to find out who that is."

"You make it sound easy. I think it's going to be tougher
than that."

"Giving up already?" she teased, a smile on her face.

"Not even close," he said grimly. This was an opportunity
they hadn't even dreamed of. "But let's not lose sight of the goal
here – the truth. And it won't be in that folder he gave you.
Whatever is in there is a distraction to send us down the wrong
path. He wants us out of the way."

She tapped the file sitting on the seat between them. "This is
either useless or filled with lies. It doesn't matter which one or
both. I won't be run off."

He wouldn't either but he had a feeling they should be
scared. A vast, wealthy secret society that wanted to run the
world. He and Willow just might be roadkill on the way to that
goal.

Chapter Six

THE "SWEEPER", A short man with a receding hairline who mumbled to himself, had a neat stack of listening devices – bugs – on the kitchen island when Willow and Josh returned to her home after picking up the dogs. Josh counted out eight, which meant that they'd been spread around the house to pick up every word spoken. Willow was visibly upset as she studied the pile, finally reaching out and picking one up to examine it more closely.

"Where were they?" she asked, her voice shaky.

The Sweeper, whose name they didn't have because of "reasons" Ellis wouldn't go into to, listed them off. "The kitchen, the dining room, the living room, the study, the master bedroom, the poolhouse, and the back patio area."

"That's seven locations," Josh pointed out. "But there are eight bugs here."

"There were two in the living room since it's so large. These aren't that effective much past ten feet or so."

"Even outside?" Willow sat heavily onto a barstool. "We went to such trouble to stay outside when we found the first one but they were way ahead of us."

Josh placed his hand on her shoulder, hoping to reassure her. Give her some sort of strength because he had a feeling things were only going to get worse before they got better. This was probably only the tip of the iceberg.

"Then there were the cameras," the Sweeper continued as if she hadn't spoken. "There was one here in the kitchen and one in the living room. I disconnected them and I'm having my team try to chase down who was uploading the footage. I can't tell how long you were being watched, ma'am, but I can tell you that the camera had almost a week of footage that was ready to be sent to whomever planted it."

Josh sat next to Willow as her skin paled. This was what she'd been afraid of. Cameras. God knew what she did when she was all alone, but apparently God wasn't the only one now with that knowledge. "Son of a bitch. Those perverts were watching me. That's sick. I guess I should be grateful it wasn't the bedroom."

Hating to ask but needing to know, Josh turned his attention back to the man. "Did your associate find the same at Ms. Scott's home and Ms. Nelson's?"

Willow seemed to be holding her breath waiting for the answer.

The Sweeper nodded. "They did. About the same number of devices and cameras although there was one difference. There was a camera in Ms. Nelson's bedroom."

"I'm glad Peyton isn't awake for this," Willow muttered under her breath. "How on earth are we going to tell her?"

Josh held out his hand. "We appreciate your help and how

quickly you got here. Ellis said you would be taking these bugs with you so you could have a further look?"

"I will. If I see anything distinctive about them I'll let you know."

"Wait," Willow said before the man could leave. "Where were the cameras hidden in our houses?"

The man smiled and pointed to a framed black and white photo on the wall of Clearwater Beach at the turn of the century. Willow had these old Florida photos all over the house.

"Good question. They were hidden in the pictures." He walked over and pulled the photo from the wall and set it down on the island. "Look here. There's a small hole in the photo. A dark area, of course. The camera was positioned behind it and attached to the frame. Fairly standard and not very imaginative. I found it in the first fifteen minutes. They even hacked your WiFi password and used it to send the video to their servers. You need to get better security, Ms. Vaughn, and stop using your dog's name as a password. I could have all of your banking and shopping information within seconds."

Josh rolled his eyes and Willow gave him an indignant look. "I have a bad memory, okay? Using Scout or Brodie's name is just easier."

The Sweeper laughed. "If it's easy for you, it's extra easy for a hacker."

"Believe me, I've learned my lesson."

"Where were the cameras located in the other homes?" Josh asked. "Frames again?"

The man checked some notes on his clipboard. "They were only slightly more imaginative elsewhere. In Ms. Scott's home, one camera was hidden in a small sculpture and the other was mounted on a frame just like here. In Ms. Nelson's house, she had one in a painting, one in a lamp, and the one in the bedroom was mounted on the drapery rod."

Rubbing her temples, Willow sighed. "I'll have to ask the girls if we all use the same decorator. This is too creepy to be believed."

The smile the man wore fell and his expression turned somber. "Ms. Vaughn, you need to wake up and believe this. Someone or several someones have gone to a great deal of trouble to put surveillance on you and your friends. This is not your run-of-the-mill cheating spouse investigation, which means they aren't going to take my cleaning them out lying down. They're going to do everything they can to infiltrate your life again. Every pizza you have delivered, every box from your online shopping, every person that comes on this property has to be looked at closely. Until you find out who this is, trust no one in your home. Whoever did this was someone you knew and trusted. They have access to you and they won't hesitate to use it again and next time they'll make my job much tougher. I have one more request before I go."

Visibly shaken, Willow nodded. "Of course. What can I do for you?"

"Can I pet your dogs?"

Willow glanced at Josh but nodded. "Sure, they love the attention and they're friendly."

The Sweeper scratched their bellies and allowed himself to be licked on the face. Josh thought the guy was simply a dog-lover until he ran his fingers around their collars and onto to the tags.

"Is this a tag you placed on their collar, Ms. Vaughn?"

The Sweeper pointed to a tiny silver circle that was sandwiched between the county tag and the microchip tag. Frowning, Willow crouched down to have a closer look.

"No. No, that's not anything I've put on their collars. Where did it come from?"

The man smiled and reached for a pair of metal clippers in his tool bag, quickly removing them one at a time and then tossing them on the pile of bugs.

"The same place these others came from. Where do you have your dogs groomed? Do you have a dog walker?"

The Sweeper slapped the stack into a black box and locked the lid. "They're going to be mad. Upset. They're going to come back. They know that we know. Call me if you have any more trouble. I'll be in touch."

Just like that, the little man was out of the door without another word. Josh watched as his van disappeared at the end of the driveway before turning back to Willow. She needed him. Clearly trembling by what he'd found, she was simply sitting on the barstool staring at the window.

"Honey, are you okay? Let's talk about it."

She turned to him then, her gaze stricken. But there was more, she was scared. "How can I not trust anyone? I'll never look at another human being the same. I've always talked to strangers, Josh. I've gone out of my way to help old women cross the damn street but now how do I know if they want something from me? And for the love of God, what do they want? They're the ones with the secrets, not me."

It wasn't the best time to bring it up but it had to be done.

She was already upset and shaking like a Chihuahua so unless she fainted or puked it couldn't get much worse.

Josh slid the file folder closer to Willow. "Maybe it's time to see what propaganda Archer Caldwell wants us to know. Let's see what wild goose chase he wants to send us on."

Sucking in a breath, Willow bravely nodded.

"How bad could it be? At one point I thought Alex was a murderer. But first, I'm going to fix us a drink. I don't care that it's the middle of the day."

Was there anything worse than a killer for a husband? They were about to find out.

WILLOW SET TWO highball glasses and a bottle of Jameson's on the kitchen table where Josh had settled. He'd lifted his eyebrow when he saw she was serious about the drink but he didn't say a word.

"When you find out that creepy people are listening and watching your life like a twisted *Truman Show*, I think you deserve a drink. Or three."

"I think you're right," he agreed. Calm as usual. She was freaking out but then she was the one they'd seen naked. Not that several citizens hadn't seen her unclothed before she met Alex. They had and she wasn't ashamed of what she'd done. But she'd done it willingly. Frankly, this was something entirely different.

"I feel violated," she blurted. "Like I need to scrub myself fifty times in the shower."

Josh opened the bottle and poured each of them a generous shot. "You aren't the one who is dirty, honey. They are. They're the ones who should be ashamed of themselves. You're innocent."

That made her laugh and soon hysterical giggles had given her the hiccups. She had to get a glass of water from the sink and gulp it until they went away.

"I never realized I was so damn funny. Want to share?"

She flopped back into the chair, a smile still on her face. "It's been years since anyone has described me as *innocent*. I'm not sure I even remember that time in my life. So thanks for the laugh, I needed it."

"You're welcome." Josh was watching her closely, probably waiting for her to faint or cry. She was long past that. "You know, we can do this another time. We don't have to look at this now. You could lie down for a while or we could take the dogs for a walk."

Both of those ideas sounded infinitely better than what they were about to do but sometimes a woman had to buckle down and do things that weren't pleasant. Today was one of those rotten, lousy days. Better to get it all over with and then move on to better things.

"Let's do this and then take the dogs for a walk. Or better yet, since it's so hot, let's take them into the pool. They love to swim."

And it would distract her.

Josh's hand was splayed on top of the file. "Do you want to do the honors? This file belongs to you."

"And Bailey and Peyton. But let's not kid ourselves that it's real. It's probably a bunch of falsehoods created by Evandria."

She flipped open the folder. There were three stapled sections. One for each husband, she presumed. Alex was on top and she set that aside, picking up Frank's and handing it to Josh.

"I'll work on Alex while you read through this."

At first, Alex's file was fairly boring. He was recruited at eighteen and agreed to work in the Environmental Unit, promoting responsible use of natural resources.

Since when had Alex given a furry rat's ass about the environment? She didn't think he even knew there was an Earth Day once a year. He didn't even like to be outdoors. He had a massive garage full of gas guzzling cars that emitted carbon monoxide and she knew that wasn't healthy. This had to be a cover on Evandria's part. Whatever he'd actually volunteered for, they didn't want her to know.

His unit director was one Bernard Baldwin, a man Willow had met many times. CEO of an oil company, he threw lavish parties on his private island. And this was who Evandria put in charge of the environment? No conflict of interest there.

Alex had paid his dues each year without fail.

He'd also been called in front of Evandria's disciplinary board a over a dozen times for alcohol and drug abuse plus "conduct in conflict with the organization's values." Whatever that meant. Willow was pretty certain it meant all the whoring Alex had done. He liked them young, big-boobed, and to disappear before morning. He wasn't the cuddle and make them breakfast type.

He'd tried to keep that part of his life out of Willow's face but every now and then it bled over and she'd see just how far her knight in shining armor had fallen. He'd beg for forgiveness and for some stupid reason she'd give it. He'd seemed so helpless at those moments, like a scared child. She'd seen the fear in his eyes and it was more than just about her leaving. He'd lived his entire life terrified of something. Maybe growing up? Being an adult? Commitment? Evandria? She didn't know the answer but it had tortured him for years, unrelenting until the day he died.

Turning the page, she found a long list of fines he'd incurred. Alex wasn't much of a rule follower so that wasn't a surprise. The next page detailed his assets and she was surprised to see a trust she hadn't known existed. All assets within had been left to Evandria on his death. They were welcome to it. He'd left her filthy rich, a state which hadn't gone unnoticed in the community. They hadn't much liked how she'd come about her money. Too bad she didn't care what they thought.

The last few pages were medical reports of some sort and her heart skipped a beat as she quickly scanned the forms, thinking Alex might have been ill. That would be a very legitimate reason to act out.

Her trembling fingers skated along the page and flipped to the next form, and then the third. Acid rose in her throat and it was only by sheer will that she didn't lose what little she had in her stomach. She must have made a sound because Josh had abandoned his own pile of papers and was looking at her.

"Did you find something?"

Swallowing hard, she pressed her palms to the cool oak of the table. She'd known she would find out things about Alex but she'd never imagined something like this. She pushed the forms closer to Josh and sat back in her chair as he read through them, his expression changing from curious to anger. She just might see Josh pissed off.

"I have to tell you I didn't like your late husband before this but now I really think he's scum." Josh flipped the pages shut. "I take it you knew nothing of this."

She didn't know whether to laugh or cry so she did a little of both. "Are you asking whether I knew that Alex had a half-brother the family didn't acknowledge? The answer would be a resounding no. I had no idea. His father was a real piece of work though so I can't say that I'm shocked."

Josh gulped down his whiskey and she did the same, feeling the burn all the way to her belly. "These forms look legit. There are lab tests that prove paternity. I wonder if this guy ever received any money from the father?"

She refilled their glasses. "From what I've seen with that family, I doubt it. Poor kid. Alex shouldn't have inherited everything. Now I have what's his. I should share some of this with this kid."

Josh held up his hands. "Now hold on. First of all, he's not a kid anymore. He's around your age so he's a grown adult who for whatever reason never went after Alex's dad for money. Hell, Willow, he might not even know who his real father is. This paternity test was done at birth, honey. He might have no idea. Secondly, remember Archer Caldwell. He wants you to go down this rabbit hole. We don't even know if any of this is true. Smoke and mirrors. Don't be fooled. This guy might not even really exist."

She massaged her temples and nodded. "You're right. Caldwell wants us to head in another direction. It's been years so I guess this can wait until later. Nothing is going to change between now and then."

She hoped.

"Anything interesting in Frank's file?"

Josh shook his head. "Not really. Frank was recruited to the Financial Division and his director was Nigel Holmwood, but we knew that. Bailey is looking for him. Nothing disciplinary. He paid his dues every year and left part of his estate to Evandria. This part is kind of interesting. Frank's family built their fortune bootlegging, a little fact they've spent the last hundred years or so covering up. Their story is they made their money in cattle and lumber."

"That's it?" Willow asked. "Just some bootlegging? Did they work with Capone or something?"

Josh tossed the papers aside and reached for Greg's set. "It doesn't say so but I doubt it. If they had that kind of dirt, I think they'd put it in the file. Assuming any of this is real, of course."

Josh scanned Greg's papers. "Political division. His director was Darius Cameron. Why does that name sound familiar?"

"You don't follow politics, do you?"

Making a face of disgust, Josh shook his head. "Honestly it makes my blood pressure go up. So much stupidity and not a lick of common sense."

That was true. "Darius Cameron used to be a senator and then the Secretary of State. I think he's one of those television news commentators now. They bring them on during conflicts or scandals."

Josh whistled. "Guy Eckley wasn't kidding when he said that Evandria had infiltrated the government and the financial markets. Its members are some heavy hitters."

"What else is there?"

Josh turned the page. "Greg has a long list of disciplinary actions. Gambling, women, and alcohol. Wow, this list is long. I can't believe he didn't get kicked out."

Willow shrugged. "If they kicked out every horndog and boozer they might not have too many members left. Is that all?"

Checking the last page, Josh stiffened next to Willow. He'd gone quiet. Too quiet. In the time he was taking to answer her question, he could have read the page several times.

"Josh?" Willow prompted. "What are you seeing?"

"It's probably all a lie."

Hopefully all of this was but there might be a grain of truth in these files. "What did Greg do?"

Josh pushed the stack of papers toward Willow, but kept his hand on it so she couldn't pick it up and look. "Before you look, you need to know that this is something we are going to have to look into. We have to know what to tell Peyton."

Archer Caldwell wasn't stupid. Not by a long shot. He had them running in circles, chasing their tails.

"Let me see it."

He removed his hand and sat back while she turned to the last page.

Wife.

Kids.

Willow's heart hurt for Peyton. They'd all known what their husbands were but this was the kind of secret that could rip someone's world to shreds.

"He had another wife," Willow said shakily. "And two kids.

Jesus, how are we going to tell Peyton this? He was an asshole and she knew that but this is a whole different league of jerk. He not only had secrets, he had a secret life."

If it was even true.

"Damn you, Caldwell," Willow bit out between clenched teeth. "Damn you to hell if you're lying to us. There won't be a safe place in the world for you to hide from me."

Chapter Seven

WILLOW HAD BEEN dreading this call all day. She'd put it off as long as she could but when Bailey and Chase called her and Josh, there was no delaying any longer.

"They found listening devices and cameras in all of our homes," Willow said, sitting next to Josh on the patio as they spoke to their friends. "They're clean for now but we need to be careful as to who or what we let into our house. Packages, friends, really anything could potentially bring them back in."

"Are you as creeped out as I am?" Bailey asked, a shudder in her voice. "I lead the most boring life on the planet. Why would they care about what I do?"

"I've been asking myself that very question all day."

Josh leaned forward to speak into the phone. "I believe Evandria is all about having information. They collect it all, the trivial and the critical. Having it is the asset."

"Still creepy," Bailey said. "I'll have to tell Peyton when she wakes up. There's a good chance that might be tonight or tomorrow. She was moving her hands and legs today and muttering in her sleep. The doctor said that's a sign that it will be any time now."

A weight that Willow hadn't even known she'd been carrying around seemed to fall from her shoulders. "That's the most amazing news. I can't wait to talk to her."

Josh elbowed Willow gently and she nodded. She knew what he was trying to tell her.

"There's something else we'll have to tell her as well."

"What's that?"

"I told you what was in Frank and Alex's files but I didn't say what was in Greg's."

A sigh on the other end of the phone. "She knew about the affairs. She knew he was a womanizer who drank and gambled too much."

This entire situation sucked.

"He had another wife. Another family."

Silence.

Then rustling in the background.

"Willow, are you there?" Chase asked. He must have taken the phone from Bailey or maybe she'd given it to him.

"I'm here. Is Bailey okay?"

"She's fine," Chase assured her. "She just needed to sit down for a minute. I think I need to ask for a clarification. You're saying that Greg, Peyton's husband, had another wife?"

"Yes, and two children."

"Children? You're sure?" pressed Chase.

Josh held out his hand for the phone and Willow gave it to him gratefully.

"Chase? It's Josh. No, we're not sure of anything in those files. I wouldn't put it past Archer Caldwell to fabricate all this crap to send us on a wild goose chase. It's clear to me that they don't want us digging around. That's why they've invited us for the weekend. They want to keep an eye on us."

"This is a bunch of shit," Chase ground out. "The files have important information. If they're true. But we don't know if they're true unless we investigate. He's got us over a goddamn barrel."

"He does," Josh agreed. "Listen, we're going to continue here as if these files don't exist. This weekend when we're at The Retreat I'm going to try and get some real information about the men. These people were their friends supposedly. Someone must know something."

"That sounds like a good plan," Chase said. "We can't let them divert our attention from where it needs to be."

"Exactly. Before we let you go, I wanted to ask you about Nigel Holmwood. Any leads on his whereabouts yet?"

"None. He's not answering his calls, his emails, and even his assistant isn't answering the phone. Unless we hop a jet to London, I'm afraid we've hit a dead end on that."

Another one.

"Do you think your friend Daniel Ford can get you in to talk to Darius Cameron? He was Greg's division director."

"Darius Cameron? The former Secretary of State? Are you joking?"

Josh grinned at Willow. "Apparently I'm not. I didn't recall Cameron's name until Willow reminded me. If we can't get to him, then that's okay. He may not even know Greg. This file could be all fantasy."

For Peyton's sake, Willow hoped it was.

"I'll see what I can do." Chase sounded dubious. "We'll look him up. He retired from the public eye a few years ago."

"Thanks. Call us if Peyton wakes up."

"Will do."

Josh hung up and handed the phone back to Willow.

"How about that swim? After that call, I think we need to relax a little."

"I couldn't agree more. I'll change into my suit."

Josh gently captured her wrist before she could escape upstairs. "Then we'll need to sit down and decide where we go from here. The list is long and we need to prioritize."

Willow wrinkled her nose. "Remind me to kick Archer Caldwell right in the balls next time we see him."

Josh laughed, his blue eyes alight with mirth. "I'll make a note of that."

"I'm serious. That man just made our lives exponentially more difficult and he did it on purpose. He's not trying to help us, I know that for sure."

But he knew what he was doing. Willow wanted to know if the information in that file was the truth. That's what he'd been counting on.

JOSH DOVE IN the deep end and swam to the other side where Willow was sitting on the pool steps with a dog on each side. She didn't actually do much "swimming", instead floating around, throwing a small football for the dogs to retrieve, then retiring to sit in the waist-high water while he swam laps.

The physical exertion was something he'd sorely needed, not just his body but his mind as well. He was thinking and then over-thinking, making himself crazy. This was simpler, more straightforward. Move. Kick. Glide through the water. It was basic and his brain could quiet down and take a rest.

"You're making me tired," Willow said, sipping at her water bottle. "I thought you wanted to talk."

"After we swam. Looks like I'm done, and the dogs are finished. What about you?"

"I'm not a strong swimmer. I can dog paddle but that's about it."

His gaze ran down the sleek lines of her body, lingering on her long, shapely legs. The legs of a dancer. She'd told him and Chase what she did before she met her late husband and it was easy to see how she'd caught his attention. She was a beautiful, sexy woman who was also smart and kind.

And rich as hell. She wouldn't be interested in a simple guy like him. He wasn't poor but he wasn't wealthy. He came from a normal, middle class family. He liked pot roast and mashed potatoes. There was nothing special about him.

"I can teach you," he offered. "You have this great pool— you should know how to swim, if only for your own safety."

"I'm more of a lounge-by-the-pool-and-look-glamorous type," she laughed. "But I do appreciate the offer. I think you would have made a good teacher."

He couldn't imagine a career he was less suited for. "A teacher? Why?"

"Because you're calm. You would have kept your cool when some kid was being a smart aleck."

She didn't know him as well as she thought she did. "I doubt that very seriously. I work with animals because they're easier than actual people. As for kids, well, I don't have tons of patience so I can't see me in the teaching profession. What about you?"

Willow scratched the dogs behind the ears. "What about me?"

"Do you have patience for children?"

She shook her head. "I don't think so. Alex never wanted kids and I was fine with that. I always thought that I wouldn't want to bring children into this crazy world. After seeing what Evandria is trying to do, I'm more sure than ever."

Evandria. They needed to make some decisions.

He sat down next to her on the pool steps. "Have you given any thought to what you want to do?"

"It's just about all I've thought about."

"Come to any conclusions?"

Ruffling the dog's fur, she sighed in resignation. "I think we need to ignore what was in the files. For now, anyway. I think it could take us in the wrong direction. We should concentrate on learning more about Evandria and Alex's real assignment, not that fiction that Caldwell was trying to feed us."

"I agree but I know it wasn't easy for you to make this decision."

"It wasn't," she conceded. "But we need to stay focused."

He was glad to hear that because he had a few ideas as to how to proceed.

"Good. Let's talk about Alex's personal effects. You said you cleaned out most of them from the house but are there places you didn't touch?"

Frowning, she chewed on her bottom lip. "We have an apartment in New York but we didn't keep much there to begin with. There's also a condo in Vail. He liked to ski but there's nothing there but sweaters. And then there's the garage."

"The garage? Is it near here?"

She nodded. "We have some land up in Pasco County. He had a huge garage built for his car collection."

"And you didn't clean it out after he died?" Josh pressed.

Levering up from the stairs, she grabbed a towel lying on the lounge chair. "There was nothing to clean out. It's all cars and car parts. He didn't have any personal items there."

It was a long shot but worth the effort. "Take it from a guy. An automobile is personal."

She rolled her eyes and held out a towel for him. "I don't think you know how pathetic that sounds."

He took it from her and wrapped it around his waist. "I do but that's not the point. We'll start there."

"It's a waste of time."

It might be. Probably. Most of their investigation had been up to this point.

"Got a better idea?"

Her smile fell. "No, I don't. I guess it's worth a look but I want to go on record that I think it's a waste of time. It's a bunch of cars."

Not much enthusiasm but he'd take it.

At this point, he'd try anything. Everywhere they looked, they came up empty.

Chapter Eight

WILLOW TRAILED AFTER Josh, muttering under her breath as he pushed open the door of her late-husband's luxury garage. Josh was a lovely man but he had a problem listening to her when she spoke. For example, she'd told him there was nothing to find here, but he'd completely ignored her and came out here anyway.

Typical male.

Okay, maybe not so typical. For one, he was more laidback than most of the men she'd met. In the last few days, she'd made a concerted effort to get a reaction from him that wasn't an easy smile and a good-natured shrug. Basically, his attitude was *whatever makes you happy*. Frankly, it was a little unnerving.

"There's nothing here to see," she repeated again, knowing it wouldn't make a bit of difference. Josh was also a trifle stubborn, and when he got something in his head it wasn't easy to change his mind. At dinner the night before he wouldn't even take a bite of the fresh calamari, instead cringing in his seat in horror. The waiter had trouble hiding his grin of amusement as Willow assured her dinner companion that it did not taste like a rubber band. He hadn't believed her.

Turning on his heel, he was wearing that smile again. The one that said he only wanted to make her happy *but on this one little thing he was going to do whatever he damn well pleased.*

"You've made your objections clear. Loud, clear, and frequent."

Throwing up her hands, she perched on a stool next to a storage cabinet. "Go ahead. It's your time to waste. But I'm not too nice to say 'I told you' so later."

His brow went up, looking way too handsome at this particular moment. She wanted to be annoyed with him. "I'm shocked, Will. Shocked, I tell you."

It was hard to stay mad at Josh. Not only was he easy to be around most of the time, he was easy on the eyes as well. Dark hair cropped short, a strong, square jaw, piercing blue eyes, and a body that spoke of regular, hard workouts. He had a small scar on his upper lip that she'd been dying to ask him about but she didn't want him to think she'd been looking.

"The mechanic kept things here," Willow explained patiently as he began to walk the expansive garage in a grid fashion. Alex had collected automobiles and this building housed twenty-five of them, along with cabinets full of spare parts that he had picked up for vehicles he hadn't even purchased yet but wanted to. Spic and span, a person could eat off of this floor. It was a car junkie's wet dream. "So I doubt Alex did."

Josh looked over his shoulder. "The cars are still here."

"So? I never sold them because the accountant said they were a good investment. Do you think there's some hidden message in the letters and numbers on the license plates?"

"I never thought of that. It's an interesting theory."

Crossing her legs and huffing in frustration, she controlled the urge to hurl a wrench at his back. "It is not an interesting theory. It's a stupid theory and I was only joking. Don't patronize me, Josh."

He walked from the far end of the building to stand in front of her, his cool gaze taking her in from head to toe and making her warm in response. "I was not patronizing you, Will. I was being serious. He may have requested certain plates for these cars. It's something to look into, especially if we run out of leads."

"We don't really have any now. Only that we need to investigate the Evandria Council, and we'll get to do that this weekend."

"We also know that Evandria is some spooky shit," Josh replied. "New world order stuff. Anytime I hear someone tell me they want to change the world for the better I always worry. What do they think is better and what are they willing to do to make it happen?"

That was the million dollar question. Did Evandria have anything to do with Alex's death, and those of his two friends?

"Some people will do anything they can," Willow said, recalling a few of the customers that used to come into the nightclub where she'd danced. "And some won't do anything at all. The secret is to know the difference."

She'd learned fast. Who would be ruthless and cunning, men to stay far away from, and others who were kind and gentle. Those were men she felt comfortable with. When Alex had come into the nightclub that evening, he'd been somewhere in the middle. Handsome and dashing, he was no milquetoast but he wasn't callous or brutal either. Just enough of a bad boy to catch her eye, but romantic enough to capture her heart.

Hands on his slim hips, Josh surveyed the cars all neatly lined up in five rows of five. "So tell me about these vehicles. Which ones were Alex's favorite? Which was he thinking of selling? Are there any with funny stories attached to them like they belonged to someone famous?"

Standing, Willow studied the filled garage, trying to remember anything Alex might have said. "We didn't talk about them much, to be honest. Cars aren't exactly my thing." She wandered down one aisle and up another. She stopped at a baby blue T-bird, year unknown. "His favorite color was blue. I remember when he bought this one. He was excited."

"Good enough for me. I'll give it a go-over."

She didn't know what that meant. Everything except registration had been taken out of these vehicles. Maybe the original tire jacks and spares remained but unless Alex had been using them to send surreptitious messages, they were out of luck.

Josh grabbed the cart from the wall and used it to slide effortlessly under the car. "You see, Willow, a man who loves a car this much has an obsession. He put this collection together carefully, thinking about each and every acquisition. But I also bet he didn't let anyone around these cars unless he trusted them, am I right?"

She knelt down to peer under the car but all she could see were Josh's legs and the bottom of his khaki cargo shorts. "He had one mechanic he let work on the cars. He'd take his friends in here but he kept the place locked up if that's what you mean.

Not that I cared one way or another. It wasn't like I was dying to hang out here and discuss chrome."

Sliding back out, Josh grinned. "Once again, I'm shocked, Will. You don't have to stay for this. I have twenty-four more cars to check. This could take awhile."

"What are exactly are you even looking for? Maybe I can help."

"I don't know. I just know that these cars are pretty much all we have left of Alex's belongings. Bailey found the newspaper clippings in Frank's possessions…I was thinking maybe we'd find something in Alex's."

It made sense. Kind of. "So you're checking under the car? Do you think he wrote something on the exhaust pipe?"

"I'll say it again, I don't know. What I do know is I can't sit here and wait for something to happen. I won't let you get blown up like Peyton. We have to be proactive and that's what I'm trying to be."

She couldn't fault him for that. Technically, he was risking his life by guarding her. The package bomb that had put Peyton in a coma hadn't been an accident.

"Then I need to help. Tell me something I can do."

"Check the interior of every car. Not just the glove compartment but under the dash, in between the seats and in the trunk. I realize this is a long shot but I can't just sit idle. All the cabinets and drawers need to be checked as well."

"Then that's what I'll do." She pointed the cabinets behind her. "I'll start over there."

They had to start somewhere and it was as good a place as any.

"MY BACK IS killing me," Willow groaned as she finished checking the interior of the last car hours later. "And I found nothing. Can I say 'I told you so' now?"

Josh wiped his hands on a rag. "No, because I'm not done yet. And you shouldn't look that happy about it, by the way. We want to find something, remember?"

"I remember," she grumbled. "I wish we had found something. Honestly, I do."

"As I said, I'm not done yet. I have two more cars to check underneath. It's a real shame you don't drive any of these. They're just sitting here and rotting."

Maybe she should sell them, investment or not. He was right. There was probably a collector out there who would think they'd gone to heaven to have these cars.

"I have someone come in and start them on a regular basis."

"It's still a crime. These were meant to be driven, even if only on a track. I'm not suggesting you drive down to the drug store in it."

Confession time. "That's good because here's the thing…I'm actually a pretty awful driver."

He playfully winced. "Don't tell me you like to talk or text on your phone. That will get you killed."

"I don't," Willow said defensively. "I just don't like driving on busy highways. Local is all good though."

"I wouldn't suggest taking these cars on the freeway either."

He rolled under the last car and she was quiet while he finished. It had been a long evening and although she'd warned him they wouldn't find anything, she was glad they'd tried. It was better to be proactive than sit around waiting for someone to try to kill her. He came back out and hopped to his feet.

"I guess if we had found something it would have been too easy." Josh's gaze wandered around the large space. "I really thought something might be here. It would be the perfect place for a man to have personal things. A place his wife never goes, friends rarely visit. A man cave of sorts."

"It was his man cave. He liked to come here and sit in the cars. He said it helped him think."

"Where did he sit?"

She pointed to the Cadillac convertible. "He sat there, I think. That's where I found him once anyway."

Josh slid into the driver's seat of the automobile. "Like this?"

She nodded, not sure where he was going with all of this.

He ran his fingers around the steering wheel and across the arm rest. His other hand ran up and down the leather interior.

"Actually, he reclined the seat," she said. "Is that important?"

"I have no idea," Josh declared. "I'm just trying to become Alex, to think like he might have when he sat here."

Other than a Y-chromosome, Josh had little in common with Alex. Getting into his head wasn't going to be easy, if possible at all.

Reclining in the seat, he was now staring at the top part of the windshield and visor. His fingers plucked a garage door opener from the passenger visor and held it up.

"Do all the cars have these?"

"Uh, I don't remember. Hold on." She quickly walked up

and down the aisles. "No, none of them do but that would make sense if that was the car he drove most often."

"Let's see what it does."

He positioned it in front of the garage door and pressed the button.

Nothing happened.

"It probably needs new batteries. I saw some in one of these drawers when I was here before. Can you check what it needs?"

"It's probably double-A." He popped the back off and smiled. "Or not. Take a look at this."

Instead of batteries, there was a small gold key nestled there.

"I'll be damned," Willow breathed. "You were right. Something was hidden here."

"A man's cave is his castle." His fingers had to wiggle it to get it loose from where it was wedged. "He wouldn't hide anything where you could find it."

He held up the key for her inspection.

"What is it to?" she asked, taking it from him and checking it for markings.

"That's an excellent question, Will. Alex didn't want anybody to find the key but he also wanted to keep it close. We just have to figure out what it opens."

Chapter Nine

WILLOW HELD UP the key in her left hand as she munched on a slice of pizza with her right. They'd taken a break to have a late dinner and knowing they wouldn't sleep, they planned to try and find what the key might open even though it was getting quite late.

"It's small," she said, turning it over in her palm. "Too small to be to a door or a vehicle."

Josh reached for it and held it up to the light. "I think it's too small to even be to a locker at the bus station or a safety deposit box."

"You've seen too many movies. The hero and heroine find a key that fits a safety deposit box and all the answers lie within." She snorted. "We should be so lucky."

Setting the key on the table between them, Josh reached for another slice. "I wouldn't be upset if that were the case but you're right, things are rarely that simple. We need to look through Alex's possessions again."

"We already did," she pointed out. "And came up empty."

"But we didn't know what we were looking for and now we

do. We need to find something that has a small lock on it."

"Maybe he had one of those diaries with the tiny lock on the outside. 'Dear Diary, I kept more secrets from my wife today. She suspects nothing. Ha Ha.' How about that theory?"

"You're angry with him."

Tossing the crust back in the cardboard box, Willow took a drink of her wine. "Duh. I'm livid. I was his wife and he shared nothing with me. His whole life is a black box and I'm on the outside looking in. I always was, if the truth be known. I was never an insider at any time of my life. I think that's why I chose Alex. It was something I knew and was familiar with, orbiting around him like he was Louis the Sun King."

"Did he ever tell you anything about his life?"

She shrugged, pushing the pizza toward him, her stomach satisfied. "Sure, some things. His family traveled quite a bit so a lot of the furnishings in the house are from those trips. He had a story for each one that usually included a luxury resort and a phalanx of servants. Sometimes he'd talk to me about his so-called business deals. He was sort of an errand boy for his father and he'd have meetings all over the world. Funny what a person remembers years later. He always talked about the people or the place. He never talked about the business. I didn't care at the time because I thought it was boring."

"Maybe that's why he didn't tell you?" Josh suggested. "He knew that it wouldn't hold your interest."

"I always assumed it was because he found it so boring him-self. He didn't like working in general."

Alex had complained about it constantly as if he was digging ditches for a living.

"Must be nice not to have to," Josh laughed. "Anything else?"

"Not really. He told me just enough that I didn't find it strange but not enough that I knew a lot about him."

She'd been rather naive about a lot of things when she met Alex despite her profession. If she'd met him now, she doubted seriously that she would have given him the time of day. She'd come too far in her life to go back to what she had.

Closing the pizza box, Josh stood and placed it in the trash. "Those items he brought back from his travels, do you still have them here in the house?"

Where was Josh going with this?

"Sure, they were nice pieces. Alex let me decorate any way I wanted to so I haven't done much to the house since his passing."

"Let's take a look at them."

Wiping her hands on a napkin, she stood from her chair. She'd been looking at these items for years so she wasn't sure what Josh was going to find. "Okay, we'll take the tour."

Their first stop was a painting of a sunset in Bali that Alex had picked up when his family visited there when he was a teenager. Josh took it off the wall, checked it front and back, even checking the accent light above it. Nothing.

The second and third pieces were no better. Gorgeous pottery from New Mexico. However, they were simply vases. No locks to be found.

The fourth piece was a sculpture he'd picked up in Paris on a business trip about a year after they were married. It was hand-carved wood and depicted a man and a woman in an embrace.

Not as racy as Rodan's *The Kiss*, but sensual enough that Willow had loved it the moment he brought it home and set it on the table in the hall.

Reaching out, Josh's hand hesitated for a moment. He'd asked permission to touch each time she'd showed him an item and she appreciated his manners. "Yes, go ahead and look at it. But be careful, the housekeeper says it's heavy."

"You've never picked it up?"

He lifted it, running his fingers over the spine of the woman and around every inch of the statue. She inwardly shivered at the thought of those fingers caressing her own flesh. "Why would I? He bought it to put right there on that table and Fran dusts it once a week. I've never needed to move it around."

"Damn, it is heavy." A smile bloomed on his face and he turned the statue upside down. "If you had moved it, you would have seen this. Alex was all about the things he loved."

A lock. There was a small door on the base of the sculpture.

She hadn't known her husband at all. "Alex was a sneaky shit."

"Do you have the key?"

She'd tucked it in the pocket of her shorts and she pulled it out now, handing it to him. He held it up in front of him. "Here goes nothing."

At first it didn't fit, but then he turned it over and it slid in easily. He twisted the key and the door popped open. "Let's take this into the living room and see what's in it."

She had to practically run to keep up with his long strides. He might be acting all cool but he was as excited as she was and couldn't wait. They sat on the couch and he reached into the cavity and pulled out a black velvet bag, tied with a drawstring.

He handed it to her but her fingers were shaking so much she had trouble opening it, finally untying the knot and pouring the contents on the table. Four gold coins rolled out and she checked the bag to be sure it was empty.

"That's it. Coins."

Josh picked one up and examined it. "French coins, to be exact. Twenty francs, and I think that's Napoleon."

Picking one up, she felt its weight in her hand before taking a closer look. "I don't know what Napoleon is supposed to look like so I can only say that it just might be. It could also be Danny Kaye from that Christmas movie with Bing Crosby. I can't tell. Are they valuable?"

Josh chuckled and produced his phone from his pocket. "I don't know but we can check. I'm guessing they're worth something if he kept them hidden."

He held up the phone so she could see the screen and she leaned forward to get a better look. "I guess they are worth some money but not as much as I would have thought. We have more expensive pieces in plain view. Why did he hide these?"

Another mystery or had Alex overestimated their value?

Josh reached his hand into the cubby again. "I don't have the answer for that so let's see if there is anything else."

He pulled out a piece of paper in a messy, handwritten script. Three names along with addresses and phone numbers.

"That's Alex's handwriting," she said, reading through the list. Two of the names were familiar but one jumped out at her. "Look, here's Nigel Holmwood with an American address and phone number. I wonder if Bailey has tried this one."

"We'll send it to her. Do you recognize the other two?"

She sighed in frustration. Nothing about this case was ever easy. "They sound familiar but I don't know from where. I only know I've heard them before but it could be anywhere. From Alex, from his family, at a party. I can't remember."

Josh placed his warm hand on her knee. "Relax, honey. It might come to you later when you least expect it. But this is interesting in and of itself. Three people, who I assume are Evandria members, and their contact information. These might be homes no one knows about."

Maybe. Or maybe her late husband was simply weird. He hadn't been thinking too clearly during their marriage. Too much drugs and alcohol.

"I'm afraid to get my hopes up," she admitted. "We've hit so many dead ends."

He smiled and nudged her leg with his own. "Then we're due for some good luck."

Another optimist. They were going to drive her to drink.

He was reaching in again and pulling out another piece of paper. This one looked like a copy of an official government document, the photocopied seal at the bottom.

"It's a birth certificate," Josh said unnecessarily. She'd quickly figured out what this was. "Is that Alex's father's name right there?"

She nodded, emotion pouring through her veins. Alex had known about his half-brother and never said a goddamn word. "Ambrose Vaughn. That was Alex's father."

"Grant Daniel Hollister," Josh recited. "Born in Savannah thirty-eight years ago. Looks like he and Alex were born closely together."

Willow was shaking with anger. "I don't know whether to be more pissed off at Alex or his dad. Alex never mentioned a word and neither did Ambrose. And his wife must have known too. What a cluster."

Josh set the certificate down on the table and put his arm around her shoulders. She allowed herself to lean on his strength, wanting nothing more than to offload all this bullshit.

She couldn't do that, however.

This was her problem. He might be helping her and offering a shoulder to cry on but ultimately it wasn't his issue. He could get up and leave at any time, and hadn't her mother taught her that?

You can't depend on anyone to take care of you. You have to learn to take care of yourself.

She'd never forgotten that lesson. It had been the driving force behind her when she'd taken the job at the strip club. It might not have been the classiest career but she stood on her own two feet and paid her own bills. She didn't need some loser in her life. When she'd met Alex, she hadn't married him for his money. She'd married him because she'd fallen in love.

No fool like a fool in love.

"The rich are different," Josh said matter-of-factly. "That's what you said. Maybe this isn't a big deal to them. But it does mean one thing…that file Archer Caldwell gave us was right."

She groaned and let her head fall back so she was staring at the ceiling. "That means that Greg might truly have had another wife and kids. Shit. Just shit. We're going to have to tell her. I can't keep this from her."

"You will tell her. When the time is right. In the meantime, I'll get Ellis working on finding out who these two other people are. Maybe something he finds might jog your memory of where you heard their names."

Willow's phone buzzed and she grabbed it from the table. Bailey. Just in time to hear what they'd found and learned.

"Hey, I'm so glad you called. Josh and I have so much to tell you."

Bailey was breathing hard as if she'd run a long race. "That's great but first I have to tell you...Peyton is awake." The last part was delivered in more of a squeal than actual words. "She's groggy and kind of disoriented but she remembers her name, why she was here, and where she was when the bomb went off. The doctors say everything looks good for a full recovery."

"That's wonderful. Amazing."

It was. More than great and such a relief. Peyton was going to be fine and that was the best news Willow had heard in days.

It also meant that clock was ticking much faster than Willow had envisioned. She'd have to tell Peyton everything. And soon.

Chapter Ten

JOSH HESITATED AT the door of the exclusive clothing store. Willow had insisted he needed more than jeans, shorts, and t-shirts for their weekend at The Retreat but he wasn't sure why he had to buy his new wardrobe here. A shirt probably cost as much as his last mortgage payment.

"Can't we just go to the mall?"

Shaking her head, she nudged him through the entrance. "No, we can't. If these people are anything like the good citizens of Midnight Blue Beach that I've been dealing with all these years, they will be able to tell where you purchased your clothes. They care about these things so whether you like it or not, you have to care too."

"I don't like it," he replied stubbornly. "I hate shopping and this sounds even worse."

Willow sighed heavily. He felt a little guilty about how he was acting. She was trying to help but this seemed over the top.

"I get that. I understand that this won't be fun but please listen to me. If you look out of place with these people, they aren't going to trust you. They aren't going to treat you as one of them, and that means they won't talk to you. We won't learn anything and this will be two wasted days."

Dammit.

He couldn't argue her logic. It made perfect sense. But it didn't make it suck any less.

His gaze took in the sparse racks of clothes. This didn't look like any store he'd ever been in. They barely had anything to sell. Maybe this wouldn't take too long.

"What did you have in mind? What do I need?"

Another sigh. "Pretty much everything. A tuxedo for dinner and the party. A few shirts, a few pairs of pants, a pair of shorts, some tennis gear, and a few pairs of shoes. I think that's the minimum. I'll see what else as we go."

Whoa. Wait a cotton pickin' minute.

"That much?" he asked aghast. "I thought it would be a shirt and some pants. I don't need a tux, Willow. Hell, those can be rented."

Her eyes widened and she shook her head. "You cannot show up at The Retreat in a rented tuxedo. Let me repeat myself. They will be able to tell. You have to blend in, Josh. I respect that you like to be casual but this weekend isn't about what you – or I – want. This is about the case."

It was in his nature to go with the flow when the battle didn't seem worth fighting and today was no exception. He wouldn't win anyway and if he did, she would still be right.

"Fine," he conceded grudgingly. "This little vacation I'm taking is costing me a fortune."

She grabbed his arm and gave his shirtsleeve a tug. "This trip is on me. It's the least I can do."

Before Josh could reply, a man wearing an elegant suit seemed to float out of nowhere. "Mrs. Vaughn, how lovely to see you today. You look gorgeous as always. How may I help you?"

Willow smiled and accepted the air kisses on each cheek from the male who must work in the store in some capacity. "It's so nice to see you, Orsini. We're here to pick up a few things for Josh and myself. We have a weekend at The Retreat."

Instantly Orsini stood taller, his chin lifted. "Of course, we can handle that. Everything you'll need is here. If you'll just follow me back to the fitting rooms, I'll bring in a selection for you to try on." His gaze flicked to Josh. "I have your measurements but we'll need to take the gentleman's."

Willow nodded. "We'll be right back there. Can you give us just a minute?"

Orsini smiled cordially. "I'll be in the back. Take as long as you need."

Turning to Josh, Willow gave him a tight smile. "I'm paying for all of this."

Fuck, no. What did she take him for?

"I'm no kept man," he said softly, not wanting Orsini or anyone else to hear this conversation. "I pay my own way through life, Will."

"I know you do and I appreciate you wanting to. But let's be real here, the clothes here are insanely expensive and you don't want them anyway. Add in the fact that you're doing me a favor with all of this and I think I owe you. If I was paying someone to protect me it would have cost me thousands, and you cannot put a price on taking a leave from your own life to help me. Let me do this, Josh."

He didn't like this, not one little bit. "You wouldn't owe me as much as you're planning on spending today."

"Maybe. But we don't know how long this is going to go on, nor can we measure how much danger I've put you in. Just that alone is worth a few changes of clothes. Don't make this a bigger deal than it is. We need you to look a certain way for this weekend and I'm buying you the uniform. That's all it is...a uniform. If you joined the military they'd give you an outfit."

Shaking his head, he chuckled at her comparison. "Are you truly equating government-issued pants with whatever they have here?"

"It's the same idea," she insisted. "Aren't men all about the right tool for the job? This is the right tool."

Rolling his eyes, he groaned in defeat. "I don't suppose any of this is returnable?"

"You're going to love the clothes so much you won't want to return them."

She knew better than that.

"No, I won't."

"No...you won't," she laughed, linking her arm with his and leading him toward the back of the store. "Thank you for doing this. When we get there, you'll be glad you did."

The Retreat. That's what was important.

They might only have this one chance and they had to make the most of it. Somewhere inside The Retreat was the truth.

SHOPPING, AND ALL that went with it, took the better part of the day. By the time they returned back to the house they were hungry, tired, and in Willow's case, a little grumpy. She retreated to the back patio to make the call she'd been anxious for since last night.

For someone who had been in a coma not long before, Peyton sounded quite coherent and sharp. Bailey and Chase had brought their friend up to date on the happenings and she was anxious to be discharged from the hospital and come back home. For more reasons than she was sick of hospital food.

"My family showed up today," Peyton said. "I love them but they're already driving me crazy. Mother wants me to move into the family home when I get back. You know, until I feel better which she thinks will be about forty or fifty years from now. There's no way I'm doing that. I let myself get under their thumb one more time I'll never wriggle free."

There was a long story there that neither Willow nor Bailey had heard but would eventually. They'd known the relationship was fraught with tension but it appeared to be even more than that.

"You can stay with me," Willow offered. "I've got lots of room."

"I might take you up on that." A slight pause. "Would there be room for Ellis too?"

Now wasn't that interesting.

"Ellis? Is he coming down here as well?"

"He wants to make sure I'm protected until this is all over."

Willow had a feeling Ellis wanted Peyton as well. Whether the grouchy cop should have her was another matter altogether.

"He's welcome to stay too," Willow offered. "Lots of guest

rooms. I'd love to have you here. In fact, maybe Bailey and Chase should stay here too. All of us in one place might be easier to protect."

"Not a bad idea," Peyton replied, excitement in her voice. "I can't wait to come home. I'm so tired of being in the hospital and I was asleep for most of it. They've already taken blood from me twice today. They're like vampires in teddy bear scrubs."

"Do you know when they'll let you out?"

"A couple of days, and even then they want me to take it easy after that. Swelling of the brain isn't something you shake off quickly from what I've been told."

"No mountain climbing for you," Willow teased. "Maybe it's time to learn to knit."

"I already know but there isn't much call for knitted wear in Florida."

That was true. It was almost a hundred degrees outside with abysmal humidity.

"I'm just so glad to talk to you. I can't tell you how worried we all were."

"I'm glad to be talking," Peyton laughed. "I can't wait to hear about The Retreat and I can't wait to get down there and help. Just lying here is driving me crazy."

This simply wasn't the moment. Peyton had barely woken and to throw a spanner in her happiness was something Willow wasn't willing to do. Not yet. Let her be for another day. Tomorrow was good enough.

"Don't overdo it. Follow doctor's orders and you'll be up and around in no time. I'll call you tomorrow, okay?"

"Sure." There were low voices on Peyton's end of the phone.

"Wait, Ellis wants to speak to you."

Willow waited, listening as Ellis excused himself from Peyton's room.

"I have some information for you. Let me step outside the hospital for a minute where there's some privacy."

"Did you find Grant Hollister?"

There was a part of her that was hoping he might not actually be real and all of this was an elaborate hoax.

"I did and I've sent Josh all the particulars by email. But I wanted to let you know that he does exist. He lives in Savannah and is one of those genius millionaires. He invents things that people need like a better vacuum, but in his case he invented a better oil extraction method. Oil companies had a bidding war for his method and here's a fun fact…guess who won?"

Willow was heartily tired of weird coincidences. "The Vaughn family?"

"You bet," Ellis cheerfully agreed. "They leased it to one of the bigger oil conglomerates but there is definitely a link between Hollister and the Vaughns, and it's not just blood."

There was nothing more incestuous than big business. "I'd like to say that I'm surprised but I'm not. I have to even wonder if Grant Hollister truly came up with that idea or was this something that Ambrose gave his son so he could make money without actually having to give it to him."

"Interesting theory. It's possible."

At this point, Willow didn't think anything could shock her but she didn't want to say that out loud and challenge the universe. Not when it had been messing with her and her friends lately.

"Did you get anything on those other names?"

They had sounded so familiar but she still couldn't figure out where she'd heard them.

"Haven't had a chance, but when I get it, I'll send it to Josh. Are you two ready for The Retreat?"

Thinking back to the shopping spree she and Josh had that morning made Willow smile. She'd dressed him up and damn, had he looked fine. Handmade Italian shoes. An Alexander McQueen tuxedo that was being altered. Even a new haircut. Personally, she liked the other Josh better, the more casual one, but this new man would fit right in among the wealthy elite.

"We are, I think. We just have to tread lightly when asking questions."

"You'll do fine. Listen, I have to talk to you about something. I know you decided not to tell Peyton about the file today."

Bailey must have talked to Ellis about their decision.

"That's right. We thought she needed another day to rest up before we lay something like this on her. Why? Do you think we did the wrong thing?"

Not that she cared what Grouchy Pants thought. This wasn't his decision to make no matter what he might think. He wasn't her boyfriend or even a person in her life. He barely knew Peyton even if he had sat with her almost twenty-four hours a day while she was in a coma.

"Not at all," he assured her. "I was thinking though that maybe the news should come from me. As the cop on the case, you see. I can be more detached and perhaps keep the situation from becoming too emotional."

Willow wasn't sure unemotional was the road to go down. Peyton needed the opportunity to be upset, angry. But she also didn't need Willow's own emotions spilling out onto the situation. She had enough of her own to deal with.

"What did Bailey say?" Willow asked after a beat. Bailey was the most down to earth, common sense one of the three of them.

"She thinks it might be a good idea. Just so you know, this isn't the first bad news I've had to deliver. As a detective I've had to inform loved ones when a friend or family member has been hurt or killed."

Was she a chicken for being relieved?

"It sounds like a good idea but let me talk to Bailey first, okay? I just want to make sure we're doing the right thing by Peyton."

"Absolutely. One of you can let me know what you decide."

Willow hung up and went back inside the kitchen where Josh was preparing dinner.

"Peyton sounds wonderful and Grant Hollister is real."

Nodding, Josh minced up garlic for the pasta sauce. "That's good about Peyton, and well, the other is what it is. I'm not surprised about Hollister."

"There's more about him. Do you want to hear it?"

Josh pushed out a stool with his foot without even a pause in his chopping. "Have a seat and tell me all about it."

She perched on a chair to observe his culinary skills. "Can I help?"

He eyed her suspiciously, which she knew was well-earned. She was a terrible cook.

"Absolutely not. You stay on that side of the island and I'll stay on this side. Don't touch anything. Just talk. Why don't you pour us some wine? We need to talk about the weekend too. Tomorrow is going to be a busy day getting ready for it."

The Retreat. Willow was excited to go but scared too. These people might know more about her husband than she did.

Did they know everything about her?

Chapter Eleven

THE RETREAT WAS everything and more that Willow had thought it would be. Lush green lawns. Rows of perfectly manicured hedges and flowerbeds. The sound of tennis balls bouncing against a tautly strung racquet. The scent of sunscreen mixed with chlorine and rum. The overwhelming aroma of money and power.

"Here goes nothing," Josh muttered as he pulled up in front of the large resort. "Are you ready?"

"As ready as I'll ever be. If I didn't mention it before, I'll say it now. You look great."

They say clothes made the man but Josh made those clothes look fine indeed.

"You know what they say about fine feathers," Josh snorted. "Wait until someone asks me what I do for a living and finds out I'm just a humble vet."

Honestly, Willow thought it was a terrific career and one she would have liked to have pursued if her early life had been different.

"Tell them you're the pickle king of Texas. They won't know

the difference."

Archer Caldwell was standing in front of the large resort wearing light linen trousers and a loose-fitting cotton button-down shirt. The older man smiled and waved before instructing the valet to take care of their car. He helped her out of the passenger side and lifted her hand to his lips. What was supposed to be charming came off kind of sleazy.

Ick.

"I'm so glad you could make it this weekend. The bellman can take your bags up to your suite while I give you a tour. Unless you're too tired. We can do this another time."

Willow shook her head. One of the first things she and Josh had on their to-do list was to see the grounds and now Archer was offering to help them with that.

"We'd love a tour. It's very kind of you to offer."

"It's no trouble." Archer ushered them into the resort, the automatic doors opening with a whoosh and the chill of the air conditioning bringing out goosebumps on her skin. "The fact is I love showing off the community we have here. We're very proud of it and I think rightly so."

"It's quite impressive," Josh observed. The lobby was four stories high with a large fireplace in the corner – the floors all of marble with comfortable couches and chairs scattered about. On one side was the check-in counter and the opposite end boasted a bar with a small string quartet playing background music. "When was all this built?"

"Good question." Archer slapped Josh on the back. "This particular building was completed about ten years ago but each structure on the property has its own timeline. Originally there were about a dozen bungalows along with the tennis courts and the swimming pool. The Clubhouse was completed about a year later and it is now the oldest building on The Retreat as the bungalows were torn down about fifteen years ago and replaced with a large spa and library."

Willow immediately wanted to ask for a tour of the Clubhouse but it would be a mistake to appear too eager or to have an agenda. Biding her time would be worth it.

"How many buildings are there?" Josh asked. "How much property does Evandria own here?"

"We own about a hundred thousand acres but only a small part of it is developed. There are about twenty-five buildings if you count the storage sheds and garages for the equipment. But we're always planning to improve and expand. Let me show you the rest of the resort. We have five dining rooms but there is also twenty-four hour room service."

Caldwell didn't appear to be in any hurry as they toured the resort, the pool, the tennis courts, and stables. Willow was almost vibrating with anticipation as they approached a three story brick building with white columns on the front. It was a smaller version of the main building.

"This of course is The Clubhouse. The officers of Evandria have their meetings here plus we do have a small staff that takes care of records and dues, so their offices are located here as well."

So far he'd taken them inside of every building but he made no move to do the same here. Not a shock as she'd read that most members hadn't even been inside.

Willow gave Archer what she hoped was a guileless smile. "Are we going to tour this also?"

"I'm afraid not. It's only for staff and officers. But we can walk through the spa and fitness center and get you both set up for a massage. You'll want to be relaxed for the barbecue tonight."

A massage wasn't nearly as interesting as a secret conclave but for now it would have to do. Perhaps later, when everyone was partying and they had the cover of darkness, they could sneak over and take a peek.

Josh smiled easily and wrapped an arm around Willow's shoulders. "Lead the way."

If he could play it up, she could too. "I agree. I can't wait to see the spa."

Was Archer Caldwell fooled? Probably not.

Did that mean they weren't going to try and get in The Clubhouse? No.

It only meant that they needed to be careful and sneaky. The one thing they'd learned was that Evandria was always watching and listening.

AFTER SWEATING TO death in the trousers and shirt Willow had made him wear, Josh was ready for a shower. If they just hung out in the room, maybe she'd let him wear his shorts and t-shirt.

The room. Another conundrum. While it was a suite and a fancy one at that, it had one bedroom and one gigantic bed. He wasn't sure if the couch folded out but he could always camp on it regardless. He'd slept in worse his entire freshman year of college. That bed had been pure torture. He'd almost flunked out on purpose simply so he could sleep at home and get a good's night rest. Eventually he'd figured out that he could crash in friends' rooms and apartments.

Willow went straight to the wet bar and pulled out two cans of soda. "So what's the plan for tonight?"

Josh held up his hands and shook his head, placing a finger over his lips. They had to assume they were being listened to pretty much everywhere they went except when they were outside and far away from a structure.

At first she frowned, but then understanding crossed her features and she nodded, pouring the soda into two glasses.

"What time is our massage scheduled for?" she said, a trifle too loudly which made Josh wince and Willow flinch at the sound of her own voice.

"Four o'clock. We have an hour to relax."

She handed him a glass along with a piece of paper and a pen. Smart girl.

"I might shut my eyes for a few minutes then."

He clicked the pen open and scribbled a note on the paper.

Assume we're under surveillance at all times.

Willow nodded and took the pen from him.

What about The Clubhouse?

She handed him the pen.

Tonight we'll take a closer look. Our best chance is probably one of the staff.

She reached for the pen but he stopped her, needing to say one more thing.

Your job is to talk to people and be charming. Learn what you can about Alex. My job is the covert sneaking. Don't confuse the two.

Rolling her eyes, she snatched the pen from his hand.

Bossy. If I see a chance to check things out I'm going to take it.

He didn't even bother to write down his answer, mouthing it instead. She'd understand him with no problem.

No. You won't.

Her lips turned into a mutinous line but he was having none of it. He shook his head again and tossed the paper and pen on the coffee table. Willow was a handful but he was one of six children and he'd been teased, berated, and generally harassed by the best.

She stood and stuck out her tongue. "Didn't you want to take a shower?"

"I certainly did," he replied smoothly. "You should try and catch a quick nap."

"You should too."

He bent down to whisper in her ear so no one else would overhear. "In the mood you're in, you might murder me in my sleep."

Glancing over his shoulder as he grabbed his bag and headed into the bedroom, he could see Willow was smiling and laughing, looking way too beautiful. He shouldn't be noticing things like that. He needed to keep his mind firmly on the task at hand. Keeping her safe and getting information about Alex and the other men.

A little fun in the sheets wasn't on the menu.

THIS WASN'T LIKE any barbecue that Josh had attended. There were no guys hanging around the grill drinking long necks, talking sports and girls. There were no paper plates and plastic forks and tablecloths. There wasn't a boom box plugged into the nearest outlet blasting out tunes from their youth. This was an entirely different animal altogether.

The only thing this shindig had in common with cookouts from his past was it was held outdoors. That was it. Unless you counted the plethora of cooking staff that were bustling around an outdoor grill that had to be at least thirty feet long. Maybe the smell of charred meat could be counted too.

"You were right." Josh tugged nervously at the sleeve of his tuxedo. The last time he'd worn one had been at his brother's wedding last year. It hadn't been nearly as nice as this one. "Everyone is in eveningwear. I stand corrected in ridiculously comfortable shoes."

"I told you," Willow laughed. "This little soiree is about seeing people and being seen. Mark my words, business connections and deals will be made tonight."

"Are they all like this?" he sighed, grabbing two glasses of champagne from a passing waiter.

Willow shook her head. "Not at all. Some are down to earth and you'd never know they were filthy rich. Wonderful, generous people without a judgmental bone in their bodies. It all depends. But I had a feeling that this place and this group of people...well, they're into the money and power angle. So just relax and mingle. In that tuxedo you're going to fit right in."

"You don't look so bad yourself. I think you're the most beautiful woman here tonight."

By far. Willow had an innate sense of style and she dressed to enhance her already stunning good looks. Classy and sexy at the same time, she didn't rely on hundreds of carats of diamonds and plunging necklines. Tonight she was wearing a strapless scarlet silk dress that showed off her gorgeous, long legs. Her curls were piled up on top of her head with a few stray ones framing her heart-shaped face. When she'd stepped out of the bedroom this evening, ready to leave, he'd had a hard time stopping himself from showing her just how beautiful he thought she was.

"I think you kissed a blarney stone," she joked back, but a delicate flush invaded her cheeks. She might not believe his flattery but she liked it. "There are dozens of flat-out gorgeous woman here tonight. Women who, by the way, hate my guts. This should be interesting."

"I take it you recognize some of the faces here tonight. But hate your guts? That sounds harsh. Why?"

"Because I'm not one of them. I was a dancer who took off my clothes and they'll never let me forget it. They think I married Alex for his money."

He hadn't known Willow long but he knew she would never do that. "But you didn't."

"I didn't," she agreed. "But I'm not going to beg and plead for their friendship or approval. I have a few trusted friends and that's good enough for me. I won't spend my time hoping for table scraps. I did that too much in my youth."

He wanted to ask her about her past but she'd been clear that it was a topic that was firmly off limits. He could respect that. He didn't like going on and on about his childhood either, although there hadn't been anything wrong with it. His was boring and normal but he had a distinct feeling that hers was not. Not wanting to bring up any bad memories, he steered the conversation back to the party.

"How many of these people do you recognize?"

She looked up at him and smiled. "About half of them. I'm surprised there's anyone left in my little town to be honest."

"It may not be like this all the time," Josh warned. "Caldwell could have invited them just because you were here."

"To intimidate me? It won't work."

Archer probably knew that too.

"Or to watch over you. Talk to you. Find out what you know and what you don't know."

Sipping her champagne, her eyes were alight with mischief. "There's one thing wrong with that theory. These people wouldn't spit on me if I was on fire in the middle of the street. They'll never come and talk to me. They wouldn't lower themselves."

He could see two couples making a beeline for them, determination all over their faces. They'd been spotted like a gazelle at dinnertime.

Here come the lions.

"Are you sure about that? Because brace yourself, honey, it looks like we have company."

Chapter Twelve

YESTERDAY THESE PEOPLE wouldn't have given Willow the time of day. Today they acted like they were her best friend.

Evandria really was powerful.

She and Josh had mingled, chatted, had dinner and a few drinks, then mingled some more. Most of the guests seemed rather benign, more interested by something shiny than by power or secrets. From the few delicate questions she'd posed, most of them regarded Evandria as a benevolent organization where they could spend time and make connections with like-minded people. When Willow casually mentioned their reputation for secrets, they simply laughed.

Josh had drifted off to freshen their cocktails when she was approached by none other than Bernard Baldwin. Now that she knew he'd been some sort of mentor to Alex in the Environmental Division, she had even less respect for the man. If that was possible. She hadn't liked him when she'd met him and now she knew why. Whatever bogus leadership he'd given Alex hadn't done any good.

"Willow," Bernard's voice boomed across the lawn, causing a few heads to whip around. "It's so good to see you. How long has it been?"

She knew exactly how much time had passed.

"Five years. Alex's funeral."

His expression turned suitably sad. "Such a sorrowful day. You were to be admired though. You stayed strong through the service, a real tower of strength."

She scrunched up her forehead and pursed her lips. "Was I a tower of strength before or after you agreed with Candace and Ambrose that they should fight Alex's will? That a greedy little gold digger like me shouldn't get a cent?"

The man should get an Oscar. He didn't even break a sweat at her sarcastic tone or words.

"I think you misunderstood the situation," he replied smoothly. "I never said that. Candace and Ambrose were justifiably upset so I was simply supporting them in their time of need. In the end, they didn't fight you and isn't that what's important?"

"No," she shot back. "That's not what was important but I don't think you'll ever understand, so let's just move along. I didn't know you were a member, Bernard, but Archer told me that you were Alex's mentor when he first joined."

He waved his half-full glass and smiled. "I would hardly call myself a mentor. I was his division head and very lucky to have him on my team. Alex was very devoted to our mission."

"And what mission was that?"

"The preservation and allocation of this earth's natural resources. He worked tirelessly toward that goal."

Funny how she never saw any of that. "What exactly did he do?"

"All sorts of things. As I said, I was lucky to have a man like him. I don't have to tell you how passionate he was about the issues he cared about."

It was as if they were talking about two different people. Two different Alex Vaughns, walking around in one body.

Willow decided to go for the jugular. She'd played it safe all night but Bernard was someone who might have a clue as to what was going on with her late husband. He'd been high enough in Evandria's pecking order to know some of their secrets.

"Was his brother Grant also in your division?"

Bernard froze for a split second but recovered quickly. This guy was good. "I don't know what division Grant joined. But you can ask him yourself if you like."

It felt like someone had taken a baseball bat to her sternum, knocking the breath from her lungs. "He's here?"

Amazingly, she sounded almost normal.

"I'm told he'll be here tomorrow," Bernard shrugged. "He usually comes in early in the morning and lands at the airstrip. He flies his own plane."

Josh sidled up next to her, a drink in each hand. "Sorry it took so long. I met Archer on the way back. He invited us to go horseback riding Sunday morning before we head back to town. I told him I had to check with you."

She wouldn't turn down any time with Caldwell. "I think that sounds like a wonderful idea."

"He said to let the front desk know and they'd get a message to him."

Josh was eyeing Bernard up and down as he handed Willow her glass. "Josh, this is Bernard Baldwin. Bernard, this is Dr. Josh Coleman."

The older man's brows went up. "Medical doctor or PhD?"

"Veterinary medicine, actually."

Baldwin nodded. "I'm told it's harder to get in veterinary school than it is medical school."

"That's true."

The conversation seemed to falter. Josh wasn't one to toot his own horn and from his stiff as a board stance he'd taken an instant dislike to Bernard. The oil tycoon scowled at his glass and then looked around, snapping his fingers at a passing waiter.

"Get me a new drink," Baldwin growled at the youth. "Scotch. Neat. And don't take all damn day."

Willow had seen this behavior from him before. He treated most people like dirt under his feet. Another reason she hadn't liked him much.

"The kid's just trying to do his job," Josh said between gritted teeth. "I've always taken the road that says you shouldn't piss off people that serve you food or drink. You might find something unwanted in that scotch, like a big wad of spit."

If anyone had spoken to Bernard Baldwin like that, it hadn't been recently and he clearly didn't like it. His expression hardened and his fingers tightened on his empty highball glass.

"Everyone needs to do their job. If they do that, they won't be in trouble."

"And your job is to tell him how to do his job?" Josh wrapped his arm around Willow's waist, his hand on her hip.

"How about a walk?"

"I'd love one." She wiggled her fingers in a buh-bye motion. "It was…interesting seeing you again, Bernard. Have a lovely evening."

When they were about twenty feet away, Josh leaned down to whisper in Willow's ear. "That guy is a real asshole. I don't know how I'm sure of that since I only spent a few minutes in his company, but I know."

"He is," she confirmed with a little laugh. "Believe it or not, that was one of his better moments. Usually he's far more insufferable and arrogant."

"How charming."

Willow stopped and pulled Josh away from the milling guests. "I'm glad I ran into him. I asked him about Grant. Apparently he'll be here in the morning."

She watched several emotions flit across Josh's handsome features, the last one resignation.

"Is there any way to talk you out of walking up to him and introducing yourself? We need to play this the right way. We don't want to put him on the defensive."

"I completely agree. I'm going to keep my distance until we decide how to approach him."

Laughing out loud at Josh's shocked expression, she turned on her heel and headed for the resort.

"Where are you going?"

After seeing that waiter, she'd had an idea. It might be a waste of time but she thought it was worth a try.

"The kitchen. Maybe someone who works here remembers Alex."

WILLOW STOOD OUTSIDE the door of the bustling kitchen, watching servers rush in and out of the swinging doors. Now that she was here, she wasn't sure how to proceed. Did she waltz in and pass around a photo of Alex? Did she pretend she needed something else, and then try and bring him into the conversation somehow?

"Ma'am, can I help you? Is there something you need?"

Startled, Willow swung around to see a petite redhead, probably in her mid-twenties, wearing a server's uniform.

"Can I help you, ma'am?" the girl repeated.

Think. Think. Think. And make it fast.

"An ice pack." Willow's fingers tightened around her purse. "I need an ice pack. My husband was playing tennis earlier and hurt his finger but only just now told me about it. You know how men can be."

The girl relaxed and smiled. "Of course we can help you with that but there is a twenty-four hour medical team on staff. I'd be happy to call them for you."

Knowing this place, it was a clone of *Marcus Welby, MD.*

"He'd be mortified if anyone knew he'd injured himself. Besides, it looks quite minor. I think some ice should do it."

"We have a first aid kit in the kitchen. I know it has an ice pack in it."

The girl moved toward the door and Willow didn't hesitate, stepping right behind her. This was her ticket into the kitchen.

Get her talking.

"I'm Willow, by the way. What's your name?"

The server led the way through the labyrinth of shelves, counters, and workers. The hum of conversation seemed to go quiet as Willow followed.

"Sherry. Willow's a pretty name. Kind of unusual."

Sherry brought them to a double sink near the back of the kitchen and dug into the cabinet on the wall.

"Thank you. Sherry is a lovely name too." Willow's gaze darted around the room, and she could feel the weight of a dozen or so set of eyes on her. It felt like every single person was looking straight at her. "Have you worked here long?"

"A few years." Sherry placed a large, white plastic case on the counter. "Now let's see. One ice pack coming up."

"Sherry!" A woman's sharp voice caught Willow's attention. Around her own age, the female wasn't in a uniform but she wasn't in evening clothes either. A blue pencil skirt and white blouse paired with sensible shoes. A scowl. Maybe the dining manager? "I'll help Mrs. Vaughn. You need to get back out to the party."

Face flushed, Sherry nodded and hurried out of the kitchen, leaving Willow with Nurse Ratchet.

"I'm sorry," Willow apologized although she really wasn't. This woman knew who she was but they'd never met. "I was hoping to get an ice pack for my husband's finger. He played tennis this afternoon and kind of overdid it. My name's Willow, by the way."

The woman didn't offer her name in return. She flipped open the plastic case and rummaged through the band-aids and burn cream. "You are supposed to call the medical office."

So much for friendly.

"Hubby was a little embarrassed, I think, and I just can't say no to him. Who could say no to this cutie?"

Willow held up her phone so the woman could see the screen. She'd pulled up a scanned-in photo of Alex, hoping to get a reaction, but the female gave it a cursory glance before turning back to the first aid kit.

Grabbing a foil pack, the woman smacked it against the countertop and then squeezed it between her fingers. "The chemicals are mixing so it should get cold."

"Thank you," Willow said, taking the cold pack. This entire field trip to the kitchen hadn't turned out quite like she'd planned. "I appreciate the help."

With one last glance, Willow turned on her high heel and exited through the swinging doors, only to find Josh waiting on the other side, wearing a worried frown.

"I was about to come in there and get you."

Rolling her eyes, she shoved the cold pack into her purse. "I was fine although I feel really dumb. I walked in there without a plan or a clue. Stop me next time I do that, okay?"

Josh snorted. "Will you listen?"

She was going to have to learn how because this had been an utter disaster. Josh was right. They needed to plan every move.

"If I don't just remind me of tonight. I'll get the message."

He was grinning, that cat that ate the canary smile she loved so much. "Are you going to ask me what I was doing while you were batting zero in the kitchen?"

Sighing, she decided to humor him. "Josh, what were you doing while I was in the kitchen? Pissing off billionaires again?"

"That was the plan," he smirked as they wandered into the lobby. "But then I saw one of the staff leave the party and head for The Clubhouse. I followed them and saw how they access the building. A key card. All we need is to get one of those and we're in."

"All we need," she repeated. "You make it sound so simple. Where do you propose we get one of these magical key cards?"

Josh tapped her on the nose playfully. "Simple, honey. We steal it."

Chapter Thirteen

"YOU HAVE AN amazing backhand. Do you play tennis a lot?"

That question was posed by a pretty redhead in a sunshine yellow tennis dress and white sneakers. She was also currently flirting with Josh, leaning over the tennis net and looking up at him, batting her eyelashes.

"When I get a chance," Josh replied. "Not as much as I would like to."

It was Willow's turn to serve in this mixed doubles match and Janice, the wife of a banker, spent much of the time in between points and games coming on to Josh. Right in front of said banker who didn't seem to care one way or the other. He had what looked like a permanent smile on his face no matter how badly they were losing or how his spouse was embarrassing him.

Janice reached up and squeezed Josh's bicep and giggled like a schoolgirl. "I don't believe it. With muscles like that, you must play every day."

Shrugging, Josh bounced a stray tennis ball on the court before tucking it into the pocket of his shorts. "I work out as much as I can. Mostly I run."

Holy crap on a cracker. Was he flirting back with this Mary Sue?

Janice's gaze swept Josh's tanned and muscular legs. "I can see that."

For fuck's sake. Were they here to solve a mystery or get Josh laid?

"Are we ready?" Willow asked, her voice sharper than she'd intended but it seem to do the trick. Janice got back into position and so did Josh, but not before throwing a quizzical glance over his shoulder.

Did he really not know why she was impatient? If they'd spent half as much time playing tennis as they'd spent flirting, this match would be done.

Even if he didn't know why, Josh appeared to get the hint. She and Josh could have creamed the other duo but Willow wasn't that type of player. They won the set with a respectable six to two.

"You guys are so good," gushed Janice as they packed up their racquets and balls. "We are definitely going to want a rematch next time we come. You are going to join, aren't you, Willow? This organization really needs someone like you. You're so dedicated to the charities you work with and Evandria can help you do that on a much larger scale."

Willow had no intention of joining unless she needed to for some reason to get at the truth, but Janice didn't need to know that. For all intents and purposes, she wanted everyone to think she was a heartbeat away from being one of them.

"I just can't believe I waited this long to join. Evandria is such an amazing organization. But of course, I'm still learning about it. What have you gained and learned from being a member?"

Janice seemed to perk right up at the question. Caldwell had paired them with her and her husband and now Willow could see it was for a specific reason. They were the rah-rah cheerleaders out to pull her to the dark side. Used car salesmen showing her the vanity mirror when she wanted to check out the engine.

"I'm so glad you asked. Being part of Evandria has exposed me to the societal injustices in our world. So many people go to sleep not knowing where their next meal is coming from while people like you and I live in luxury. We have to make sure that everyone has a chance in this world, not necessarily to become wealthy, but they need opportunities to make a good living. I want to be part of that."

It sounded rehearsed, although Willow didn't disagree with the sentiment.

The banker husband Thad finally spoke. "Evandria has given me more confidence. Because of the challenges that I've taken on through them, I've gained so much self-awareness. It's the kind of thing they don't teach in school. It can only be found when a person is placed out of their comfort zone."

"Comfort zone?" Josh repeated. "Can you expand on that?"

Thad nodded eagerly. "Some of the guys here like to go on adventures. Sort of Outward Bound kind of trips. We climb mountains and cliffs, sail, ski, hike, play cowboy and herd cattle. Anything and everything that gets us out of our business suits and the office. We challenge our bodies and our mind with survival trips. Evandria believes very deeply that challenge and sacrifice make us better people. When you complete one of these physical challenges you're awarded a gold coin as a memento."

That explained the four gold coins they'd found, although Willow had a hard time believing Alex had completed four physical challenges. Maybe it was before they'd met.

But one word jumped out at Willow. "Sacrifice? What kind of sacrifice?"

"Monetary, for one," Thad replied, stuffing his racquet in the case. "By paying our dues we are giving back to the society that has already bestowed much on us. Also, we sacrifice our physical comfort. It helps bring us back down to earth and remind us of the suffering we seek to alleviate on this planet."

Janice's expression turned serious and she placed a hand on Willow's shoulder. "I truly hope you join us here. What we are doing is so important and I'd hate for you to miss out on something this life-changing. Alex was so enthusiastic and a great asset to the organization. I just know you would be too."

Hold everything. This is not a drill.

"You knew Alex? Did you know Frank Scott and Greg Nelson too?"

Janice was nodding but Thad stepped in between her and Willow. Janice must have gone off script.

"Everyone knew Alex," he said simply. "He was a great man. Now how about we go get some drinks?"

Willow and Josh politely declined, feigning a business call that needed to be made. They headed back to the room but didn't say anything until they were in the elevator.

"We actually do need to call Peyton," Josh reminded her.

"Ellis will have told her by now."

Willow rubbed her temples. "I wasn't kidding about the headache either. Just listening to them spout memorized propaganda is enough to make me nauseous."

The elevator doors slid open. "We were set up with them for a reason, that's for sure. Archer wants you as a member."

They walked down the hall to their room. "Why? Because of my money or to shut me up and keep me from finding anything?"

"Maybe a little bit of both."

"Have we bitten off more than we can chew here, Josh?" They halted outside of their room. They wouldn't take this conversation inside where there might be listening devices planted. "Evandria has their fingers in the pockets of many of the most influential people in the world."

Josh rubbed the key card between his fingers, clearly deep in thought. "Do you know how they finally got Al Capone? What finally brought him down?"

Al Capone? What did this have to do with anything? If they'd talked about him in history class, she hadn't been paying any attention.

"Bootlegging or murder, I would assume."

Josh shook his head. "Tax evasion. They had an FBI agent who was an accountant. This guy combed through Capone's books and found that he hadn't been reporting his income. It's in the movie *The Untouchables*. You've never seen it? Sean Connery and Kevin Costner? Fantastic movie. You have to see it."

"I'll put it in my Netflix queue. Now what does this have to do with Evandria?"

"Honey, a little mousy accountant brought down an organized crime empire. I don't think it's out of the realm of possibility that you and I learn a few secrets. We're not trying to destroy Evandria. We just want a little information."

Willow wasn't so sure they could have one without the other.

"ARE YOU OKAY?" Willow asked Peyton. It was later that afternoon and she'd put off calling her friend for as long as she could. Ellis had already sent a text to Josh that he'd told Peyton everything they'd found out.

"I'm fine," Peyton assured her. "I know you probably think I'm shocked or crying or something even more dramatic but I'm actually quite calm. I'm not really all that surprised. Greg has done some really shitty things to our marriage over the years and this is just one more. If what Ellis showed me is true, I actually feel sorry for the other woman. She's not legally married to him and they have children. From what I can tell, she didn't inherit any money to help raise those kids. Greg was just as much of a deadbeat with her as he was with me. Hell, maybe more."

It didn't go unnoticed by Willow that Peyton said Greg had done bad things to "their marriage" and not to her specifically. Peyton had the good sense to separate herself from her late husband's behavior. It didn't matter who Greg was with, he would have acted that way no matter what.

"I'm glad you're taking this so well. Honestly, I didn't want to tell you because you've been through so much lately and this was one more piece of crap that you didn't need."

"Greg lived for himself and his pleasures. Drinking, gambling, women, and painting. He was the quintessential tortured artist who thought that he was owed something by the world because he suffered for his art. Only he made others suffer around him. The fact that he was selfish enough to involve two women and by God, two small children into his games sadly doesn't shock me in the least."

"Do you want to find her and talk to her?"

A heavy sigh on the other end of the phone. "That's the big question, isn't it? I don't really have the answer yet. I think I should do something for those kids. Set up a trust fund or buy them some stocks. Something that a father would have done if he'd had the sense God gave a goose. Greg wasn't a person who thought about tomorrow much. He lived entirely in the present."

"You're taking this way too calmly."

Peyton laughed. "Probably. Maybe I'll have some sort of breakdown later but I'm just so happy that I'm gaining strength and getting better that I can't be all mad. Surviving a bomb blast gives a person perspective. Greg had been lying to me for years. All this does is up the ante a little."

It was an interesting contrast. Alex had done his dirty deeds pretty much out in the open in their little town. Even if he had tried to hide them, he wouldn't have been able to. The gossip mill was ruthless and Willow had heard her share of raunchy tales starring her one and only beloved.

Greg, on the other hand, had tried to hide what he was doing. Making up stories, lying about every little thing, and yet feeling as if he was due the life of debauchery he had lived.

Both men had a warped sense of entitlement while Frank, Bailey's husband, had pulled away from people. Kept to himself and never reached out to other human beings.

These three men had once been like brothers. They still didn't know what had pulled them apart. Another mystery to solve.

"All I know is if I were in your shoes I'd be pissed off. Of all the secrets our husbands kept from us, this one is pretty crappy."

"No, what he did to those kids was crappy," Peyton said. "I can't even imagine what he was thinking having children. He never wanted kids with me and he made that clear from the day we met practically. Were they both accidents?"

"Too much wine and no drug store nearby? Probably."

Willow sounded cynical but after her years with Alex, it sometimes reared its ugly head.

"He liked his wine," Peyton laughed. "And he loved the attention from women."

"All men like that. You should have seen Josh this morning on the tennis court lapping up the giggles and batted eyelashes of some redhead. It was nauseating."

There was a beat before Peyton replied. "Oh really? Now that is interesting. Was she attractive?"

Willow shrugged, even though Peyton couldn't see her. "I suppose so, although I think she might have had too much Botox."

Clearing her throat, Peyton choked out a laugh. "Catty. Are you sure you aren't maybe a little jealous that he was enjoying her attention?"

"I was not. No way."

"You know, it's okay to be attracted to a man," Peyton explained, patience in her tone. "From what Chase has been saying Josh is a great guy. He'd never treat you like Alex."

There it was. The elephant in the room that had been nudging her with its trunk. She didn't want a repeat of her marriage. She simply could not do that again.

"I'm sure he wouldn't but I'm not interested. Josh is not my type."

There was a clearing of a throat behind her and Willow whirled around to see Josh standing there in his khaki shorts and blue t-shirt. His own clothes. He must have snuck them into his suitcase when she wasn't looking.

He didn't say a word, simply walked round the sofa and heading straight for the wet bar where he grabbed a beer from the little refrigerator. Feeling her cheeks suffuse with heat, she spun back around so she was looking out of the windows where a few raindrops were beginning to fall. Summer in Florida. Sunny one minute, rainy the next.

"Peyton, I need to go. I need to start getting ready for the party tonight."

"Have fun. Ellis and I are going to watch some television. You know, he's not the asshole we thought he was. I think he's just sort of a social misfit."

No, he was a jerk but he was a nice jerk. He wasn't mean, just grouchy.

"Get some rest. I'll call you and Bailey tomorrow."

Hanging up, Willow snuck a peek at Josh who was now sitting at the table drinking his beer and reading the paper. He looked completely unperturbed and a few days ago Willow would have bought the facade. But now that she knew him better, she could feel the hurt practically radiating off of him. She'd hurt his feelings and she felt like a total bitch. Here he was risking his life and she'd basically said he wasn't good enough for her, which wasn't it at all. Now what?

She could pretend she'd never said anything and let this whole situation blow over. Sort of *The Less Said, Soonest Mended* adage.

Or she could talk to him and tell him why she couldn't ever be interested in him or anyone else. It was something she barely understood herself but it would require talking about her past and that was something she wasn't prepared to do.

Decision made. She'd ignore the hell out of it and hope for the best.

Chapter Fourteen

WILLOW WAS TIPTOEING around the suite as if Josh was going to roar like a lion. Sure, he'd heard what she'd said to Peyton and it had hurt. There was no denying that. But it was par for the course with this woman. Two steps forward and one step back. Skittish and scared, with good reason, she wasn't going to run willingly into a relationship with anyone.

Least of all him.

He wasn't like the men she socialized with. He wasn't from money. He had an excellent education but he didn't play the stock market like Chase or hunt down bad guys like Ellis. His life was quiet, tame, and filled with fur and slobbery kisses. He liked it that way but Willow had to decide if she was okay with that. Right now, it looked like she wasn't but her fear was blinding her to what they might be able to have together. If she could conquer that then maybe she could make a real decision.

He set the paper down on the table. "I have good news."

Popping the top on a can of soda, she gaped at him. "You've been back for fifteen minutes. When were you planning to tell me?"

"The plan was to tell you the minute I saw you but then you were acting so strangely I decided to see what was up with you."

It wasn't often Willow was speechless so it was fun when she was. Her mouth opened and closed a few times but nothing came out. She was going to try and pretend he hadn't overheard her with Peyton and that was fine with him. Until she was ready to face the attraction they had for one another, it was the best course of action.

"Cat got your tongue? Maybe this will loosen it. I have two pieces of news. Let's step into the bathroom and I'll tell you."

That had been one room that hadn't been bugged in any of the homes so they'd decided to risk talking in the suite as long as they were in that room. Luckily, it was large and spacious. Willow perched on the edge of the huge tub and Josh leaned against the vanity.

"The first is that I saw Grant Hollister. He was coming in from a round of golf."

Her eyes round, she blew out a breath. "You saw him? How did you know it was Grant Hollister?"

"I overheard one of the resort employees greet him."

"Did you talk to him?"

Josh shook his head. "I couldn't think of a good reason to speak with him. I guess I could have made something up on the fly but I was so surprised that nothing came to me. James Bond, I'm not."

She wasn't saying anything, just staring off into space, her thoughts somewhere else.

"Honey, are you okay?"

Her gaze came back to him and she nodded. "I am. I was just

wondering…does he look like Alex? Even a little bit?"

Josh had only seen pictures of her late husband so he wasn't the best judge of whether they resembled one another. Plus it bugged him that she was even asking. Did it matter? Was she hoping that the birth certificate wasn't real?

"Not to me, but I only saw him for a few minutes and I have only looked at photos of Alex. I think you might want to see for yourself. I'll point him out at the party tonight."

Actually, it was a ball. In a ballroom. Willow had an elaborate dress and jewels. He would get to wear a tuxedo again, but this time the suit with tails that Willow had forced upon him. Lucky him. He was now the proud owner of not one, but two expensive tuxedos. Just what the overworked veterinarian needed in his life.

"Good. That's good. What's the second thing?"

He dug into his pocket and pulled out a key card, holding it up for her inspection. "This is what made this trip worth the hassle."

"A key to our room? Or is that a key to Archer's room? I'd love to see what he has hidden."

Josh smiled, a surge of triumph running through him. He might not be Ellis but he'd managed to pull this off and he was damn proud of it.

"Better. This is a key card to The Clubhouse."

She blinked a few times, her mouth hanging open. "What? How on earth did you get a key to The Clubhouse?"

"I went for a jog around the property and decided to run by The Clubhouse. A woman was exiting the building so on a whim I followed her. She went up to the resort for a drink and I sat down at a table next to hers so I could hear her phone conversation. She told whomever she was talking to that she was done working for the weekend and she would be headed home in a few minutes. It sounded like maybe a friend or roommate on the other end. They have plans to go see a band tonight."

"And you stole it," Willow interjected, a smile of glee on her face. "Did you bump into her and pick her pocket?"

"I'm not the Artful Dodger. No, the original plan was to talk to her and find out about The Clubhouse so I approached her and asked her a question about the building in progress that I'd passed. She was open to talking so I offered to buy her a drink. Things progressed from there and soon we were talking about her job with Evandria."

Josh had thought Willow would have been thrilled but instead she looked furious, her cheeks pink with anger. Was she upset that she hadn't been there? It had been completely fortuitous.

Her fingers drummed on the porcelain. "Progressed from there? You bought her a drink and she just spilled her guts about her job? It must have been one hell of a cocktail."

"She had iced tea, and she didn't spill her guts. I think she thought I was a member so it was fine to talk to me. She works as the office manager in the Administration department and she's been here two years. That's pretty much all she said other than she likes the outdoors, camping and hiking."

Willow snorted and rolled her eyes. "I'd bet cash money that she doesn't. Not really. Girls always say that to a guy but it's not really true. She was only trying to impress you."

Josh wasn't sure how to take that remark.

"Because she thought I was wealthy?"

"No, because she liked the way you looked," Willow replied shortly. "Plus you were all charming and sweet. Just like you were with Janice this morning. Laughing at their jokes when they aren't even funny."

Janice? What did she–

A grin broke out on Josh's face and his heart beat a little faster. His sweet Willow was jealous as hell. He tossed the key card on the marble vanity. He could finish the story later. This was going to be much more fun.

"Does my behavior with Janice and Alexa bother you?"

"Who the hell is Alexa?"

"The office manager I met this afternoon," he explained, enjoying this more with each passing second. She had her arms crossed over her chest and her lips pressed together. The only thing missing was a stamp of her foot and then she'd be having a tantrum fit for a toddler. "Do you even want to hear how I got the card?"

"I don't need to. You seduced it out of her, clearly. Whatever, the ends justified the means, although I thought you of all people would be above that."

"Me, of all people? You mean you thought I was too socially awkward to flirt. That I was only comfortable with animals."

"That's not what I meant. I just thought you had too much integrity to flirt you way into her pockets."

"Integrity? You're questioning my integrity? If you want to know what happened, Willow, I'll tell you. Her friend worked in the kitchen and asked her to taste something he was trying out for the first time. She excused herself and said she'd only be a moment, leaving her purse with the key card tucked into an outside pocket on the table. I thought it was the universe talking to me so I snatched it. When she came back we chatted some more and then she told me she had to leave. End of story."

Looking somewhat mollified, Willow sipped her ginger ale, holding her head up like she was wearing a tiara. "That's good then. When are we going to check out The Clubhouse?"

Josh pointed to Willow. "You aren't going anywhere. You are going to keep Archer Caldwell busy at the party tonight while I check out The Clubhouse. Use your charm."

She stood and stomped over to shelves of towels, studying them like she'd never seen a washcloth before. "Maybe I will."

He didn't follow her, knowing she needed space to come to grips with her emotions. She clearly wasn't happy about what she was feeling. "We do whatever we have to, right? We're in this to get the truth and what's a little flirting in the big scheme of things."

She shrugged. "Right. It's no big deal."

"Except that it is," he countered. "You were pissed at me this morning with Janice and you're mad again now. Why don't you just admit that you don't like to see me with other women?"

He'd stepped out on the limb. Way out. Now to see if she planned on sawing it off.

"That's ridiculous. It doesn't bother me at all."

Denial wasn't just a river in Egypt.

"Are you sure? Because you've been snarling at me all day. I think you're jealous and I think you don't want to admit it because that would mean you might have some feelings for me, and you don't want that at all. Do you? You'll go down fighting, honey, but that isn't going to make you happy."

She whirled around, spitting angry. "I am happy, and I am not jealous. That's the stupidest thing I've ever heard."

Josh shook his head. He'd opened this can of worms and he was going to see it through no matter what. Ten minutes ago he'd wanted to be patient, but now it was the furthest thing from his mind.

"You are not a happy woman, honey. I wish you were but you're not. I can see the sadness in your eyes. I've seen the same fear and hope in the eyes of the animals I've rescued from abusive homes or ones that have been strays for a long time. Who do you have to care and love you, Willow? You're not exempt from having needs."

Her fists clenched and relaxed, then clenched again. "I am not one of your mangy strays, Josh."

"You're much prettier than most of the dogs and cats that come to me tired, hungry, and frightened but you're not much different. You want so badly to be loved but you're terrified of being rejected. If Alex were here I'd like to punch him right in the jaw. He did a number on you and damn if you deserved the shit he gave you."

"He wasn't that bad–"

"Don't you dare try and defend him," Josh interjected, anger churning his gut. Alex hadn't earned Willow's loyalty. He'd given that up the first time he'd cheated. "You think if you defend him that it makes you staying with him okay. You weren't stupid for not leaving him, Willow. You took vows and you kept to them. Hell, I respect you for that. But don't try and make him into something he wasn't."

Her lips were trembling and every cell in his body was urging him to go to her, wrap his arms around her and tell her everything was going to be fine. He'd take care of her.

She wasn't ready for him to do that.

Instead, she took a deep breath and turned back to the towel rack, effectively shutting him out.

"You have this all wrong. I'm happy and content with my life. Once we get the truth about Alex, it can all go back the way it was."

"You're lying to yourself and to me. It will never go back the way it was because it all has changed. You know it has. You've changed."

"I haven't." She shook her head but Willow wouldn't look at him. "You'll go back to your life and I'll go back to mine."

"Is that the plan?" Josh asked, keeping his frustration in check. "We find out who killed Alex and then we pretend we never met? I don't think I can do that, honey, because I'm falling for you. I think you're falling for me too."

She was already shaking her head in denial and putting even more distance between them. Rounding the toilet, she used it as a shield but he wasn't fooled. He'd shaken her safe little existence up but he'd gone too far to backtrack. Good or bad. Smart or stupid, he'd stepped to the edge of the cliff. He had no illusions, however, that she was going to suddenly capitulate and fall into his arms. No, this stubborn woman was going to fight until the bitter end. He might be back in Williamsburg before she admitted her emotions.

"If you want to leave, I understand." She was looking into the distance, her chin lifted in defiance. "But...I don't feel the same. I'm sorry. I certainly don't want to hurt you but I simply don't return your feelings."

It hurt, her denial. He felt a sharp pain in the vicinity of his heart as if she'd slipped a dagger between his ribs but he wouldn't let it show. She didn't need big flowery speeches and declarations. His legendary calm and cool attitude was the order of the day. It was the only thing that wouldn't spook her.

"I'm sorry too," he admitted, deliberately keeping his tone as even as possible. "But I wouldn't leave you to do all this alone just because you don't feel the same. Forget I said anything. We need to start talking about our plan for tonight."

If he was reading her right, there would be no way she could forget their conversation.

That was assuming they survived the ball. If Josh was caught in The Clubhouse, he doubted he and Willow would leave The Retreat alive.

Chapter Fifteen

"WHICH ONE IS he?" Willow asked as they walked around the perimeter of the ballroom. Both of them were dressed to the nines, Josh in his tie and tails, and herself in a crimson ballgown with a big skirt and a tight, strapless bodice.

"I don't see him yet." Josh's gaze moved from left to right. "Wait, there he is by the bar. He's with a group of three other men—do you see them?"

She did and had to hold herself back from running right into the middle of them. "Let me guess which one he is. The tall one with the short dark hair?"

Josh shook his head and chuckled. "No, he's the young looking one with the dark blond hair."

He looked about ten years too young. "That can't be him. According to the birth certificate, he's the same age Alex would have been."

Josh placed his hand on the small of her back in what felt like a comforting gesture. "Honey, Alex abused alcohol and drugs. Didn't take care of himself. I'm guessing he wasn't an accurate barometer of how someone should physically look at a certain age."

"Good point," she conceded. "I still think he looks young though. So, how to meet him? Maybe I should get us a few drinks and be clumsy and spill one on him. Then he'll have to talk to me."

Grimacing, Josh stared at the other man across the room. "I'm not telling you not to talk to him. But I am saying that I'm guessing he knows you're here. Everyone seems to know who you are so I can't imagine that he doesn't. If he knows who he really is and he wanted to meet you, he'd already have done it."

"You think he's going to rebuff me?"

"It depends on what he knows. He's not openly trying to avoid you but he's not striding across the room to make friends. This might not be as easy as spilling a drink on his tux."

There were so many things she wanted to know about Grant, Alex, and any relationship they might have had. Had they known of one another? Did Grant know he was Alex's half-brother or had he been told something completely different? If they had known one another, what secrets might he know about Alex?

"He may not know anything about his actual parentage," Willow sighed. "He may never have met Alex."

"He's worked with the family," Josh reminded her. "I think there's a decent chance they knew one another."

The entire situation gave her a headache. "This just pisses me off. We don't know that Grant knows anything about Alex and the other men. Archer could be sending us way off base on purpose."

"We can't overlook any leads." Josh nodded toward where

Grant was standing. "He's a lead whether we like it or not."

"Then there's no time like the present, is there? I'm going to meet Mr. Hollister."

With a swish of her skirts, she made a beeline for the bar, determined to introduce herself to Grant one way or another. If his tuxedo had to be sacrificed along the way, then so be it. She had to stop short when Archer Caldwell stepped into her path.

"Willow, you look lovely tonight. I hope you're enjoying your weekend."

Her gaze darted to the bar and her heart sank. Grant had moved on, but she didn't know where. "I am, and thank you so much for inviting us. We've been having a wonderful time and I'm looking forward to horseback riding in the morning."

The older man beamed. "I think you'll find the scenery more than pleasing." He leaned down and gave her a conspiratorial wink. "Have you given any thought to joining our organization on a permanent basis? You've fit in well and I think everyone would agree that you'd be an asset."

Quirking an eyebrow, she looked out over the crowd in the ballroom. "I find that hard to believe. Most of these people wouldn't give me the time of day until they saw me here. I was the town trash who married for money."

"And now they know you didn't," Caldwell said, his smile disappearing. "They know you are serious about doing good works for our fellow citizens. We can help you with that, Willow. Together there is no limit to what we can accomplish."

It was seductive. Being respected in Midnight Blue Beach instead of sneered at behind her back and yes, sometimes right to her face. Having a partner in her charitable works. There was so much need and she couldn't begin to fill it all herself.

Am I really considering this? Wake the hell up.

She inwardly slapped her own face. "It's something I'm considering, Archer. You make a very good case."

The smile was back. "We're trying. Just tell me what else we need to do to convince you and we'll do it."

She looked up at him from under her lashes and gave him her best flirty look. "A drink would certainly help your cause."

Throwing back his head and laughing, he placed a hand on her elbow, leading her to the bar while she looked around frantically for Grant. "Then we must get you one immediately."

She spotted her prey sitting at a table near the orchestra, only one other person with him. She'd get her drink and begin moving that direction. Everything was going as planned.

WILLOW WAS GETTING a drink with Archer Caldwell by her side while the guests laughed, danced, ate, and mingled. Since Josh was simply Willow Vaughn's guest, no one was paying any attention to him. It was the perfect time while the party was in full swing.

He slipped out of one of the ballroom French doors to the outside, making sure to stay in the shadows as much as possible. The possibility of cameras watching the property was high. He zigzagged through the trees, never walking on the pathways. The Clubhouse was about a mile from the resort and while that wasn't far to walk, it was a long way to try and stay concealed. Luckily, it appeared all the guests were attending the ball and the staff was busy there as well. He didn't see anyone on his way. There was nothing outside but him, some crickets, and maybe a few deer.

When The Clubhouse came into sight, he halted under the cover of a large maple tree and pondered his relatively few options. He could stride right up to the front door in full view of the windows and whatever cameras there might be. He could round the building and hope for a back door where it was darker. Or he could...

He really only had two plausible options. He wasn't Spider-man.

Crossing his fingers, he headed for the back of the building where there were few lights. As he turned a corner, a small, empty parking lot came into view and he gave a mental fist pump. If this was where the employees parked, then there had to be a card-activated entrance in the back.

If I were going to put cameras out here, where would I put them?

On the little concrete path from the parking lot to the entrance so they could see who was approaching.

He could see a small overhang where the door should be. There were no lights illuminating it so it appeared that the staff didn't work much – if at all – at night. Good news. There was less chance of him running into someone inside the building.

Reaching up overhead, he jumped and grabbed onto a slim branch and pulled down with all his weight until he heard the wood creak and snap, leaving him with a stick about three feet long and about an inch and a half around.

It would have to do.

Ducking his head, he pressed himself tightly against the building, his abdomen scraping the stucco. If anyone did see him, it would be difficult to tell who he was from the back in the dark. All the men tonight looked exactly the same. It was an advantage Josh hadn't expected but deeply appreciated.

As he got closer to the overhang, he caught sight of the camera bolted to the underside. It was pointed directly onto the path. So far, luck was with him tonight. He still had to go into its path, however, and that was what the stick was for. He stepped closer and reached out with the slim branch, nudging the camera slightly so its line of sight was farther toward the parking lot. Not much, just a little. He only needed a few inches of clearance. If a security guard monitored this camera, hopefully they wouldn't notice the change until morning.

If the camera had been a different type that didn't move so freely? He would have been screwed. He'd have to brazen it out, pulling his coat over his head to cover any distinguishing features and dart to the door, praying no one actually watched the feed. This was much better but he didn't hold out hope that things were going to continue to be this easy.

Standing in front of the door, he reached into his pocket and pulled out the key card. He held his breath as he placed it next to the reader, not daring to move a muscle as he waited for the light to show red or green. He could hear his blood whooshing in his ears as his heart thudded against his ribs. It was go time. He could have explained away his presence on the outside of the building as curiosity.

The ballroom was stuffy and I went for a walk to clear my head. How did I end up here?

I'm fascinated by the building's architecture. When was this built?

I'm how far from the resort? Wow, I've had way too much to drink.

Once he went inside, however, there was no pretending he was drunk and lost. He'd stolen a key card and broken into a secret building that even most members didn't get to see. Archer Caldwell probably wasn't going to let that go.

Green.

The fucking lights flashed green.

Exhaling slowly, Josh slowly opened the door waiting for an alarm to go off or a net to come down on him.

Nothing but the hum of the air conditioner.

His gaze darted around his surroundings, a small lobby that led directly to two elevators, looking for more cameras but he found none. Hopefully now that he was inside that would be the case everywhere. Did they trust their employees? Did they trust anyone? Josh was pinning his hopes on the officers wanting as much privacy as possible when they arrived for their meetings.

Eyeing the elevators distrustfully, he looked for a doorway to the stairwell. It would be quieter and more out of the way. Maybe. Frankly, he didn't want to be surprised if the elevator doors slid open and there was someone standing there waiting for him. Like in a horror movie.

He finally spotted the door to the stairs in the far corner. Carefully pushing it open just enough to slip through, he closed it softly behind him and bounded up the stairs two at a time. His destination? The third floor. He'd start at the top and work his way down.

As quickly as possible, before anyone noticed he was gone.

Chapter Sixteen

ARCHER HAD TO have planned this. For the last hour Willow had been trying to get within three feet of Grant Hollister and had failed. Each time she thought she was close someone would step in and divert her until Grant had moved on. It was maddening, frustrating, and her patience was stretched beyond its breaking point. It was only years of iron self-control that kept her from stomping her foot like a three-year old and throwing a tantrum.

She was back at the bar getting a fresh drink and regrouping. Clearly her original plan wasn't going to work. She needed to figure out a new way to meet him, and soon. He might leave the party and go to his room at any moment.

Keeping an eye on Hollister out of the corner of her eye, she accepted her martini and stepped away from the bar, murmuring greetings to a few guests that she'd seen in town but had never spoken to. They'd always turned up their noses whenever she'd walked by. They certainly weren't doing that tonight. There had been a great deal of ass kissing and Willow couldn't help but wonder how much any of these people truly knew about Evandria. Would they blindly do whatever Caldwell asked them to? Was the "mission" that important to them or was it something else? The power and prestige. The connections. It had been made quite clear to her tonight that if she decided to join she could expect her fortunes to do nothing but rise.

"Where's your friend, Willow?"

She whirled around to see Archer standing there, a highball glass in his hand. He appeared perfectly sober but he'd had a filled glass as an appendage all evening. It might all be for show and that could be the same drink. A man like Caldwell wouldn't get drunk in front of others. She knew his type from her dancing days. He was a man that took his pleasures in private, keeping the facade up in public.

"Josh? He ran up to the room for a moment to take a call. He should be back soon."

She was turning into a big liar and she had the sweat on the back of her neck to show for it. She'd never pass a polygraph but all she had to convince was this man right here.

Where was Josh anyway? She'd known he would go off to try and break into The Clubhouse but he'd been gone much longer than she'd expected. She'd been too busy stalking Hollister to worry but now that she'd glanced at the clock, he had been missing a little too long. Archer had noticed.

"I hope he doesn't miss the rest of the party. These things don't really get going until after midnight."

"That's far past my bedtime," Willow giggled and took a sip of her fresh drink. "Little girls should be tucked in by then."

"We wouldn't want you to turn into a pumpkin."

"I think my fairy godmother might drink," she confessed

with a sly smile. "She's probably somewhere in this crowd doing body shots off of a waiter's abs."

Archer's brows rose and then he threw his head back and laughed, his palm pressing his stomach. "You are quite something. I do hope you decide to join our group." He glanced at his watch and tapped the face of it. "If you will excuse me, Willow, I need to duck out of the party for a few minutes. I have some business at The Clubhouse."

There was no way she could allow him to go there. Not yet. She used the one thing that had always been powerful with men.

She ran her hand up Archer's arm and batted her eyelashes. "Just a few more minutes? I have so many questions and frankly, you're the only one I trust to answer them. You seem to have such a...command of the inner workings and mission of Evandria. Admit it, you've made Evandria what it is, haven't you?" She leaned forward so he could catch a glimpse of her cleavage. "Don't be modest. There's an air about you, Archer. You simply exude power and control."

A slow smile spread across his features. She had him. It had been easier than she'd thought it would be.

"Do you find that attractive?"

She licked her lips and let her gaze flicker from his head to his toes and back up again.

"Very much so."

JUST ONE MORE file to photograph and Josh could get out of here and back to the party.

It had taken way too long to find the file room, located in a far-off corner of the second floor. By the time he'd found it, he'd been in the building almost thirty minutes and as far as he was concerned he couldn't get out of there fast enough.

It didn't take long to put his hands on Frank Scott's file, then Greg Nelson's, and now he was finishing up with Alex's. With nervous sweat pooling on the back of his neck and back, he snapped a picture of each page, not even bothering to read any of it. There would be time later to decide if the risk had been worth it.

He clicked the camera button for the last page, then closed the file and placed it carefully back into the cabinet.

One more precaution in case he was caught on the way out.

Quickly, he transferred a copy of each photo to Ellis. If for any reason they took his phone, his friends would still have the information. It was a paranoid move, but this was Evandria. Nothing about this organization made Josh feel complacent.

When that was done he shoved the phone in his pocket and made his way down the stairs to the back door. Hesitating there, his heart galloping in his chest, he strained to see outside before opening door. If security had seen anything on camera, there might be a welcoming committee for Josh the minute he walked out of the building.

Swallowing hard, he pushed open the door, the heavy night air hitting him in the face, no cool breeze to dry his damp skin. Cautiously his gaze darted left, right, left, and then right again, straining to see through the darkness.

No one.

Josh exhaled slowly in relief, although he wasn't in the clear yet. He still had to get back to the party without being seen. Pressing against the wall once again, he crept to the corner and paused, listening for any tell-tale sound of a footfall or the rustle of leaves. He was about to dart into the trees when he saw a shadow out of the corner of his eye near the front corner of the building.

Frozen in place and barely breathing, he waited, his heart pounding in his ears so loudly he was sure it could be heard all the way in the resort ballroom. It seemed like hours before he slowly moved to look around the building. There hadn't been a sound or any other movement.

Had he imagined it? Or was it a bird, a deer, or some other nocturnal animal that had caught a whiff of Josh's human scent? Was he silently freaking out over nothing?

There wasn't anyone else around from what he could see. He stood there for a few moments longer but that wasn't a good idea either. He needed to be on the move and back to the ball.

Taking a deep breath, he lunged forward, staying as low to the ground as possible until he was under the cover of the thick branches. From there it was easier, staying out of sight and avoiding any people. By the time he reached the door of the ballroom, his body was covered in sweat and his tuxedo stuck to his flesh as the blast of the air conditioning made him shiver. He'd find Willow and signal to her that they needed to leave. Anyone taking one look at him would wonder what he'd been up to.

Patting his pocket where his phone was safely ensconced, he finally spotted Willow near the bar. Her head was thrown back and she wore a huge smile on her face that Josh instantly knew was fake. Her body was angled so that she was displaying herself at the most advantageous angle for...

Archer Caldwell.

A twinge of jealousy ran through Josh but he sharply reminded himself that her smile wasn't real. She was flirting with the bastard for some unknown reason but it couldn't be because she had any real feelings toward the man. There had to be an explanation.

Pulling his phone from his pocket, he sent her a text to meet him in the room.

They needed to look over what he'd found.

He wouldn't mind knowing why she was laughing at that creepy guy's jokes either. Josh didn't trust Caldwell any farther than he could throw him, and he sure as hell didn't trust the guy with his Willow.

His Willow?

Ah hell. That was another problem, and he had enough of those already.

Such as whether that shadow had been an actual person.

Chapter Seventeen

WILLOW METHODICALLY KICKED off her shoes before working on her jewelry. First the earrings, then the necklace, and last the bracelet. She'd done this exact same routine after every party for years. It felt soothing and familiar at a moment that was anything but.

A scowling Josh was pacing behind her, a bottle of water in one hand. Every three steps or so he'd stop, look at her, and then continue his relentless assault on the marble tiles of the large bathroom. Finally she could delay it no longer.

"What is your problem?"

He stopped again, his scowl cutting grooves into his handsome face. "Are you kidding me?"

She sighed, utterly exhausted after the evening she'd had. "Sadly, no. Now tell me, why are you so upset? You should be celebrating. You succeeded. Now are we going to look at the pictures?"

It was his turn to sigh. "It may not have been the success that you think. I saw a shadow."

"A shadow?" she echoed. "Can you be more specific?"

"No, I can't because that's all I saw. It might have been an animal, or it might have been a person. I really don't know. The whole operation may not have been as clean as I'd hoped it to be."

His mood made sense now. "That explains why you're so unhappy. Don't worry about it. You were right that this was the perfect night to do this. All the men are dressed the same. If anyone says anything we deny it. Simple."

He shrugged off his jacket and tie, draping them over the edge of the bathtub. "Honey, that is not why I'm upset."

She was tired of playing this game. She wanted to see the photos but dammit, she wasn't going to take his crap to do it. At this point, she'd rather call Ellis, the grouchy cop.

"Well, get over it," she snapped. "I'm going to change. I'll be back in a few minutes."

She strode into the bedroom and slammed the door shut behind her in a most satisfying way. Five minutes later the gown was back in its garment bag and she was wearing sleep shorts and a tank top, contemplating whether it was safe to go back into the bathroom.

What the hell. She'd dealt with ornery men.

Padding on sock-covered feet, she entered the bathroom only to see him knocking back a shot of whiskey, the bottle sitting on the vanity. That should improve his damn mood but she was getting tired of having their meetings in the commode.

"I wouldn't mind one of those."

He poured her a measure of liquor into a highball glass and raised his own in salute.

"Here's mud in your eye."

She lifted her drink and smirked. "Here's to your health, which is going to be suffering if you don't tell me what crawled up your ass and died."

Slamming the glass down on the counter, Josh took a step toward her. A muscle worked in his jaw and his chest rose and fell rapidly. "You let him put his hands on you."

At first, she had no freakin' clue what he was talking about but then a light came on. Archer Caldwell. Jesus frog in a pond, that's what all this was about? She'd been saving his sorry ass.

"He intended to go to The Clubhouse, the one place in the world I couldn't allow him to go. So yes, I let him touch me. I danced with him and I let him flirt with me. He only touched my arm and my back. It's nothing to get upset about. I did what I had to do."

So help me God, if he asks if I enjoyed it, I'm going to knee him in the balls.

"I didn't like it," Josh stated, snapping his teeth together. "I don't like him and I don't like him touching you."

Men and their egos. "I wasn't all that fond of it myself but what was the alternative? Let him find you pilfering the files? Would you rather I'd have done that? Because next time your ass is in trouble I'll do nothing if that's what you'd prefer."

Groaning, he scraped his fingers through hair that was already standing on end. "You make me crazy, woman. I think you do it on purpose."

"I don't even know what I'm doing. You're pissy about something so trivial I can't even muster the energy to defend myself. We should be talking about the files, not this petty bullshit."

But it wasn't petty to him. She could see it in the tense line of his shoulders.

Josh was jealous, and he had no reason to be. Yes, he was being unreasonable but her denial of any feelings had pushed him into this corner. She'd been the architect of this little mini-tirade. After all, hadn't she been a jealous shrew this morning?

"Fine," he said flatly. "Let's talk about something else."

For one brief moment, she almost stopped him and insisted that they clear the air. But that was going to bring up a boatload of other issues that she wasn't quite ready to talk about yet. He deserved the truth after all he'd put himself through for her. Could she muster the courage and tell him her story? Tell him why she was pushing him away?

Because she did care for him. Too much. He was the kind of man she'd dreamed about when she was younger. Strong, steady, smart, and handsome. He made her laugh and he made her think. He challenged her on a daily basis but not in a bullying manner. He was the knight in shining armor she'd fantasized about all those nights she'd lain awake in her bed, huddled under the covers, scared and alone.

His phone on the vanity lit up and buzzed, Ellis's face appearing on the screen. Josh reached for it and swiped at the screen, looking relieved at the distraction.

"Talk to me, bro. What did you see?"

Of course. Ellis had received the files even before Josh had left The Clubhouse.

"There wasn't much that was new, but there were a few interesting items. The program all three men volunteered for was called the Arsenal. There are no details at all about it but they all three signed waivers that were, between you and me, something I'd never in a million years place my John Hancock on. The waiver basically said Evandria wasn't responsible for any injury, illness, or death that may result from their assignments for Arsenal." Ellis paused. "Here's the fascinating part. The waiver actually recommends that members of the Arsenal never marry or have children as emotional ties complicate their assignments."

"What the fuck?" Josh exploded. "What philanthropic group needs an Arsenal? Are they some sort of spy?"

That waiver explained why Alex hadn't wanted children. Maybe it explained his alcohol and drug use too. Had he been so conflicted he'd self-medicated to ease his conscience about marrying her?

Her hand shaking, Willow steadied herself, her fingers curling around the edge of the bathtub. She needed her friends and she needed them soon. Josh was wonderful but there were things only Bailey and Peyton would understand.

"When are you coming down here?" she heard herself asking. "When can you travel?"

"Good question and we have an answer. Peyton got the all clear today from the doctor so we're going to head down tomorrow along with Bailey and Chase."

Good. That was good.

"I'll send the jet."

"You don't have–"

"I'll send it," she interrupted. "Peyton shouldn't have to deal with the hassle of flying commercial. This will be easier for her and she'll be home more quickly. I'll text you once I have the details."

Willow knew what buttons to push on the police officer. When Peyton's well-being was mentioned he immediately gave in, agreeing that his charge shouldn't have to worry about a busy airport and crowds.

"Is there anything else?" Josh asked. "We'll look at the files ourselves of course."

"Not that I noticed but we'll look at them again," a voice piped up in the background. It sounded like Bailey. "Wait, Peyton found something. The department head for the Arsenal? Nigel Holmwood."

His name kept coming up and that couldn't be a coincidence either.

"We have to find him. Did you have any luck with the addresses that we found in the sculpture?"

"The address for Holmwood doesn't exist from what I can find," the cop sighed. "That street isn't in that town. As for the other two, we can't find any record of the people or the addresses. It was like they were completely made up."

Josh frowned. "Do you think it's some kind of code maybe?"

"I think we're all paranoid as hell," Ellis replied. "It could be a code. It could be a mistake. Hold on. Peyton says that she's good at puzzles. She'll take a look at the names and addresses."

"We have to find Nigel," Willow pressed. "Has Bailey had any luck?"

"It's like he's fallen off the face of the earth. She's even tried his friends. They said he's on holiday in Greece but they don't know exactly where or what hotel he's checked into. I've got a buddy at Homeland Security who said he'd check into Holmwood's passport and see if he's left the UK."

Josh rubbed the back of his neck. "We have to find out what the Arsenal program is."

Willow shrugged. "We're horseback riding with Archer in the morning. We could just ask."

It was a horrible idea but she was out of good ones.

"Sure, we could also end up dead," Josh retorted. "They gave you those made-up files for a reason. Arsenal must be a big secret. Big enough to keep it from you."

"Whatever it is, I think it got Alex killed," she said quietly. "I think it's the reason all three of them are dead."

Despite the tension between Josh and herself, he placed a comforting arm around her shoulder and pulled her close to his warm body. Deliberately ignoring the risks of her action, she allowed herself to lean against him, letting him be the strong one. She was so goddamn tired of chasing ghosts.

"I'll ask my Homeland Security friend if he's ever heard of anything called Arsenal. I doubt it but you never know. The FBI keeps track of all sorts of weird shit." Willow heard Peyton's voice in the background, soft and urgent. "Uh, Chase just got a call. Stephen Baxter is dead."

He'd said he didn't kill Alex or his friends.

Would they ever know the truth?

Chapter Eighteen

THE ILLUMINATED RED numbers on the bedside clock read two-oh-three. Willow had been awake, tossing and turning for hours, and she couldn't lie there any longer. She had allergy pills in her purse that would knock her out and she was desperate enough to take them even knowing how drowsy she might be in the morning.

Throwing back the covers, she slid her feet into a pair of slippers and didn't bother with a robe. She would take the medication and go right back to bed. Hopefully it wouldn't take long to kick in. Her purse was on a chair in the bedroom so it took no time at all to dig out the tablets but a glance around the room told her she'd forgotten to bring in a bottle of water when she went to bed. She'd have to grab one from the wet bar.

Not wanting to wake Josh who was camped out on the couch, she carefully opened the door, the hinges squeaking slightly. During the day she wouldn't even have noticed, but at night with nothing but silence surrounding them it sounded like a jet plane landing in the living room.

"Shit," she muttered under her breath and froze, hoping Josh hadn't heard anything. Her hopes were dashed, however, when his head popped up from the sofa. He didn't look like she'd woken him at all. There was no yawning, no sleepy-face, no rubbing sleep from his eyes. Josh had been awake.

"Are you okay?" he asked, standing quickly, his entire body tense. "Do you need something?"

It took every ounce of willpower she had not to answer that she needed him. More than she'd ever thought possible. Instead she held out her hand, the pills nestled in her palm.

"Water. I can't sleep. I guess you couldn't either."

He shrugged as she rounded the wet bar and opened the small refrigerator. "It's my job to keep you safe. Sleeping heavily isn't the best way to do that. I caught a nap earlier but I set my alarm so I get up every hour or so and walk around, make sure everything is still secure."

Willow had no idea he'd been doing that. Her mouth hung open in shock that he would forego his own health and comfort for her. No one ever had before. Not someone she wasn't paying.

"That's what they do to torture prisoners when they want them to talk. Josh, get some sleep, for Christ's sake."

Shaking his head, he paced to the windows, pushing back the drapes and looking out. "I can't. After what I did tonight, I'm paranoid as hell. What if they saw me? What if they came here in the middle of the night and took you away from me? What if I wasn't there when you needed me?"

Emotion so strong welled up inside of her at his words. So simple, yet so powerful for someone like her. She'd been playing it safe for so long, keeping her armor in place as protection. She'd told herself it was to protect others but that was a lie. She was protecting herself. This man had blown her defenses to smithereens and he didn't have a clue. He'd affected her more in the few weeks she'd known him than anyone else she'd ever met.

"Then you'd be like everyone else in my life. I wouldn't say that I've ever inspired protective feelings in a man before."

He strode over to the bar and she caught a whiff of his body wash, sharp and tangy. After his shower, he'd put on a pair of pajama pants and a t-shirt that looked as if it had been washed several hundred times. Her arms itched to curl around his muscular frame and trace his spine with her fingers. She wanted to live in his arms, luxuriate in his strength. But that little girl who had always been disappointed kept her standing exactly where she was.

Pouring himself a whiskey, he didn't acknowledge her statement right away. He took a sip before turning back to her.

"Careful, honey, you might reveal something personal about yourself. We can't have that, now can we?"

The bitterness in his tone was easily recognizable. He was frustrated with her but no more than she was with herself. Her heart was pushing her to tell him, talk to him. Her head? That was another matter entirely.

"Josh," she began tentatively. "I just–"

"Don't," he cut in harshly. "Don't tell me how much you like me or that you care or, God fucking forbid, tell me you're grateful. I don't want you to trust me because you think you have to, I want you to trust me because you want to."

Just once in her adult life she wanted to trust someone and not regret it later.

She wanted to trust him.

Settling on the couch, she reached out a hand to him so that he was sitting next to her. "Will you tell me about your childhood? Your family? Growing up?"

He frowned but didn't say no. "What's this all about, honey?"

Exhaling slowly, she shook her head. "Can you humor me? Please? Tell me what Josh's family life was like."

He looked confused but he nodded in agreement. "There's not much to tell. I'm one of six kids, two older siblings and three younger ones. Three boys and three girls. We used to get teased we were like 'The Brady Bunch'."

Willow had watched that show in re-runs as a child so she knew what he'd referred to.

"And were you? Like 'The Brady Bunch', I mean? Were you close like that?"

"You mean did we have innocent adventures and form a pop singing group to buy our parents an anniversary gift? Hell, no. My brothers and I were little hellions and came home caked in dirt every day. After six kids, my mother only got upset if there was a lot of blood. A little didn't even register on her radar anymore."

"Was she a good mother?"

"Yeah…sure she was, although I'm not sure what your definition is. We were raised what they might call old-fashioned these days. We had to be home by dark. We hung out in the neighborhood with all the other kids. We ate what my mom cooked for dinner or we didn't eat, period. With five brothers and sisters, you had to eat fast or you were shit out of luck when it came to seconds."

That explained why he finished his food so quickly.

"Are you close to your brothers and sisters?"

"Yes, although I don't see them much. We all have our own lives. Jobs, families, that sort of thing. But I see them on holidays which is more than a lot of people."

She splayed out her hands on her thighs, studying each tiny freckle that marred her skin. "It sounds very nuclear family suburbia to me. Very 'Leave it to Beaver'. You were lucky."

"It wasn't all perfect," he protested, his brows pulled together. "With so many kids, we didn't get much one on one time with our parents. There was never enough money to go around either. I knew if I wanted to go to college I had to pay for it myself. Mom and Dad couldn't have swung tuition for six of us."

College. Willow almost laughed.

"Did you ever go hungry? Did you have clothes?"

"Sure, we had the necessities."

It was then that what she'd been tiptoeing around seemed to dawn on him and his shoulders slumped as he reached for her hand.

"What about you, honey? Did you have enough?"

JOSH SHOULD HAVE expected this. He'd known she was a dancer – a stripper – since the day he'd met her, but somehow he'd fooled himself into thinking she'd chosen it from a wide array of possible professions. He had to face the grim truth that she'd picked it because it was better than the few options she'd had.

"There was never enough food," Willow said simply but with a smile that he was sure wasn't real. "There was never enough of anything. My mother was an alcoholic. Not the kind that staggers out of a liquor store and turns tricks to make a buck. She was what they call a functional alcoholic. She held down a job, married and divorced soon after, had a child – that would be me. She appeared normal to her friends and the people of the community. It was at home that the cracks showed. She was pretty much drunk every night and when that happened, no one else mattered. The only thing she cared about was that next drink."

He hated thinking about the little scared girl she must have been. He hated how vulnerable she was and how he wasn't there to protect her. The shell she'd built up made sense now even more than it had before.

"I'm sorry." He rubbed his chin and smiled sheepishly. "I guess it's not a surprise. I kind of assumed you had a tough upbringing."

"The cliché of junkie parents, foster care, and teenage promiscuity?" she taunted. "It wasn't quite like that, although I suppose I could have gone that direction eventually. Lucky me, huh?"

That brittle force field was in full glory, keeping him at arm's length even as she revealed what he doubted she'd told many people. Had Alex known? Josh sure as shit wasn't going to ask. He didn't want to talk about her late husband any more than necessary.

"You said there wasn't any food," he prompted gently. "But

she had a job?"

Willow nodded. "She was an administrative assistant and she didn't miss too many days of work, thanks to me getting her up every morning and pushing her into a shower. We had an apartment that was nice but she spent most of the money on booze. But even if she hadn't, she often simply forgot to go shopping. I have no memory of her cooking a meal for me. When I was little she'd hand me a Pop-Tart. Eventually as I got older, I learned to go into her purse for money and go to the store myself. She never noticed it was gone and I learned to make microwave dinners. That explains why I can't cook."

"You took care of your mother."

She rolled her eyes. "Someone had to. I'd wake her up in the morning and help her get ready before I went off to school. After work, she'd go have drinks with her friends. That would start the ball rolling for her evening. By midnight she didn't know her own name, let alone mine most of the time."

"How did you…you know, end up dancing?"

She smiled at that question. It probably wasn't the first time she'd heard it.

"You mean stripping? Because that's what I was. A stripper. A damn good one too." She sighed and slumped against the cushions of the couch. "I never got really good grades in school. When you don't eat or sleep well it's hard to concentrate about algebra and the history of the Revolutionary War. So when I graduated I didn't have much going for me. I had a high school diploma, which meant nothing when it came time to get a job. I worked as a waitress and did okay but I was going nowhere fast. Then a guy came in one night with his wife. They owned a dance nightclub in Tampa. He said I had the right look and that I could make a lot of money."

"And you believed him? He could have been a human trafficker, honey."

Willow laughed. "He could have been but I was already cynical for my age. I only even talked to him because he was with his wife. He gave me his card and the next day I went to see him with my biggest badass friend that worked the grill in the restaurant and two more friends out in the parking lot. The man's name was Gary and he thought it was cute that I came with protectors because he took the safety of his girls seriously. I worked there until I married Alex, and I still think Gary is a good guy. He was the first person to really give a shit about me in my life."

Josh wasn't as convinced. This Gary might simply have wanted something from Willow so he'd pretended to be what she needed. A father figure.

"Did your mother find out?"

Her little chin lifted. "Hell, yeah. I didn't try to hide it. I've never been ashamed of it. She slapped me and said I was a whore, but I didn't care what she thought. I moved out a few weeks later and shared an apartment with one of the other dancers. I didn't talk to my mother until I married Alex and had the money to get her a better life. Get her into rehab."

"Is she…?"

"Still alive?" Willow finished for him. "No, she died about seven years ago. Her heart gave out. She'd abused herself too long. By then I had her in a nice place to live with the best doctors in the world but it was too late. She just couldn't get sober and frankly, I don't think she wanted to. She once admitted to me she liked to drink because it made her forget."

"What did she want to forget?"

Shrugging, Willow shook her head. "I don't know. She never said. Whatever demons drove my mother she took to the grave. Just like Alex." Laughing, she took the highball glass from his hand and drank the last of the whiskey. "Isn't that a kick in the ass? I picked a man exactly like my mother. Falling for Alex was no accident. I couldn't save her so I tried to save him. I failed – spectacularly – both times."

Josh wouldn't allow her to think like that about herself. "You didn't fail. None of this was your fault. They didn't want to be helped, honey. Their failings had nothing to do with you."

"I tell myself that all the time."

"It's the truth," he urged, lifting her fingers to his lips, but expecting a rejection. But this time she didn't pull her hand away. "Why are you punishing yourself? Because you didn't save them? Is that why? You think you don't deserve to be happy but you do. Shit, honey, it doesn't have to be with me but cut yourself some goddamn slack. You were just a little kid."

She tapped her temple. "I know everything you say is true. Up here. But down here—" She moved her hand to her heart. "It says that I failed the two people who needed me most."

He tried another argument. "What about what they owed you? They failed too. A hell of a lot more than you did. It was your mother's job to take care of you and she failed to do even the most insignificant tasks like feeding you. Alex had a husband's duty to love, honor, and cherish you. Did he do that? From what I can see the answer is no. If you failed them, they failed you first, and much worse."

Fingers plucking at the hem of her tank top, she avoided his gaze, not addressing what he said. "You wanted me to trust you tonight but that wasn't the problem."

He swept back her hair from her face but she shied away from looking at him. "I trust you. I do. It's me I don't trust."

"If it makes any difference, I trust you."

She finally looked up at him, her eyes soft with the emotion she worked so hard to hide.

"It does."

He held out his arms and for once she didn't argue with him. She settled against his chest, her warm body cuddled up with his, her silky hair draped over his shoulder like a curtain. Tomorrow she'd be back to her prickly self but tonight she'd let her guard down.

It was a start.

Chapter Nineteen

T HE NEXT MORNING Josh somehow found himself on the back of a horse that had been described by Archer Caldwell as "gentle and mild."

That was an understatement.

Pixie, as she was called, didn't even want to move down the riding path that had been carved out beneath the shade trees. Josh had only ridden a few times in his life so they'd wanted to give him a beginner mount – one that was used mostly by the children – but this was a tad too far. He was trailing the group of riders by at least twenty to twenty-five feet because Pixie didn't like being in a crowd. She didn't like turning left. Or right. Or going forward. Mostly she liked to stand still in the pasture and munch on grass. He was afraid to ask how old she was but it couldn't be less than double digits.

If Archer knew Josh had been in The Clubhouse last night perhaps this was his way of killing him. Abandoning him out in the middle of nowhere with nothing but a bottle of water and a horse who should have been retired to a petting zoo.

Urging Pixie to catch up, his attention was caught by Archer leaning down to speak with Willow. The older man's expression had turned serious and Willow's looked surprised for a moment but quickly schooled into something more neutral. Whatever it was he'd said, she hadn't expected.

They meandered down the path and the quiet gave him a chance to review the eventful night before. He'd thought getting into The Clubhouse would have been the pinnacle of his day but Willow opening up to him had changed everything. He thought they'd be back at square one this morning but she'd been as open with him in the light of day as she'd been under the cover of darkness. This was a real turning point for their relationship. For the first time, he felt like they might have a chance.

His mind was far away, curled up with Willow on that couch last night when he heard it. At first he thought it was the backfiring of a car or truck but there were no vehicles allowed up there. By the time he realized it had been a gunshot, Willow's horse had reared up, its front legs pawing wildly in the air as she held on for dear life. A scream had escaped her throat as it lifted from the ground once again, its massive body twisting to one side and dislodging her from the saddle. His heart and breath stopped in his chest as he helplessly watched her fall from the horse to the ground with a sickening thud. The horse, however, hadn't registered his success at getting rid of his rider and he continued to rear and paw at the ground mere inches from Willow's vulnerable body.

Archer lunged from his own horse and managed to grab the reins even as Josh jumped down and raced to where Willow lay unconscious, dragging her away from the spooked horse. Her lids fluttered open as he inspected the warm blood pooling on the back of her head.

"Ouch," she hissed when his fingers probed a particularly sensitive spot. "That fucking hurts."

"Stay still," he commanded as a crowd began to form around them. Everyone had dismounted from their horses now that Willow's mount had been calmed. He looked up but didn't address anyone in particular. "Call an ambulance."

"I don't need an ambulance," Willow protested weakly, batting at his hands that were running up and down her arms and legs checking for injuries. "I think I'm okay. Just bruised."

"You don't mess with a head injury. You'll get checked out."

Archer was kneeling on Willow's other side. "Jesus, are you okay? I don't know what happened. Joker is usually better trained than that."

"I'm fine. I just got the wind knocked out of me."

"You're bleeding," Josh growled. "You need to get checked out."

Archer had pulled his phone from his pocket and was now speaking urgently to someone on the other end. Josh stayed by Willow's side and held her hand, keeping her still. He hadn't wanted to move her in the first place but he'd had to get her away from a stomping horse.

"Is Joker okay? Is he hurt?" she asked.

"He's fine," Archer assured her. "Just scared."

Josh smoothed back Willow's damp hair from her face. "It sounded like a gunshot."

Brows pulled together, Archer shook his head. "Couldn't be. There's no hunting allowed on Evandria property. It had to be a car backfiring."

"Why would a car be up here? There are no roads."

"Maybe a landscaping truck. Or a construction vehicle."

Landscaping? In the middle of the trees? And the construction was at least four miles away. Plus it was Sunday. Archer's explanation was flimsy at best but Josh didn't press. The suspicion that this might not be an accident was beginning to take root inside of him.

"It will be faster if we can take her to the infirmary. Can you travel, Willow?" Archer asked, pausing his phone conversation. "You and Josh can ride together."

Willow nodded and tried to sit up but struggled until Josh placed a steadying arm under her torso. As stubborn as she was, it would be a waste of breath to try and convince her to do anything else. "I can travel."

As carefully as he could he lifted her to her feet, holding her steady until he was sure she wasn't going to faint or keel over from dizziness. She did, however, lean against him as he walked her back over to the horse that Archer had been riding previously. He'd indicated that he would be riding Joker back, not Willow.

Both men helped her into the saddle and then Josh mounted up behind her, wrapping his arm around her waist to keep her steady. The ride back to the infirmary seemed like it took forever but it was probably less than half an hour. Some of the riding party and galloped ahead but the rest stayed with Willow at a more sedate pace. Her head couldn't take much jarring or bouncing. He kept his arms tightly around her and talked to her about anything and everything in the most soothing voice he could muster. Whatever he could do to try and keep her mind off of the pain in her head and the myriad of bruises she was going to have head to toe. She didn't seem to mind but she only responded back a few times. Once to tell him he was an idiot and another time telling him he was wrong about whatever it was he was saying.

It meant that she was awake and alert, so he'd take it.

When they reached the small clinic, he slid off the horse first and then lifted her down. She was stiff and wincing but this time she was steady on her feet and was able to walk inside with only his arm for support. He would have carried her but she might have kneed him in the balls.

"Do you want me to go back with you?" he asked and received the answer he'd expected. She scowled and shook her head as a nurse took her other arm and led them toward an exam room. He was being unceremoniously dismissed. She might have made herself a little vulnerable last night but she was going to tough this accident out without his help.

The door closed and Josh settled into a chair opposite it, pulling out his phone to tap out a text to Chase and Ellis about what had transpired. They were supposed to meet their friends back at Willow's house early in the afternoon but this might make them late.

"Can I get you anything?"

Josh lifted his head to see Archer hovering nearby, shifting back and forth on his feet.

"I'm good but once we get back to the resort we're going to need to pack and check out quickly."

"I can have one of the maids go in and pack for you."

I just bet you would. You want to see what we have. Go right ahead.

"That would be great. I'd appreciate that."

If Archer was surprised that Josh had agreed, he didn't let on. Instead he made a quick call, then came to sit down next to him.

"Listen, I said this to Willow on the ride but I'll go ahead and tell you now. I think I'm getting very close to finding out who killed her husband. I've got a few suspects and it's only a matter of time before I'm sure."

Now this is interesting.

"That's great, but I guess I'm confused. If it was this easy to find the killer, why wasn't that done a long time ago?"

"That's a good question."

That's why I asked it, asshole.

"It just seems like it shouldn't be that easy. The men's deaths were made to look like accidents, after all."

"They were and I think that was intentional. As for what took so long, my predecessor five years ago buried their files and the circumstances. If three of our brothers had died on the same exact day, and they were well-known to be close friends, then their deaths should have been looked into. I don't know why that didn't happen but I'm hoping to right that wrong now. Evandria takes care of its own."

Josh tucked his phone back into his pocket. "Stephen Baxter is dead."

Not a flicker of surprise crossed Caldwell's face.

"I'm sorry to hear that but from what I'd heard he was in rather dire straits. There wasn't much hope he would pull through."

Josh was definitely ready for his tinfoil hat. He wasn't sure if

Willow's accident was truly an accident. He wasn't sure that Baxter's death hadn't been helped along. He sure as hell wasn't positive that Archer was being truthful when he said he had the suspects narrowed down. Josh and his friends had been working on this much longer than Archer and they weren't close to finding out what had happened. Every time they thought they'd learned something it only brought out more questions.

"It's too bad. He might have been able to answer more questions for us."

Archer shrugged. "At least his friends and family won't have to face a trial for what he did to his sister Gwen. They'd be devastated if he was imprisoned for life."

Would they? They hadn't given a shit when their daughter was murdered in cold blood.

"Depends on how you look at things," Josh conceded. "And if Gwen was the only other person he'd murdered."

Caldwell didn't take the bait, seemingly content not to say anything more about his own investigation. An investigation as phony as those files he'd given Willow.

Time dragged on as they sat there, barely speaking, waiting for Willow to come out of the exam room. When she finally did, the tension was so thick Josh jumped out of his chair and rushed to her side, anxious to get as far away from Archer Caldwell as possible. The guy gave him the willies.

The first words out of Willow's mouth were, "I'm fine. No concussion."

The elderly doctor with a gray mustache and beard smiled and patted her on the shoulder.

"She's absolutely right. No concussion. She is, however going to have a nasty headache today and probably tonight. Also, quite a few aches and pains for the next few days. I'm recommending rest and fluids, plus ibuprofen." The doctor turned to Willow. "No horseback riding for at least a week. You need to ease back into your usual activities. Let this nice young man take care of you."

Grinning, Josh took her arm as she glared up at him. "Doctor's orders, honey. Now let's get you home."

Archer waved an arm toward the entrance. "I have a golf cart here that will take you back to the resort and I'll have valet parking pull your vehicle up to the front. The maids should be done packing your things. I'm so glad you could join us this weekend and I'm just sorry that things took such a turn. I hope this doesn't put you off our organization. I still think you'd be a major asset to Evandria."

Willow was feisty and she'd had a crappy morning but she mustered a smile for the creep.

"You've certainly given me a lot to think about."

"If you don't mind I'd like to call you in a few days to see how you're doing."

Willow nodded in agreement, although her grip tightened on Josh's hand. "That's very thoughtful of you. I'll look forward to it."

Like a root canal.

Caldwell gave them a salute and headed out the back door of the clinic, possibly to the stables to check on Joker. Josh and Willow went out the front entrance where a young man in the Evandria uniform was waiting for them with a large golf cart. They both climbed and it jerked into motion, slowly rolling forward on the wide sidewalk. As they passed the corner of the infirmary building, Willow's eyes went wide and she clutched his arm, surprisingly strong for someone so small.

"Look there." She elbowed him hard in the ribs. "It's Grant Hollister. He was watching us."

Josh's head whipped toward where she was nodding and indeed, out of the corner of his eye he could see Hollister standing there watching them pull away. Josh didn't know whether to tell the driver to stop or to jump out while the cart was still moving and run after the man but it was quickly a moot point. Hollister turned on his heel and strode away, disappearing behind the building. Heading in the same direction as Caldwell? How had Hollister known Willow was even at the clinic? Had Archer called him at some point? Or was he there for a completely different reason?

Once again, more questions than answers. Only this time, it had almost managed to get Willow killed.

Accident? Maybe.

Chapter Twenty

"**Y**OU AND CHASE look really happy," Willow said as the three women huddled at the kitchen island in her house, a margarita pitcher between them, although she was only sipping hers. Her head still hurt from her fall this morning and she had a feeling she was going to be black and blue tomorrow. There was also way too much food spread out in front of them, courtesy of Chase and Ellis who had run out for some lunch. Apparently, Josh had informed them that Willow wasn't allowed to cook in her own kitchen.

The men had decided to sit outside on the patio and eat their lunch so the ladies could talk and catch up. It felt like she hadn't seen these women in forever, which was funny considering a month ago she hadn't even known them. Bailey smiled and waggled her brows. "We're happy but we aren't the only ones. Have you seen the way Ellis looks at Peyton? Like she's the centerfold in the latest issue of *Grumpy Detective Magazine*."

Peyton elbowed Bailey. "Hey, he's not that bad. If he's grouchy it's because he has a reason to be. He has a difficult and stressful job, you know. Give him a break."

Willow giggled as she slid into a barstool between them and popped a fry into her mouth.

"I'm just happy that you're all better. I need both of you down here. This mystery keeps taking strange twists and turns."

Bailey pointed a fry at Willow. "What about you? According to Josh, you took quite a spill this morning. How's your head?"

Willow tapped her temple. "As hard as ever. Seriously, I have a little headache when I move my head a certain way and I'm going to be sore when I wake up tomorrow but I got lucky."

Peyton shook her head. "Lucky? Are you sure? Because it sounds like that fall might not have been an accident. Do you think Grant Hollister did it?"

"Why would he try to injure me? It doesn't make any sense."

"You're a threat to him," Bailey pointed out. "He might not want anyone to know he's part of the Vaughn family. He might have set you up for that fall."

"We don't know that it wasn't an accident," Willow argued. "A skittish horse could happen to anyone."

Ellis strode into the kitchen and stole a fry from Peyton's plate. "But it didn't happen to anyone else, did it? It happened to you. On a horse that Archer Caldwell chose. That makes him a suspect in my eyes."

Peyton shooed Ellis's greedy fingers from her lunch. "What about Hollister? Watching them is suspicious behavior."

He nodded and refilled his margarita glass halfway. "Agreed. But that could be just because he wanted to get a look at Willow."

Slapping down her glass on the marble countertop, Willow huffed in disgust. "He could have come up close and personal last night at the ball. I tried to get near him for two hours and every time I was intercepted by someone. No, he didn't want me around."

Ellis rubbed his chin. "Or Archer Caldwell didn't want you two to speak."

"Maybe. I definitely got the creepy vibe from him. Plus we know that the files he gave us were bogus. He wants us to go off in another direction. Did you find out anything about the Arsenal?"

He shook his head. "Not yet. I called my contact and he said he'd look into it. I'm not hopeful. Evandria is not on any watch lists. Frankly, if as many powerful people are members as we believe, I doubt the government watches them at all."

Bailey frowned. "Wouldn't it be the other way around?"

Ellis laughed. "Not if the powerful people are the ones that do the watching. According to the research we've done, most of the government and Wall Street belong to Evandria. But maybe that's just an urban legend. I'm getting just like Josh. Paranoid as hell."

"It isn't paranoia if they're really out to get you," Peyton said grimly, echoing Ellis's earlier words. "And I do think that the more we learn, the more they want us out of the way. Whatever secret our husbands held, they don't want anyone to know."

"No one is getting near you," Ellis growled, bringing a smile to Willow's face. He was protective and she liked that. Peyton would be safe with him. Just as she was safe with Josh. "They'd have to go through me first."

Willow hated to ask but she had to know. "Do you think they'll try again?"

Ellis nodded, his face a mask of anger. "I do but we aren't going to let our guards down for a moment. They won't get to you."

"If what we've learned is to be believed, they can get to anyone," Bailey objected. "They got to Stephen Baxter."

Whoa. "Are you sure about that?" Willow asked. "It did cross my mind but do we have proof?"

Bailey rolled her eyes. "I wish. All I know is that the doctors were pleased with his progress and they thought the police could finally talk to him. That night he died. I'm sick and tired of using words like coincidence and suspicious. Maybe I'm paranoid as hell too but in my mind he was murdered because they were afraid he'd say something."

Ellis nodded in agreement. "He might not have known anything but he was a loose end that needed tidying up. He might have been able to give us a nugget of information that would have put us back on the right path."

This wasn't helping Willow's headache. "What path are we on now?"

"The right one," Ellis declared with more fervor than she had expected. "We know they were involved in something called Arsenal. We know Nigel Holmwood was in charge of that program. We know that Caldwell doesn't want you anywhere near Hollister. And we know that Hollister is at the very least interested in you in some manner. That's a hell of a lot more than we knew just twenty-four hours ago. You and Josh did good, although I'm not sure you truly realize just how dangerous of a situation you were in."

Willow had thought they had but it was nice of Ellis to

acknowledge it. "I think we did know how dangerous it was but we didn't think about it too much. Otherwise we might have chickened out."

Peyton's expression sobered. "If Josh had been caught breaking into The Clubhouse…"

Willow didn't want to think about that. "But he wasn't."

"That we know of," Ellis pointed out. "Josh admitted that he saw something as he was leaving."

"It could have been a deer."

"It could have been a human," Ellis shot right back. "Hell, it could have been Hollister. I wish Josh had pulled his file. I wonder if he's in Arsenal too."

"It wasn't Grant Hollister." Willow shook her head. "He was at the party."

"Then Caldwell."

"He was at the party as well."

Ellis quirked an eyebrow. "You saw him the entire time?"

Thinking back to Josh's pissy attitude after the party, she was positive. She'd made sure Caldwell didn't go to The Clubhouse. "He was there. I was with him a good part of the evening and at the time Josh would have seen a shadow. No, I think he saw an animal."

"For all our sake's, I hope so."

A phone chimed and Bailey quickly straightened as she checked the screen. Her eyes widened and she began wildly waving her arm. "It's Uncle Nigel. He's finally called me back. Go get Josh and Chase. I'll put the call on speaker so stay quiet."

Everyone went silent as Bailey accepted the call. Her hands were wrung together tightly but her voice sounded normal.

"Uncle Nigel, it's so wonderful to hear from you. I was getting worried. Where have you been?"

"Just a small holiday and I'm as fit as a fiddle, my darling girl." Nigel Holmwood had an upper crust tinge to his British accent. "I needed a little break from work. How are you? Your messages sounded urgent."

"I'm fine. Good. But I really need to see you. Are you in America?"

"As a matter of fact, I am. Are you at home, love?"

Willow noticed that Nigel hadn't revealed exactly where he'd been or where he was now. He kept redirecting the conversation to Bailey.

"I'm here in Midnight Blue Beach but I can come wherever you are."

"No, that's not necessary. I'll come to you. But I am concerned about you, darling. You sounded quite upset in your voicemails. Has anything happened?"

Ellis had scribbled something on a scrap of paper and he pushed it in front of Bailey who nodded.

"Kind of." She paused, her gaze searching Ellis's one more time. "I know about Evandria."

A bigger pause. This time on Nigel's side.

"It wasn't a secret, my child. If you'd needed to know, Frank would have told you, of course. It's not a big deal."

More scribbling from Ellis. Bailey's brows raised when she read it but once again she nodded.

"I know about Frank, Alex, and Greg. I know their deaths weren't an accident. They all died on the same exact day."

"That doesn't mean their deaths weren't an accident, Bailey.

Frank's passing was a great tragedy and I can see that you're having trouble moving on."

Bailey's jaw tightened but she took a breath before speaking. "That's true, Uncle Nigel. I am having trouble moving on. I have all these doubts about what is true and what isn't. I really need to see you."

Willow had to give credit to Bailey. She was staying calm and composed.

"And you shall, child. How about we have lunch tomorrow at the Midnight Blue Beach Farmer's Market? They have that lovely cafe with the outdoor seating. We can chat and catch up. I've missed you so very much. You know, I feel like your doubts are all my fault. If I had been around more these last few years, I could have helped you with this earlier."

Ellis shoved another note under Bailey's nose.

"Tomorrow? Then you're close by? Are you already here?"

"Close enough. I'll see you tomorrow around noon. I'm so looking forward to this, love, and I'm glad you called. It's been far too long."

"I'm excited about it too. I guess I'll see you tomorrow."

The call ended and Bailey groaned. "I'm sorry, Ellis. I couldn't get him to say where he was."

"That's okay. It was a long shot but I wanted you to try."

"What would you have done with the information?" Willow asked. "Do you think he's in Midnight Blue Beach?"

Ellis grinned. "I wanted to know for two reasons. The first is that wherever he is might be important to the case. Does Arsenal have a base of operations? Maybe he's there and that's a location we should check out. Second, I wanted us to go do a little snooping ahead of time and perhaps gain an advantage. I want to see who he might be with. His Evandria contacts could be helpful. I don't for one minute think he's been on a vacation."

Josh snorted. "I'll wholeheartedly agree with that. I also think it was mighty convenient that he called today after we just left The Retreat. Even if no one saw me leave The Clubhouse, they're concerned about what we know. They've sent in good old Uncle Nigel to find out."

Wincing, Willow rubbed at her aching temples. "I need some more ibuprofen."

Josh shook his head and jumped to his feet. "I'll get you some but you also need is to lie down and rest for awhile. Remember doctor's orders."

She would have normally argued but she was tired and her whole body needed to be soaked in a hot tub. "Fine. I'll rest. But don't do anything important without me."

Bailey and Peyton giggled as Josh placed an arm around her waist and led her upstairs.

"Honey, nothing important could possibly happen without you. Now would you like me to run you a nice, hot bath?"

Fighting her instincts to tell him exactly where he could stick that hot bath, she instead nodded and let him guide her to the bedroom. Last night she'd let Josh in, made herself vulnerable, and he hadn't run away screaming into the night. There might be hope for the two of them. If she could continue to open up and trust him. It wasn't easy for someone like her but nothing worth it ever was. If she wanted a future like other people had, she was going to have to do some work.

"YOU'LL NEVER FIND a better man," Peyton declared as the women soaked in the jacuzzi. They were keeping Willow company while she soothed the aches and pains she was sure to have after her spill off the horse this morning. "He's willing to die for you, girl. Grab him up."

Willow had been having exactly the same thoughts although slightly more cautious. She wasn't the grabbing type.

"You could take that advice yourself," she pointed out to Peyton. "Ellis is definitely the jump-in-front-of-a-bullet kind of guy. He growled at my mailman this afternoon."

The sun was setting on the horizon but the summer air was still warm and humid. They men could be seen in the kitchen through the large picture windows, huddled over the files and clues she and Josh had collected. Ellis was quite interested in Grant Hollister and was having him checked out by his FBI connection.

"Maybe your mailman looked shifty," Bailey laughed. "But you are right, Ellis is over the top protective while Josh and Chase are a little more laid back about it."

"I didn't see Chase relaxing when he rushed Taylor and the gun. That's proactive in my book," teased Willow.

Peyton looked over her shoulder to the kitchen window where the three men were debating what Bailey should say at tomorrow's lunch with Nigel.

"Ellis is a detective and that makes him suspicious of people right off the bat. He doesn't trust easily." Peyton turned back to her friends. "Of course I could say that about all of us."

Rolling her eyes, Willow shifted on the hard concrete bench, the bubbling water lapping around her shoulders, soothing her aching muscles. "You can just say it. I have trust issues. There, I said it for you."

Bailey's brows went up and her lips were pressed together to hold in her laughter. "Um, I think we all do but I can see you felt you resembled that remark. Want to talk about it?"

No, I do not.

"It's just that I have lousy taste in men," Willow heard herself saying, the words flowing from her lips despite her attempt to stem the tide. "I always pick the wrong ones."

Peyton shrugged. "We haven't done much better but your luck has got to change at some point, don't you think? I mean, all men can't be bad."

Their little optimist...Peyton. She was so sweet and so naive.

"Sure they can," Willow shot back. "Movies, books, and magazines practically count on it."

"Josh isn't like that," Bailey said. "Chase went out of his way to tell me what a good guy he is. If you like him, go for it."

"I told him to back off," Willow sighed. "And then I told him about my childhood and then we slept together."

Bailey and Peyton almost came out of the water as Willow shook her head frantically. "I mean we slept. For real. Just innocent sleeping."

Peyton leaned forward, a smile on her lips. "Was it nice? Being held?"

"Yes," she admitted, remembering how warm and safe she'd felt. It was something she hadn't felt in a long time. "It was nice."

Bailey tapped the water with her fingers. "He won't make the first move. He's too respectful of the distance between you. If you want him, you're going to have to do it."

Groaning, Willow buried her face in her hands. "I have never had to make the first move with a guy in my entire life. They've always come to me. I'm not sure how to even do it."

"What do men do?" Peyton asked.

"I don't know—flowers? Candlelight? Romantic music? Wine?"

Bailey nodded in agreement. "Compliments too. And touching. Fleeting touches of your hand on his arm or his shoulder."

"Are you suggesting I...romance Josh?" Willow asked, her voice shaky at the idea. "You must be joking."

Bailey and Peyton were grinning at each other and Willow didn't like it one bit. They were plotting something without saying a word; she could practically see the light bulbs above her friends' heads. Damn.

The two women levered out of the jacuzzi and wrapped towels around themselves.

"We would never joke about this," Bailey smirked. "We're going to head home and leave you and Josh...alone. You know what to do. Music, candles, romance. He wants you, girlfriend, you won't have to try hard. Just enough to give him the hint."

After much discussion it had been decided that all of them staying in one house would make it too easy for Evandria to hurt them. Bombs. Fire. Or whatever else they had up their sleeve.

"Or after a night and day of thinking what a mess I am, he might turn me down flat."

"He won't," Peyton assured her. "He looks at you like Chase looks at Bailey."

"And Ellis looks at you," Bailey countered.

Peyton shook her head. "We're not going there right now. I just woke up from a coma—give me a break. Plus I've got to deal with Greg having another wife and kids. That's not exactly conducive to romance. In fact, it makes me more cautious than ever. Next time I fall for a guy I'm having him checked out by a private detective."

After everything they'd been through it wasn't the worst advice in the world but in Willow's case it was too late. She'd fallen, and hard.

Willow's friends were putting on their robes. They were really going to go.

"Don't leave me. I need you here."

Peyton shook her head. "We are the last thing you need. You'll be fine."

Reluctantly, Willow pulled herself out of the water and dried off. This was tough love at its finest. Could she do this? Did she even want to?

Yes, she absolutely did. Josh was the man she'd been waiting for. The kind she'd dreamed about all those years ago when she was still innocent and naive.

Seduce a man. How hard could it be?

Chapter Twenty-One

AFTER JOSH SHOWERED, he pulled on a pair of running shorts and a t-shirt and padded downstairs on bare feet to get a cold beer from the refrigerator, the dogs at his heels. Chase, Ellis, and the ladies had left rather abruptly but Peyton had been complaining about being tired. With her so soon out of the hospital Ellis had immediately stood up and bundled her into the car, Chase and Bailey on his heels.

Josh had asked Willow how she was feeling as well but she didn't directly answer the question. Instead she'd said something about the jacuzzi and wine, which didn't make much sense but he didn't press. She'd been through so much these last few days that she might simply need an evening to chill out, have some alone time. He'd grab a beer and go into his room and read, let her have her house to herself for a change. Even though she'd revealed a great deal about last night, that didn't mean she wanted him around all the time. She was probably sick of him by now. He'd give her some space.

Last night. He hadn't been able to get it off his mind. He shouldn't blow it up and make it more than it was. She'd

allowed herself a moment of vulnerability but that didn't equate to a relationship. Having feelings for him wasn't a slam dunk. She did trust him though and that was a good start. He could live with that, for now.

As he reached the bottom of the stairs, he heard the soft strains of Michael Bolton along with the flicker of candlelight. Willow had turned off the lights in the living room and lit several candles, the scent of vanilla heavy in the air. The dogs sniffed and then headed straight for their beds in the corner. It was bedtime. They had to be worn out from all the attention they'd received today. Chase had thrown the tennis ball for them until his arm was sore.

What was Willow doing? Meditating?

"Honey?" Josh called into the empty room only to hear soft footsteps behind him. He turned and the air was sucked from his lungs. Willow stood there in shorts and a halter top, holding a champagne bottle and two glasses, her eyes wide and her hands trembling. She was nervous and now so was he. This was clearly more than meditation.

"Honey?" he asked again. "What's going on?"

"Nothing," she denied with a shake of her head. "I thought it might be nice for the two of us to relax and talk. Maybe have a glass of champagne."

He hated champagne but if it would get her to open up to him he'd drink a whole damn bottle of it. "Sure, that sounds good."

She thrust out the bottle. "Can you open it?"

"Absolutely. Why don't we sit down?"

Back to the couch where they'd fallen asleep last night curled around one another. He managed to pop the cork without taking out an eye, the bubbles exploding from the top. After filling their glasses, he set the bottle aside, watching her closely. Her hands were still shaking and her knuckles were white where she gripped the crystal flute.

"A toast?" She raised her glass and he did as well. "Here's to us."

Us? There was an *us* now? He sure as hell wasn't going to argue. Holy shit, was that what this was all about?

"Willow," he asked gently after taking a sip of his champagne and placing the flute on the coffee table. "What's going on here, honey?"

She shifted on the cushions, her gaze everywhere but looking at him. Yep, something was going on, all right. She was the kind of woman that looked a man in the eye. "Nothing. What did you think was going on?"

Her bottom lip was trembling and he had to squelch the urge to capture it with his mouth. There was talking to be done.

His gaze flickered around the room. "Candlelight? Music? Michael Bolton? Honey, are you trying to seduce me?"

WILLOW WAS SO bad at this Josh didn't even recognize what she was trying to achieve. This was past sad and well on its way to pathetic.

"No," she replied immediately, then hated that it was a big, fat lie. She was a person who believed in honesty, especially after her marriage to the king of secrets and lies – Alex. "Maybe."

His handsome face split into a grin. He was either happy about it or amused.

"Honey, you don't have to go to such trouble." He indicated the candles and champagne. "For you I'm a sure thing. Just crook your finger and I'll drop everything and come running."

Oh. Good. That was very good.

Her neck pooled with sweat, she lifted her heavy hair up trying to catch a cool breeze. She was shaking with nerves and she didn't seem to know what to do with her hands either, eventually placing them on her thighs and rubbing the damp palms against the material of her shorts.

"So…"

"So," he smiled and chuckled, obviously enjoying her display of tension. "How about a dance?"

He was asking her to dance for him? It was a strange request, but okay. She'd need better music than this. Before she could say so, he'd taken her smaller hand in his and gently led her to the middle of the living room where he pulled her body close, his hands splayed wide at the small of her back.

"I'm not a huge fan of Michael Bolton but I think we can make this work," he murmured in her ear as they began to sway slowly to the music.

Willow buried her face in the soft cotton of his t-shirt. "I didn't know what kind of music you liked so I chose the romantic favorites channel on the television. I think they'll play someone else eventually."

She felt his chuckle under her cheek. "I wouldn't care if they played heavy metal. I get to hold you in my arms and that's all I care about."

Her cheeks suffused with heat and her arms tightened around his waist, his flat abdomen pressed to her softer belly. How much he was enjoying this was beginning to make itself known, hard and ready against the top of her hip.

"This is nice," she said awkwardly. "Better than at the ball."

Laughing, Josh dropped a kiss onto her bare shoulder and the skin practically sizzled from the contact. "I hated that damn tuxedo. At least we're both comfortable this time."

They didn't say much of anything for the next few minutes, seemingly content to hold each other and dance, pressed so closely together. Willow took in a lungful of his heady scent, a combination of spice and citrus and male. He was so incredibly masculine without being an asshole about it, comfortable in his own skin. While she on the other hand…

Jumpy and sweating like a whore in church. She wanted him but it has been so long. She wasn't sure she even remembered what she was supposed to do. It all seemed so far away and hazy.

"Honey?" His voice in her ear sent a bolt of electricity straight down to her toenails. "I'd like to kiss you."

A kiss. Yes, she wanted that too. Tilting her head up, their gazes met and the nervousness that up to that moment had controlled her drained away, no match for what she saw. There was nothing in his eyes but kindness and adoration. No reserve or cruelty. No self-immersion. It was just Josh, his emotions laid bare for her to see and she had nothing to fear from him. She'd known that last night and she was reminded of it again tonight. This man would never hurt her.

So when he kissed her, capturing her lips with his own, she put everything she had into it. All her pent-up emotions and desire were poured into that one moment. Her fingers clutched his shoulders as the world spun on its axis. She'd had more kisses in her life than she could count but this was different. He wasn't trying to get anything from her.

He was giving.

When his tongue slid over her lower lip, she opened to him immediately, not wanting to let him go. If this could go on forever she'd be happy to let it. When he finally lifted his head, his eyes were heavy-lidded and his fingertip traced her jaw, a slow smile spreading over his face.

"That was the best kiss I've ever had," he declared with a grin. "Nothing else has even come close. Not even when Amy Camden taught me to French when I was thirteen. I thought I'd died and gone to heaven."

Giggling, she stood on her tiptoes and pressed a quick kiss to his lips. "She did an excellent job. Maybe we should do it again."

"Yes, ma'am," he breathed before capturing her lips again, this time less tentative and more…everything. His fingers caressed the nape of her neck as his mouth traveled leisurely down her cheek to nibble at her jaw and ear. Her heart stuttered and her breath caught when his tongue found the spot where her pulse beat madly, nipping the flesh with his teeth.

Lifting her into his arms, he sat down on the sofa, arranging her on his lap so she was straddling his thighs. In this position, she could feel his impressive erection press against her, and she wriggled slightly drawing a tortured moan from him. His grip on her hips tightened and he pushed her back slightly to lessen the friction.

"Honey," he hissed. "You have to go easy on me or I'm going to get the wrong idea."

Frowning, she shook her head and pressed open-mouthed kisses on his neck and jaw. "No, you have the right idea."

"Honey," he said again, his tone more desperate than before. "Let's talk about this for a second."

The last thing she wanted to do was talk. She'd made a decision here but he wasn't getting the message. Slipping her hands under his cotton t-shirt, she caressed his chest, tracing his ridged abs with her fingers. Unceremoniously, she found herself lifted into the air as Josh stood, placing her on her bare feet while Josh backed up, his hands on his knees as he took several deep breaths.

She stepped toward him but he shook his head and held up his hand in a stop sign. "No, you stay over there. I just need a minute here."

It would have been cute if this had been happening to anyone but her.

She crossed her arms and pouted. "You said you were a sure thing."

He straightened and smiled. "Honey, I am, but I think you need to think this through. You might think you're ready but maybe you're not. I don't want you to rush into something and then regret it in the morning. I couldn't take that."

"I won't regret it."

Of that, she was positive. She'd waited a long time for this moment but it had finally arrived.

"I know you think that now but tomorrow—"

"I'll be just as glad that I did it," she interrupted him. "You're treating me like a child, Josh. I'm a grown woman and

I've had sex before. I'm no virgin here. Far from it."

He walked toward her and placed his hands on her shoulders. "Have you? Since Alex?"

"No, but that's because I hadn't found anyone I could trust, plus I'm too old for casual sex. I wanted it to mean something."

His thumb traced her lips. "It would definitely mean something and it wouldn't be casual. If we do this it's because we're going to try and make this work, Willow. I don't want a few nights with you while I'm here and then leave. If I go to bed with you, I want you in my life. I'm not talking about getting married or anything like that, but I am talking about—well, being a couple."

She wanted to smack his forehead. "What do you think I'm talking about? Hit it and quit it?"

Rubbing the back of his neck, he turned away from her. "Honey, I'm just a humble veterinarian. You're a millionaire. Or hell, maybe a billionaire. I'm not sure and I don't care but I'm well aware I'm not in your league. Not even close."

That's what this was about? Money?

"I don't care," she said flatly. "I don't care about the money and I never have. I could have landed another rich man in the last five years but I never found one that made me feel a tenth of what I feel for you. Would it be terrible if I said that I'm glad that you're just a normal guy with a normal job? I don't want a titan of business. I want a man that loves me and puts me first before his career. A man who would make our relationship a priority in his life. From what I've seen since the day I met you, I think you're that man. It doesn't hurt that you like dogs as much as I do."

He whirled around and yanked her close, their bodies pressed together. Lowering his head, he kissed her, one hand cupping the back of her head and the other at the curve of her bottom. She wrapped her arms around his neck and kissed him back, putting everything she felt into it. If he didn't understand her words, maybe he would understand the emotion.

By the time he lifted his head, they were panting, their fingers tugging frantically at their clothes. For Willow it had been far too long and she couldn't wait much more. His shirt went flying over her shoulder and her hands went to the waistband of his shorts before she stopped, a slim shred of sanity still left in her fogged brain.

"We should go upstairs. There are beds up there."

Chapter Twenty-Two

CLOTHES HIT THE floor at a rapid rate until there was nothing left to take off. Willow had left modesty and shyness on the side of the road a long time ago. There had been no room for it in her chosen profession. She was accustomed to the salacious looks from the patrons but the expression on Josh's face wasn't anywhere close.

It was carnal, yes, but so much more. Loving. Worshipful.

The same way she was looking at him.

Golden skin from being outside. Lean and muscular but not overly so. He had the physique of a baseball player or perhaps a swimmer with his wide shoulders and lean hips. His abdomen was flat and her fingers reached out to brush the skin stretched taut over his torso. His hand captured hers and he lifted it to his lips before turning it over and pressing a kiss into the palm.

A wave of white-hot heat swept through her veins and her knees almost buckled from the onslaught. Backing up toward the bed, she knelt on the mattress as Josh joined her, pulling her into his arms.

"Honey, if you change your mind all you have to say is *stop* and I will."

Running her hands up his chest, she linked them behind his neck and leaned in to kiss him, nibbling on his generous lower lip. "For a sure thing, you're hard to convince. I'm not going to change my mind. I want this and I want you. Are you having second thoughts?"

The way his hands were moving up and down her body, exploring every inch of exposed flesh, was making it difficult to think clearly. All she knew was that she needed him in a way she'd never thought possible.

He shook his head and chuckled. "Are you kidding? This is the greatest day of my entire life. I just want to make sure that you're as on board with this as I am. I don't want you to regret this afterward."

She bit down on his shoulder, drawing a groan from deep in his throat. "Again."

"Again?"

"That's the only thing we're going to be doing afterward." She trailed her tongue down his chest and flicked it over a flat male nipple. "We're going to do this again."

That seemed to be the right thing to say because she was quickly pushed onto her back with his much larger body hovering above her, his gaze raking her from head to toe. He dipped his head and lapped at an already hard nipple before sucking it into his mouth. A rod of arousal went straight to her core and her nails dug into the muscles of his shoulders. He repeated the action on the other side before kissing a wet path down her abdomen, pushing her thighs wide apart.

Her legs quivering in anticipation, the heat from his warm

breath ghosted over her clit sending shivers up her spine. The first touch of his tongue was electric and her body arched as the breath was pushed from her lungs. She moaned his name as he explored her slit, his tongue everywhere, teasing and licking, but never giving her what she needed to go over.

Josh pressed two fingers inside her, finding that sweet spot that had her writhing on the bed, the sheets clutched between her fingers. Panting, she squeezed her eyes closed as her orgasm overtook her, pleasure washing over her like warm waves on a sunny beach. She rode his fingers until it was over, her entire body limp but not satisfied. She needed him.

"Josh, I need–"

As she reached for him, he resisted her efforts to pull him up her body, instead taking his time and kissing the inside of her thighs, her hipbone, her ribs, and then her collarbone, each tender brush of his lips turning her bones to jelly. Her fingers wrapped around him, hot and hard, and he groaned as his own hand covered hers, staying her movements.

"Easy, honey. As worked up as I am, this could be over before it begins."

Positioning himself between her legs, he guided himself toward her core but then froze, his face contorting into a mask of what appeared to be excruciating pain. "Shit, I don't have any condoms."

For a moment, she panicked too, and then remembered a gag birthday gift she'd received from another girl at the animal shelter where they both volunteered. Willow had laughed it off and then shoved them in her nightstand drawer. Unless the cleaning crew had moved them, they were still there. Thank heaven.

Reaching with one hand, she tried to open the drawer but her arm wasn't long enough. Luckily, Josh seemed to get the hint and did it for her, ripping the small box apart in his haste and tearing the wrapper before tossing it on the floor.

Quickly and efficiently, he rolled it on and took his place again, probing her drenched slit. Slowly, aware that it had been a long time he pressed forward, pausing every now and then so she could be accustomed to his invasion. She began to move experimentally, swaying her hips side to side and sending a clear signal that she was ready for more.

His thrusts started easy and soft, but as she wrapped her legs around his hips he sped up as they found the rhythm she craved. The coil in her abdomen tightened with each delicious stroke, his groin rubbing against her clit until she was seeing stars. Her climax ripped through her like a freight train and she cried out his name as the room spun and tilted like a carnival ride. His own orgasm had him burying his face in her neck as he plunged himself inside of her one last time.

Their skin was covered with sweat as they collapsed, Josh rolling off to the side but tucking her into the curve of his body to keep her close. With a kiss to her damp forehead, he whispered silly, romantic things, telling her how beautiful she was and how amazing she made him feel. It was only words but somehow he made her believe every one of them.

"Wow," she said when she could form sentences again. "That was amazing."

Chuckling, he ran his hand down her back to rest possessively on her bottom. "Damn right it was, and it's only going to get better."

"Braggart," she teased, pressing a kiss to his chest, the skin salty on her tongue. "So much for modesty."

"I was talking about you, honey. You're the amazing one. I was just along for the ride."

Hardly but she'd take the compliment. Giggling, she ran her fingers through his silky hair and then tugged on the ends. "I meant what I said. I want to do this again."

"My God, woman, I'm going to need a few minutes to recover."

He didn't sound all that outraged though. In fact, he sounded...glad.

"Take whatever you need. We've got all night."

With any luck, they had more than just tonight.

IN A GROUP this small there was no such thing as a secret. From the way Chase, Ellis, Bailey, and Peyton were staring at him and Willow, they knew exactly what had been going on last night. Bailey and Peyton couldn't seem to stop smiling and giggling, and Chase and Ellis kept slapping him on the back and grinning.

Jesus, it was like high school but with better hairstyles.

They were all gathered in Willow's kitchen to prepare for Bailey's lunch with Nigel Holmwood, Ellis barking out orders as usual as if they were troops ready to storm the castle. It had been decided that Willow was going to go with Bailey so she wouldn't be alone but Peyton was going to stay with the men. They didn't want to overwhelm Holmwood or scare him off, but this way if he took Bailey off track, Willow would be there to get the questions going again.

"Use the recorder on your phone and turn it on before you sit down," Ellis said. "Just put it on the table like it's no big deal. He won't suspect anything."

"If he's truly part of this organization, he might," Josh observed. "There are several reasons for him to be paranoid as hell. The first is that we're finding out some of their secrets, the second is that he has to answer to Archer Caldwell."

"You assume he does," Ellis shot back. "For all we know, Caldwell is a figurehead and the real power lies somewhere else."

Chase chuckled. "You're both paranoid. I'm not worried about who's after Holmwood. I'm worried about the safety of Bailey and Willow. That's plenty to keep us busy today without adding to our problems."

"Good point," Ellis grunted. "We keep the ladies in our sights at all times. We never take our eyes off of them. I don't trust this guy."

Peyton snorted. "You don't trust anyone, so what a shock."

Ellis turned toward the woman he'd been protecting for days now. "Give me one reason why I should trust this guy and I will. Just one."

The room was silent and finally Bailey sighed. "How about he was good to me and Frank?"

Brows raised, Ellis shook his head. "Sorry, no can do. It's nice that he was but it's not enough for me to think that he's some great guy who is going to have your best interests at heart. Right now, I consider him the enemy."

Willow poured herself more coffee, her expression pensive.

"Is that what this is now? They're the enemy? Is this a war?"

"I hope not," Josh said, wrapping his arms around her waist from behind. She rested her head back on his chest. "I truly hope not."

Where there was war there were casualties.

Chapter Twenty-Three

S WEAT TRICKLED DOWN Willow's back underneath the cotton of her sundress. She and Bailey were winding through the crowds at the Midnight Blue Beach Farmer's Market while the midday sun beat down on them relentlessly. It had to be over ninety degrees with at least eighty percent humidity. Nigel Holmwood had to be a little insane to want to sit outside and eat in this blistering Florida heat.

Bailey had her phone to her ear and was talking to Chase, Ellis, and Josh, who had spotted Nigel parking his vehicle on a side street. They should all arrive at the cafe about the same time.

Switching off her phone, Bailey sucked in a breath and blew it out slowly. "Are we ready for this? Do we know our parts?"

Willow nodded, energy coursing through her veins and an anxiousness gnawing at her stomach. She needed answers and was impatient to get them. If Nigel had information, she wanted it.

"If we don't by now, then we never will. I think the important thing is to keep him talking. Let him ramble and maybe he'll reveal something by accident."

"Maybe," Bailey conceded. "Although I've never thought of him as the rambling type. He does love to tell stories though about his childhood growing up in London. Very entertaining. He's led a fascinating life and traveled to some remote areas."

Bailey waved her arm and smiled, nudging Willow next to her. "There he is. We're on."

No one had described Nigel Holmwood to Willow so she hadn't known what to expect. Her imagination had built him into an urbane British gentleman in a tweed suit, smoking a pipe, and looking a little like Higgins from "Magnum PI".

He didn't look anything like that. Tall, thin, and pale, Nigel was wearing light khaki trousers and a navy blue golf shirt with a brown pair of hurachi sandals. He looked every one of his supposed sixty-eight years with gray, thinning hair on top, wire rim glasses, and a hardly noticeable limp. He was, however, also wearing a huge smile and waving back at Bailey.

Opening his arms in welcome, he beckoned to Bailey to come in for a hug. "My sweet girl, it has been far too long. You look beautiful, as always, if a trifle tired. Have you been getting enough rest?"

The voice matched what Willow had heard on the phone, upper class and cultured. The old friends hugged and he kissed Bailey on each cheek, European style.

"I'm fine, Uncle Nigel, maybe a bit tired though. I've had so much going on." Bailey turned to Willow. "Nigel, I'd like you to meet a good friend of mine, Willow Vaughn. Willow, this is Sir Nigel Holmwood."

Willow held out her hand. "It's nice to meet you, sir."

Nigel shook it heartily and then pulled out a chair for each of them. "It's nice to meet you too, Willow. Such a lovely name for a lovely woman. Now, please call me Nigel. Any friend of Bailey's is a friend of mine."

The three settled at a table and the waitress came and took their drink order. Bailey waited until the young woman was a few feet away before speaking.

"We need to talk to you, Nigel. That's why I brought Willow with me. We know about Evandria."

Nigel shrugged carelessly. "Evandria isn't a secret, my sweet girl. It never was."

"Then why didn't Frank ever mention it?"

"Perhaps it wasn't important."

Willow gripped the arms of the wrought-iron chair trying to calm the butterflies in her stomach. "Frank, Alex, and Greg were all members of Arsenal. You led that division."

Nigel's attention swung to Willow, but his expression gave nothing away. "Yes, they were all in my section. Good men. I was sorry to hear of their passing. They were loyal to the mission."

"Did they give their lives for it?" Willow asked bluntly. This was exactly how they'd rehearsed it but she hadn't been prepared for the overwhelming anger that she felt toward this man. He'd known things about her husband that she hadn't, and wouldn't have if she hadn't met Bailey and Peyton.

He didn't answer as the waitress brought their drinks but the tension in his shoulders gave him away. He hadn't liked that question. Nigel's gaze skittered away and then back to the two women. "The honest truth is I don't know."

"You don't know," Bailey repeated. "Or you don't know…for sure?"

"I don't know for sure."

"They were all killed on the exact same day and in ways to make it look like an accident," Willow said. "On the anniversary of Evandria's founding. That's kind of a strange coincidence, don't you think?"

Bailey wrinkled her nose. "We're getting to hate that word. So many coincidences that they cannot be called that anymore."

Crumpling his napkin, the knuckles on his lined hands were white. "If you must know, ladies, I don't think it was a coincidence. I've never thought Frank's death was an accident, Bailey. That's why I've been looking for the killer all this time."

That statement was quite a bit to take in. Willow took a sip of her water in case she was delirious. "Wait, you're looking for the killer? For the last five years?"

He nodded and sighed, looking unutterably sad. "You must understand. Frank, Alex, and Greg were like sons to me. I've never had children of my own but if I did, I'd want them to be just like those young men. I'd known them since they were children. Watched them grow up and take on adult responsibilities. You could not ask for three better men in all the world. They deserved better than what they got and that was my fault." He leaned forward, his hand reaching out for Bailey's. "It's my fault they're dead. I'm so sorry, my sweet girl. I'm so very sorry."

Her heart in her throat, Willow choked out a reply. "How is it your fault, Nigel? Do you know who killed them?"

He shook his head. "I have suspects but I've never been able to prove anything, sadly. Now at my age and with my health, I may never know."

"We're going to find out," Bailey said. "But we need your help, Uncle. Will you help us?"

"This entire situation is too dangerous for you and I feel responsible. If they hadn't joined Arsenal, this wouldn't have happened."

Bailey had gone off script slightly and it was Willow's job to bring them back. "What is Arsenal exactly and how did it get them killed?"

"Arsenal is an intelligence gathering initiative within Evandria. Believe me, we are well aware of what power can. The kind of power that Evandria bestows on people can become all-consuming. Arsenal is our efforts to ferret those people out and reveal them to our leadership committee."

Bailey's eyes had gone wide. "You mean they were like secret agents?"

A smile flickered over the older man's face. "That's one way of putting it. It was their job to investigate members that we felt were at risk and to report on them. Frankly, it's a dangerous job and because of that we only take volunteers."

"And Alex volunteered?"

Nigel nodded. "He did. Your husband was a devoted man."

Had Nigel actually ever met Alex Vaughn? It was like they were discussing two different men.

"Then that would have been the only thing he was ever devoted to," Willow replied bitterly. "Other than his own pleasure, that is. Nigel, my husband was a womanizer, a drug addict, and a drunk. Whoever killed him knew that because they used his vices to cover up his murder."

Wrapping his hands around his iced tea glass, Nigel's gaze dropped. "I'll admit the men had their issues. Knowing they were in danger and could die does have its effects on some of the volunteers. They react in different ways. Alex reacted by self-medicating but he told me that he loved you."

He'd told her that as well but she'd given up believing it. She'd learned that love was more than words you say. It was the everyday actions of two people building a life together. He might have loved her, but he hadn't acted like it. That made all the difference.

Bailey brushed a tear from her cheek. "Frank pulled away emotionally. I could never get close to him."

Nigel shook his head. "They should never have married. We recommend that they don't. It's a testament to how much they loved you that they ignored us."

Willow wasn't too sure of that. If Alex had truly loved her, wouldn't he have wanted the best for her? Even if it wasn't him? Looking back, his actions seemed selfish. He wanted what he wanted and her happiness be damned.

Or maybe she was simply bitter.

"You said this job was dangerous but I'm not sure I understand why," Bailey said. "Supposedly Evandria is a philanthropic organization."

"It is," Nigel agreed with a bob of his head. "But it's also so much more than that. The connections and friendships one makes in a group like Evandria can take a member from a law office to the Supreme Court. Some people shouldn't have that kind of power. We try to be careful when it comes to our members and that's what Arsenal is all about. But remember the

MIDNIGHT OF NO RETURN

old saying – Power corrupts, and absolute power corrupts absolutely."

Willow sat back in her chair. "So you're saying there are people in Evandria that would do anything for power? Even kill?"

Nigel rubbed the back of his neck. "Yes, and we're aware of the problem. Arsenal has existed since the day Evandria was formed but modern times have only made the schism in the organization worse. Those that want power in this world, whether it be financial or political, are willing to do just about anything to get it. We need to bring those members out and expose them to the light. It's the only way not to be taken over by them. We have to hold strong. Otherwise…"

"They could take over the world," Bailey said softly.

Nigel didn't respond, instead drinking deeply from his glass as rivulets of sweat beaded on his forehead.

Needing clarification, Willow pressed for more. "So let me get this straight. Evandria is at war with itself. It has good members and evil members and since the 1860s you have had a civil war within your ranks for control and power. Alex, Frank, and Greg volunteered to be secret agents and report on the evil members who want to take over the world. Someone found out what they were doing and killed them on the group's anniversary. Is that about right?"

Nigel nodded. "Yes, that's right. I'm sorry you ladies have gotten yourselves caught up in this. For your own safety you need to step away from this, Bailey. You need to leave this alone. Nothing good can come from this. You're risking your life."

No one knew that more than they did. Peyton had almost

paid the ultimate price.

Bailey shook her head. "I can't stop, Uncle Nigel. We need to know who killed our husbands. We have to know the truth."

Draining his glass, he signaled to the waitress. "You may never find out who did it, and does it matter anyway? You know why they were killed. Isn't that enough?"

"It wasn't enough for you," Willow pointed out. "You said you've been chasing their murderer for the last five years."

"And I've had little luck with that. With all my resources in the organization I haven't been able to find the perpetrator. If I can't find him or her, I doubt you could. You're wasting your time. Move on with your life and know that they were truly good men."

If only she could, but they'd come so far. She couldn't give up now.

"Archer Caldwell," she said instead. "Which side is he on? He gave me fake files for the men."

Nigel smiled and chuckled as the waitress refilled his iced tea. "Don't concentrate on Archer, my child. He's a figurehead. The real power in Evandria is behind the scenes. Men and women that don't show their faces. He's a puppet and does as he's told."

"Who tells him what to do?" Bailey asked. "The good or the bad?"

Shrugging, Nigel laughed. "Both, I imagine. Archer is all about Archer. He likes the power and as long as we keep him in check everything is fine."

Willow could taste the acid in the back of her throat. The whole thing made her sick.

"And if you don't keep him in check?"

The older man stared at his hands for a long moment before answering. "Then we deal with that. Evandria knows how to deal with its own."

"Stephen Baxter," Bailey said suddenly. "Did Evandria have him killed? He was recovering and then he was dead."

"I shouldn't be telling you this. Any of it." Nigel shook his head and pulled off his glasses, wiping the lenses with the shredded paper napkin. "It is very possible that Stephen Baxter was killed by Evandria but not by the regular members—by the rogues who are seeking more power. You see, Stephen Baxter was being investigated by Arsenal and had been on our radar for years. He might have known things certain people didn't want the police to know. Having known Stephen for many years, I can tell you with utmost certainty he would have sold out every member of Evandria without a second thought if he thought he would spend one less day in prison."

"More secrets," Willow said, mostly to herself. She had another question, although her gut was telling her the answer already. "Nigel, you said Baxter was being investigated by Arsenal. What agent was assigned that case?"

Replacing his glasses, he cleared his throat. "Grant Hollister. He's one of my best men. Smart, fearless, and devoted to Evandria."

Floored was the only way to describe her emotions. So shocked, she had to take a moment before she could even reply. She'd assumed Alex had been assigned the case.

"He's Alex's half-brother. Does he know that?"

Giving her a strange look, Nigel nodded. "Of course he does. We all know. But I'm guessing you didn't." His phone buzzed and he checked it with a rueful glance. "I'm afraid I must be off. If you have any more questions just give me a call. But I want to reiterate my plea for you ladies to leave this alone. It's dangerous and I'm not just saying that. These are not people to be trifled with, Bailey. Their thirst for power is unquenchable. If they think you are trying to interfere with that they won't hesitate to hurt you."

They all stood, and Nigel hugged Bailey and shook hands with Willow before tossing some bills down on the table. They watched as he disappeared around the corner, not saying anything until he was out of sight. Bailey was probably as stunned by the revelations as Willow was.

"I'm going to the ladies' room real quick." Willow placed her hand on Bailey's arm. Her friend seemed miles away. "I'll be right back, okay?"

"Sure. Yes. I'll wait here."

It only took a few minutes for Willow to find the restroom, freshen up, and mop away the sticky sweat from the back of her neck. Feeling cooler and more put together, she pushed open the door of the ladies' room and headed down the corridor to the main part of the cafe. She was almost at the end of the hallway when she heard someone calling her name.

"Willow Vaughn."

The voice was soft but masculine and she whirled around toward the sound. Rooted to the spot and her breath caught in her throat, Grant Hollister stood there in the alcove to the family restroom. Of all the people in the world, she hadn't expected to speak to him today. Or ever, after the way he'd avoided her at the ball and then again at the clinic.

"Grant Hollister," she heard herself say and he nodded, beckoning to her. She followed numbly, a little voice inside of her screaming that going anywhere with him wasn't a good idea, but her curiosity won out and she found herself alone with him in the small bathroom, the door locked behind them.

"You can't trust him."

Those were the first words from Grant's lips and she had no idea whether he'd meant them to be ironic or not. She wasn't sure she could trust *him*.

"Who can't I trust?"

Chapter Twenty-Four

"NIGEL," GRANT SAID urgently, his hand on her upper arm. Willow didn't shake it away, that sixth sense she'd honed as a dancer telling her that he meant no harm. She'd learned to trust it and it hadn't failed her yet. "You can't trust Nigel. He's part of the rogue organization."

Shaking her head to clear her thoughts, she tried to focus in on what he was saying and what she needed to know. This was no time to be dizzy and confused, no matter how shocked she was.

"He talked about a rogue part of Evandria. He says they want power."

Grant snorted and rolled his eyes. "Power? They want to rule the world and not in a benevolent, let's hold hands and sing kind of way. They'll do anything and kill anyone to get what they want. They killed Stephen Baxter."

Ah yes, Stephen.

"Nigel said that you were investigating Stephen for Arsenal. Is that true?"

Grant leaned back against the tiled wall in the tiny room.

"No, it is not true. Stephen was in Arsenal too. He was Nigel's favorite. No way we would investigate him. Listen to me, you can't believe anything Nigel tells you. He's lying to you to get you to stop digging into Evandria's affairs."

That Willow could believe. Holmwood had definitely been trying to persuade them to give up the investigation.

"Why is this the first time I've ever met you? Why didn't Alex tell me about you? Nigel said everyone knew you were brothers."

Grant shook his head. "I told you. You can't believe everything Nigel tells you. As for why you've never met me, well, that's the way Alex and the family wanted it. They helped me financially and put me through college as long as I kept my mouth shut. They've never acknowledged me openly. I'm a close family friend if you ask them. Suits me just fine. I don't have much regard for my biological father."

"He's an asshole," Willow said dryly. "A grade-A son of a bitch."

Grinning, Grant shifted so they were standing toe to toe. "You've got that right. When you inherited everything, I thought he was going to have a stroke. He was that angry."

"I still don't understand. Alex has been gone for five years and you have your own fortune now. Why didn't you contact me then?"

"And say what? Your husband was a big fat liar and he kept all sorts of secrets from you? No, that's the last thing you needed. I've kept my eye on you and watched you come out the other side of your grief. You didn't need me. At least, you didn't need me then. You need me now."

She did need him now. "You've known all along that Alex was murdered, along with his friends."

He shook his head. "Not right away, but eventually."

"Archer Caldwell is trying to find out who did it."

Hands on her shoulders, he gave her a little shake as if to bring her to her senses. "No, Willow. Archer is not helping you. He's fucking with you but he's not helping you. You can't trust anything he tells you."

"He's rogue too? The only person that I'm supposed to trust is you? That's convenient."

Willow was tired of being lied to and played for a fool.

"I don't know if Archer is rogue but I do know he can't be trusted. He has two goals. The first is to protect Evandria at all costs and the second is to protect himself. You and your friends are a threat."

"Because Evandria killed Alex? We know or at least we think we know that Evandria had them murdered. What we don't know is who did it. Do you know?"

"Archer Caldwell murdered Alex and his friends." His arms dropped away and his hands tightened into fists at his side. "It's taken me years but I finally have the evidence."

Staggering back, she grabbed onto the sink for support. "Archer. I guess I'm not surprised. Why? And how? He's one man and there were three murders."

"He may not have done all three personally but make no mistake, he was the assassin carrying out the orders. Archer Caldwell is guilty as hell and Nigel has been blocking me at every turn as I've investigated this."

She shoved at his shoulder. "Speaking of being blocked, how

about how you avoided me at the ball Saturday night? I needed to talk to you."

His expression sobered and he rubbed his chin. "That would have been the worst thing that could have happened. I needed to keep you at arm's length so they wouldn't think that I would try to help you. If they had seen us talking, I don't think you would have left The Retreat alive."

Charming. She was also getting tired of being in danger.

"Do they want me dead?" she asked bluntly. "Do they want Peyton and Bailey dead? Did they blow up Peyton at the hotel? Did they plan for me to be thrown from that horse?"

If he'd been keeping an eye on her, he had to know about the package bomb at the hotel in Williamsburg.

"They want you out of the way. Alive or dead is fine. The horse accident was meant to be a warning as was the package bomb."

"Hell of a warning. People were hurt. Peyton could have died."

"You don't get it." He turned his back to her and scraped his fingers through his sandy blond hair. "They don't care about people. They only care about power."

Her head was beginning to hurt from all the circular talking, first with Nigel and now with Grant. "Archer? The rogue organization? Who runs it?"

He whirled back around and shrugged. "I think you're getting the idea that Evandria is about secrets and the rogue organization is a big one. Archer is simply a puppet for someone bigger and much more ruthless. I don't have a clue who truly runs it and if I did find out, I'm sure I'd be dead within twenty-four hours. Personally, I like being on the green side of the grass."

That matched what Nigel had said. Archer wasn't the real power.

"So you're telling us to back off too?"

He smiled and reached for the door knob. "I'm telling you to leave this investigation to me. You'll only get yourself killed if you continue with this. I have enough friends in Evandria to protect me somewhat. If you let this alone, they'll forget all about you. You can go back to living your life."

"Why should I believe you? Trust you? How do I even know you're telling me the truth? Maybe you're the liar."

His expression softened and she could see his resemblance to Alex at that moment. The kindness she'd first seen in her husband the night she'd met him.

"I'm not lying. Alex asked me to watch over you if anything happened to him. He knew his association with Arsenal was dangerous. He wouldn't want you to risk your life for this, Willow. He loved you."

A tear slipped down her cheek and she dashed it away with the back of her hand. "Funny way of showing it."

"Let me protect you, Willow. Let me keep my promise to my brother. I loved him too, you know. We have that in common."

So many emotions were twisting inside of her – love, betrayal, hurt, anger, and even a little forgiveness.

"If you want me to believe what you say, I need to see your evidence. My friends need to see it too."

She didn't have any intention of stopping but Grant didn't know that. At this point, she needed to bring him into the fold and see how he could help them.

"Fine," he nodded. "But not here. We can't be seen together. And not at your house. I'm sure it's been bugged."

That made her smile. "We found those."

"Still, it's not safe." He frowned, and pursed his lips. "There's an old dive bar out by the turnpike called Roy's. Can you meet me there at midnight tonight? It will be packed and no one will notice us. I'll bring the evidence and you and your friends can judge for themselves. But if you believe me, then you have to back off. It's too dangerous for you, Willow."

"Fair enough. We'll be there."

He twisted the doorknob and they cautiously exited the restroom, Grant in the lead and Willow right behind. It was a trifle ridiculous to be skulking around the bathroom, but if Grant thought it was necessary she'd go along with it. She was too excited that she'd finally met and spoken with him to be nervous about who might see them together.

"Shit," he hissed, coming to an abrupt stop at the end of the hallway. "He's here. I'll see you tonight. Get back to your friends right away, Willow."

She didn't know who "he" was but Grant appeared pale and afraid. He darted into the side door of the kitchen and disappeared, leaving her standing alone. One glance toward the door of the restaurant though told her who "he" was.

Archer Caldwell.

He was hiding behind a column but she easily recognized him. His gaze was sweeping back and forth across the dining room, clearly looking for someone. Her? Nigel? Grant?

Dammit, she needed to get back to Bailey. Her friend had to

be wondering if she'd fallen into the commode. Her heart in her throat, Willow darted across the corner of the dining room to the door to the outside dining area, not caring much if Archer saw her. In all probability, he already knew she was there with Nigel.

And maybe Grant.

Bailey was taking care of the check when she returned, tucking the receipt in her purse before looking up with an expression of annoyance.

"Where have you been? I was about to send out a search party."

"I'll explain when we're away from here."

Grabbing Bailey's arm, Willow hopped over the short, wrought iron fence that separated the diners from the rest of the bustling crowd, dragging Bailey right behind her. Protesting and tugging at her arm, Bailey was finally able to pull it from Willow's grasp but not before they were away from the restaurant and in a crowd of people.

"Have you lost your mind?" Bailey looked at Willow as if she'd gone crazy and perhaps she had. All the fear and paranoia was beginning to catch up with her. "Why did you do that?"

"I'd like to know too." Josh stood just behind Bailey wearing a puzzled expression. "I was keeping an eye on you and all of the sudden you bolted from the restaurant as if someone was chasing you."

They might be.

"Archer was in the restaurant looking for someone." Willow kept her voice low. She didn't know who was around that might be listening. "Grant Hollister was there as well. He intercepted me on the way back from the bathroom and we talked. He told me Archer is the killer and he has evidence. He's going to show it to us tonight."

Mouth hanging open, it took Bailey a minute to respond. "Okay, that's a good reason for leaving me at the table. We should go get the guys and tell them."

Rubbing his chin, Josh gave them a grim look. "They'll be interested in hearing this but they're a little busy now. You see, after Nigel left the cafe they saw him talking to Archer and they took off following them. They were headed over to the side street where Nigel parked his car."

Frowning, Willow retrieved her phone from her purse to check for a message from Ellis. "Except that Archer was in the restaurant so he must have doubled back. Are they still following Nigel?"

The sound of an explosion tore through the air and the shock waves under the ground almost rocked them off their feet. Josh pushed both women against a large oak tree and covered them as best as he could with his body, his entire frame tense as they waited for a second explosion. Willow could hear the rush of blood in her ears as they stayed there, frozen for long moments even as the sound of screaming and running footsteps filled the air. All those noises seemed far away as she waited, barely breathing, for the next explosion to be even closer. Grant and Nigel had warned them.

A buzzing from Josh's phone brought them out of their trance and he cursed softly before answering it, the conversation short and to the point. He hung up and stepped back, still keeping his body in front of theirs.

"That was Ellis. The explosion was Nigel's vehicle."

Chapter Twenty-Five

"DID HE GET in his car or not?"

Bailey's tortured tone did nothing to calm Willow's frayed nerves as they sat in her kitchen a little over two hours later. They'd hung around the site of the explosion for awhile, hoping to catch a glimpse of Archer again or maybe hear the rescue squad say something that might be helpful but eventually they'd returned home empty-handed.

Willow ran her fingers over Scout's silky coat and nuzzled her nose against his cold, wet one. After the day she'd had, all she'd wanted was a cuddle with Scout and Brodie. Somehow they always managed to make her feel better. They'd been her constant companions since Alex died.

"I don't know." Ellis ran his fingers through his hair for the hundredth time. At this rate, he was going to be bald by the time they solved this mystery. "They both darted into the crowd and we lost them. Archer obviously went back to the cafe and Nigel must have gotten into his car. I'm guessing the explosion was tied to the ignition switch. I'm sorry, Bailey. I think he's dead."

"He's dead because he tried to help us," Bailey whispered.

"Archer Caldwell killed him."

Ellis shook his head, his lips a flat line. "We don't know that. It could have been Grant Hollister—he was there too. Or someone else we don't even know about. Fucking Evandria."

Willow didn't want it to be Grant. She'd liked him and her gut told her to trust him.

"It doesn't make sense for Grant to have done it," she argued, shifting the dog slightly on her lap. "Why bother to sneak into the cafe to warn me not to trust him if he was only going to kill him a few minutes later?"

"To discredit Nigel," Bailey said defensively. "He's trying to make him out to be the bad guy."

"Maybe he is the bad guy." Willow didn't want to hurt Bailey's feelings but she had to express her own. "The whole reason he talked to us was to get us to back off and leave Evandria alone. And he lied about Stephen Baxter. He was in Arsenal too."

"Says Grant," Bailey flung back, a few tears slipping down her face. "I'm not sure we can trust him. He wants us to stop investigating too. He could be lying through his teeth about Archer being the killer."

"So could Nigel. But Grant is offering us proof—that's more than Nigel is."

Bailey sat up and looked like she was going to continue arguing but Peyton stepped between them. "Stop. Stop this shit right now. Look, now they've got us fighting with each other and that was probably their plan all along."

Ellis twisted open a beer bottle and tossed the cap in the trash. "You can bet it was. Personally, I don't think we can trust any one of these assholes. As far as I'm concerned, they're all liars until proven otherwise. But Hollister is going to get a chance to convince me tonight. Until then, nothing they said is the truth. Wait, except for one thing. We're in danger and they want us dead. Now that I believe."

"You'll all get to talk to Grant tonight," Willow said. "We'll see his evidence and you can judge for yourselves."

"Do you think he'll still show up?" Peyton asked. "After what happened to Nigel? He could be in danger too."

"He is in danger. He told me so."

Ellis's brows went up. "Did he name names as to who wants him dead?"

He hadn't except for Archer, which was a given. "We can ask him for details tonight, but I believe him over Archer Caldwell. I don't believe he's truly looking for the killer no matter what he says. He gives me the creeps."

"Doesn't make him a liar," Peyton cautioned.

Willow laughed but it wasn't funny. "Doesn't make him a truther either. The man is strange and he clearly has secrets. Lots of them. He's an arrogant SOB too."

Josh laid a hand on hers. "Let's just say that Archer Caldwell doesn't inspire much trust. He tends to not answer direct questions and he's constantly trying to turn conversations in the direction he wants them to go. I can definitely see him protecting someone in the organization. He wouldn't want a messy murder investigation ruining Evandria's reputation."

Chase threw up his hands in frustration. "Then where does that leave us?"

Josh glanced at Willow before he answered. "Right now

Grant is our only hope of getting any information. We need to question him and find out what he knows, with a skeptical eye, of course. We can't take everything he says as true but we need to listen to what he has to say. You know what that means, my friends."

Frowning, Ellis shook his head. "What does it mean?"

Josh stood and tossed his empty water bottle into the trash. "If I'm going to meet some guy at midnight, I'm going to need a nap first. I'm not twenty-two anymore. I'll see you all in a few hours."

There were some chuckles as Josh disappeared out of the kitchen and up the stairs. What was she doing sitting here? She could use a nap as well. Jumping up, she waved toward her friends.

"Make yourselves at home. Eat or drink anything you want. I think I need to rest too."

She didn't imagine the laughter as she trailed after Josh.

JOSH STRETCHED AND opened his eyes slowly, the sun still high in the sky this time of year despite the hour. It was dinnertime according to his empty stomach but he didn't immediately move to get out of bed, content to let Willow cuddle close, her head on his chest. Her hair was draped over his arm, tickling the skin whenever she fidgeted in her sleep.

Staring at the ceiling, he replayed the day in his head from the moment he'd seen Nigel Holmwood to the sound of his car exploding. The man was certainly an enigma from what Bailey had told them. A businessman who had kept most of his life under wraps. When pinned down, she had admitted that she didn't know all that much about him personally or professionally. She'd been told just enough to assuage any curiosity but no more. That seemed to be a theme with this organization.

But with the car bomb today and Grant Hollister's warning, Josh needed to put all of his concentration on keeping Willow safe. He was more convinced than ever that her life was indeed in danger and that Evandria wouldn't think twice about eliminating her if they thought she knew something they wanted kept a secret.

A sigh and her stirring alerted him that she was no longer asleep. He ran his hand down her back and pressed a kiss to her nose, watching her eyelids flutter open.

"Hi."

Her voice was soft and sleep-roughened, and his heart squeezed in his chest. He'd fallen for this woman, head over heels, and he didn't think he'd ever get out. Nor did he really want to. She was straightforward, blisteringly honest, smart, funny, and so endearingly imperfect it made him want to hold and kiss her every moment of the day. She could burn water and possibly set her own kitchen on fire but instead of finding it annoying, she somehow managed to make it cute.

The only fly in the ointment was her money. He didn't want it and honestly, it was a nuisance. It created a barrier between them that he wasn't sure how to deal with. She'd laughed at him last night as they were falling asleep when he'd admitted that he'd prefer she was still a stripper than a wealthy widow. He'd inwardly winced when he said it because it sounded horrid but she hadn't taken offense, understanding what he couldn't seem to express.

If she was a woman who had everything, what was there left that he could give her?

Of course, his sweet Willow had an answer. Love and acceptance. Those two things were something both of them could use more of.

"Hi," he echoed back. "Did you sleep well?"

"Hmmmm, I did. Too well. I don't want to get up."

"It's early yet. You don't have to, although eventually we're going to have to eat."

Propping herself on her elbow, she let out a big yawn. "Are they still downstairs?"

"I don't know. I've been awake for a while and haven't heard anything so I think they went home. I can call Chase and Ellis if you want them back."

"No." She shook her head. "I just wondered if we needed to order in some dinner for them. I know they want some alone time for themselves, especially Bailey and Chase. Maybe Peyton and Ellis too."

Josh groaned as he pictured his friend in any sort of a loving relationship. He didn't have the best track record with females. "Peyton is wise to be cautious. Ellis can be challenging to be around at times. He's completely obsessed with his work and it's been hard on the women he's dated in the past."

"He definitely seems smitten. When they're in the same room, his gaze follows her everywhere. It's like he can't take his eyes off of her, which is sweet and creepy all at the same time."

"He's a man with laser focus and right now all of his attention is on keeping Peyton safe and alive."

"For that I am grateful." She butted his shoulder with her forehead. "I'm grateful to you too."

He stretched and gave her a wicked grin. "Feel free to show me how much."

Running her fingertip over his shoulder and down his arm, she looked up at him from under her lashes. This woman knew how to flirt.

"I'm not sure I'd even know how to begin."

"I think you do."

With a giggle, she lifted the sheet and pulled it over their heads. Dinner was going to have to wait.

Chapter Twenty-Six

J OSH GROANED AS he hit the brakes again, bringing the vehicle to a complete stop. Red lights flashed on top of the emergency vehicles, one firetruck and one police cruiser that had closed down the road, causing bumper to bumper traffic. Ellis and Chase were right behind him in their own vehicles but they were definitely going to be late. It was already after midnight and Willow was fidgeting in her seat, worrying that Grant wouldn't wait for them.

At this point, everybody knew their part. The plan was in place to talk with Grant Hollister, what questions to ask, who would ask them, and even who would follow Hollister home after the meeting. Ellis had volunteered for that job and insisted on doing it alone, saying that Josh and Chase needed to stay and protect the women. They also planned to press for their own copy of whatever evidence he was going to show them. Willow desperately wanted to believe that Grant was telling the truth and that Archer had killed Alex but Josh had convinced her that they needed to be skeptical. Archer might be the killer but it just as easily could be a ruse to get her and the other women to quit digging into Evandria. While she was sure that Hollister was telling the truth, Josh was less so. Much less.

The thought they might be walking into a trap had certainly crossed their minds several times in the last few hours but this was the only lead they had. If they didn't meet with Hollister, they were at a dead end. Again.

That was why not only was Ellis wearing a handgun but Chase and Josh as well, strapped to their calves. They'd argued about whether it was asking for trouble, but in the end they'd decided it was better to be too suspicious. Walking into that bar unarmed would be stupid.

His hand went down to where the gun was situated, brushing the slight bump in his jeans as his heart thumped loudly. A simple veterinarian, he wasn't a man who dealt with danger and intrigue on a daily basis. Hell, even Ellis didn't get himself into situations like this often, growling that he dealt with paperwork most of the time but at least he'd been trained. The most dangerous thing Josh did most days was express a dog's anal glands. They didn't enjoy that and often let him know.

"Grant's not dangerous."

Willow's soft voice pulled him from his thoughts and back to the present – sitting in the car waiting for the traffic to inch forward.

"You don't know that."

"I do," she pressed, her own hands shaking slightly as she fussed with the strap of her purse. "My former profession gave me a sixth sense about men and he's a good one. I believe what he says despite what Bailey thinks. Archer killed Alex."

"Don't let him tear you and her apart," Josh warned. "That's what Evandria wants to do. Get us arguing among ourselves and off on a tangent. We've been through too much to allow that to happen, honey."

"I won't but I just want you to know that I think all of this subterfuge isn't needed. I think he's telling the truth."

Josh wished he could be as confident, but he wasn't. It was his job to worry and tonight was a good reason to do it.

"Even if he is telling the truth, there's a damn good reason he's meeting us in the middle of nowhere at midnight. It means that someone is probably watching him and probably us too. This isn't a friendly drink with a long lost friend. Lives are at stake here. If Archer did do it, he's not going to be happy that Grant told you."

Josh couldn't allow himself the luxury of even one moment of letting his guard down. That's when people got hurt.

"All of our lives," she said softly. "I got you into this, after all."

"Honey, I'm a willing victim."

Josh glanced at his watch again. Twelve-ten. With any luck, Hollister got caught in this traffic mess as well. Willow craned her neck to get a better look over the cars in front of them.

"He won't wait. He'll think we aren't coming."

Josh waved a hand toward the line of vehicles they were following at a snail's pace. "He's probably up there going five miles an hour with the rest of us. There aren't any good alternative routes to this fine establishment that he chose. If we're late, he's late."

"I hope so," she muttered, her fingers twisting her purse and the knuckles turning white. "I want that evidence, Josh."

"I know, honey, but you have to be ready for him either to not have it or what he says proves Archer did it is less than spectacular. I don't want you getting your hopes up."

They were getting close to the "accident" or whatever was blocking the lanes when the police car pulled away, sirens blaring, followed by the fire engine. It appeared that it was those vehicles that had been blocking the lanes and the cars had been getting by on the shoulder. Now that they were gone, traffic quickly sped up.

"See? We'll be there in no time."

The dinner they'd eaten earlier felt like lead in Josh's stomach but there was no going back. But even in his dreams earlier he could still hear the explosion when the car bomb had gone off, the acrid smell of smoke, the screams of innocent bystanders along with the sound of their feet running away as fast as they could. That was something he couldn't protect Willow from.

The unknown.

Sure, if someone came at him with a knife or gun he could defend her and himself but the hidden threats were out there. It was a game of chance as to whether they'd find them before it hurt someone. Chances were good that they'd fail. He wasn't a pessimist by nature, generally a man who expected the best in his life, but right now he needed to be a hard realist. The odds were not in their favor. Not to solve Willow's husband's murder and maybe not even to survive the attempt. It was that attitude that kept him vigilant and might just keep them alive.

He smelled it before he saw it. The sharp smell of burnt wood came through the vents of the air conditioner but it was the bright orange and yellow shooting flames that lit the otherwise dark sky. Slowing the car down, he saw the crowd that had gathered around the burning building as the sound of sirens filled the air.

Roy's was on fire.

Quickly pulling as close as he deemed safe, he and Willow stumbled out of the car in something of a daze. The entire building was engulfed in flames. If anyone had been inside and hadn't made it out… There was no way they would have survived.

Willow began to run toward the building and he had to sprint after her, holding her tightly as she struggled against him. "Grant. Grant is in there."

She was like a wild thing, crying and thrashing against him until eventually she ran out of energy, sobs wracking her body. The other two couples had come to stand beside them, their own expressions stricken and fearful at the same time. The ramifications of this fire were sinking into their shattered consciousness.

"You don't know that, honey. You don't know that he was in there. He may have realized what was going on and turned back. But you running into a burning building isn't going to bring him back if he was."

The blistering heat pushed him back, dragging Willow along with him, his arm around her to keep her anchored to his side. While Nigel's death this afternoon had changed everything, this made it a hundred times worse. It was the confirmation of all that he'd feared. Someone was out to kill Willow and they didn't care who they took out while doing it.

Ellis had been talking to a few of the people who were watching the building burn and collapse onto itself but he came over to where they all stood silent, not sure what to say or do. Shock kept them immobile.

"I talked to a few of the witnesses," Ellis said, his fingers scraping through his hair again. "They said it was an explosion. One of the witnesses surmised it might have been in the kitchen but I think we all know that's not the case. Anyway, it happened about ten minutes ago."

Willow shuddered in Josh's arms. "If we'd been here…"

Thank god for Florida traffic jams. His heart was in his throat as his imagination took over, picturing the hell on earth that would have been. That helplessness he'd felt earlier was beginning to overtake all rational thought. He couldn't keep her safe, not from something like this. It was too unexpected, too random.

"But we weren't," Peyton said, her voice rough from the smoke blowing in their faces. "And maybe Grant wasn't here either."

Peyton was their optimist and this time Josh hoped she was right. For Willow's sake if nothing else. Grant represented the family she'd never had but might be able to. He could feel the strength of her belief. She wanted Hollister to be a brother to her.

Bailey was pacing back and forth, muttering under her breath. "I'm sick of this shit. Let's go to Hollister's house and see if he had a copy of the evidence there."

There was a decent chance that he did but it still wasn't a good idea.

"Absolutely not," Ellis cut in. "He told Willow he was being watched so his home is surely under surveillance. We cannot go there."

"We're probably all being watched," Josh agreed. "They could be watching us right now, checking to see if their handiwork did the job."

Willow and Peyton were clinging to one another, their cheeks damp with tears. Willow rubbed at her eyes, smearing her makeup. "All those innocent people are dead. Because of us."

Josh placed his hands on her shoulders so she could lean back on his chest. "This is not your fault. This is on Evandria and no one else. They're the guilty parties."

His gaze met Chase's and then Ellis's, an unspoken agreement passing between them. Evandria had to be stopped. This was bigger than who had killed the girls' husbands. This was about justice and power, who had it and who didn't.

Bailey stopped pacing, whirling around to face the others. "Then we'll go to The Retreat. We'll get the evidence and more. That's probably where Grant got it, so we go there and do the same."

Peyton was already shaking her head. "Grant was a member so he could get inside. No one would question him. But us? There's no way we would get past the gate, especially if Archer knows we're on to him."

Shrugging, Bailey was clearly on a roll. "Okay, so we sneak in. Josh did it before so we know it can be done."

Hold on. Once was enough.

"I did it and I sure as hell wouldn't recommend it to anyone," Josh growled. "It was fucking dangerous and I still don't know if someone saw me. Absolutely not. I understand that you're frustrated but barging into Evandria headquarters is not the answer."

"I think we should do it," she insisted, her cheeks red with anger. "We need to do something bold."

"This is insane," Chase hissed. "I won't let you go. It's too dangerous."

Bailey might be laid back most of the time but right now her chin was lifted and her eyes blazing. "I'm in danger just standing here apparently, so I might as well get some answers while I'm still breathing."

To Josh's utter shock Willow agreed. "I see Bailey's point. We need to go where the information is. It may be our only chance to get at the truth. The truth Grant died trying to get to us."

Peyton stepped forward and grabbed Bailey and Willow's hands. "If you guys are going, I'm going too."

Fuck, no. Things were rapidly spiraling out of control.

Ellis growled in anger and frustration, pacing the few feet between Josh and the women.

"Son of a fucking bitch, going to them without a plan is stupid. Dumb. It's like those chicks in horror movies who open the door when you're screaming at the screen, 'don't open the fucking door'. I want to go on record saying this is not in any way, shape, or form a good idea. We're going to get ourselves killed. Chase? Josh? Any thoughts on how to talk these ladies out of it?"

Chase slumped against a vehicle and groaned. "I agree with Ellis. This is a suicide mission and I like being alive."

His head aching, Josh rubbed the back of his neck where a pain was shooting down his back. This was probably the best he'd feel for the rest of the night.

"If we walk into The Retreat we're defenseless. It's dumb and we're not doing it."

Willow turned and poked him in the chest. "You can't stop me–"

"The hell I can't," he declared, with more volume than he intended as a few heads whipped their direction. "If I have to haul you bodily into the car I will. I won't let you risk your life in this idiotic fashion. I won't, Willow. I know you're upset about Grant but this isn't going to fix anything. If he were here he'd tell you the same. If you insist on doing this, I'm walking away. I'll protect you with my life but not if you're going to be stupid."

The very last thing he wanted to do was walk away from her, his heart pleading with him to stay, but he had to make a stand. He couldn't allow her to make a decision from pure emotion.

Her eyes were wide and glistening with tears, and for a moment he thought she was going to turn around and leave. Go get herself killed but then her shoulders slumped and her gaze dropped.

"I don't want you to go."

"Then stay here. What you're seeking isn't worth dying for."

"We may never get the answer if we don't go there."

That was true. But there was other truth as well.

"You may not get the answer if you go." His hands wrapped around her upper arms and he pulled her close until their faces were inches apart, needing to look into her eyes when he bared his soul. "I love you, Willow. I really goddamn love you and I want us to have a life together and that means we need to stay breathing. But if you don't love me or think that you can't move on without the answers you seek then maybe this isn't going to work. My question is…can you be happy with just me? If you never find Alex's killer can you be okay with that?"

At that moment, they were the only two people in the entire world. Everyone standing in a circle around them faded away and all his senses honed in on this one woman who could make or break his future. Her lips trembled as he waited, blood roaring in his ears. It was only his entire future happiness on the line. Was Alex always going to be standing between them?

"I can," she whispered, her voice rough. "I'm greedy enough to want you and the truth, but if I have to pick one, it's you. I love you, Josh."

The breath he didn't know he'd been holding whooshed out of him and his heart skipped several beats with relief. She was staying and she loved him. It would be enough for now.

"We'll go home," he said, crushing her against him until she squeaked for air. "We'll regroup and start again. I'm not saying we should give up."

Nodding, Willow turned to her friends. "I'm staying. Josh is right. Going to The Retreat unprepared like this would be crazy." Her gaze strayed to the building that was still burning out of control, the heat turning her cheeks pink. "I'll find another way to get justice for Grant. We'll figure something out but this isn't it."

Peyton nodded in agreement. "You've made your case. We'll find another way."

Clearly Bailey wanted to argue but Chase stood behind her, his hands on her shoulders, whispering something in her ear that

Josh couldn't hear. Whatever it was, it seemed to do the trick. She sagged against him and buried her face in his shirt.

"I don't like it but okay. We'll stay. I can't argue with the fact that we have no idea what we'd be walking into."

Josh and his friends all seemed to draw a deep breath now that the females weren't pushing to breach the gates of The Retreat. It gave them time to think their next moves through. Chase ushered the women toward the cars but Ellis hung back with Josh.

"We'll figure it out. Maybe there is a way we can get into Grant's house without anyone seeing us," Josh said, although he didn't hold out much hope. If Evandria thought Grant had something incriminating they'd go after it themselves.

"It's definitely something for us to think about. Let's get these ladies home. I don't like them being out in the open. I feel like we have less control out here."

They only had the illusion of control and not much of that. No one was going to sleep, so they might as well order pizzas and stay up all night. They were back to square one. Glancing at his watch, Josh he felt an icy fist tighten in his chest. He'd been so busy and distracted he hadn't even noticed. Josh nudged Ellis.

"Did you notice what the date is now that it's after midnight?"

At first he looked confused, then understanding, then horrified.

It was July twenty-first.

Chapter Twenty-Seven

WILLOW, BAILEY, AND Peyton were in the kitchen making up a much needed batch of margaritas while Josh and his friends talked in the living room. Quietly. Wanting to keep their thoughts and worries private, at least for now. There was no need to upset the women with talk of guns and booby trapping the lawn. After two explosions in one day, they'd become exponentially more paranoid.

The ring of the doorbell had Josh holding up his hand so they would pause. "Let me get that and then we'll get back to this."

The pizza had already been paid for by credit card so all he needed to do was sign for it. The kid at the door barely glanced at him as he shoved the stack of pizza boxes and a receipt in front of his face. Placing the pizza on the foyer table, Josh accepted a pen and scribbled his name. The kid shoved the receipt in his pocket and pulled out another small piece of paper.

"Here's your copy, sir."

Josh accepted the receipt and tossed it on the table. "Thanks."

Instead of leaving, the kid scowled. "Aren't you going to look at it?"

Josh hadn't planned on it. It was a receipt. Why did this kid even care? "Is it important that I do? Isn't it just a receipt from the register?"

"You should always save your credit card receipts, that's all. My mom says you should match them up to your monthly statement."

For fuck's sake, Josh had never done that in his entire life. He only kept receipts if he might return something. "Your mom sounds like a wise and organized woman. You should do as she says."

The kid still wasn't moving and that was when Josh managed to get a good look at him. Young, maybe nineteen or twenty, wearing baggy cargo shorts and a t-shirt. His dark hair was long in the front and wavy, his skin still sporting the teenage curse of acne. But it was his eyes that caught Josh's attention, wide and almost unblinking with brows lifted high. It was a strange facial expression for a pizza delivery guy.

Which immediately put all of Josh's senses on red alert. Keeping his gaze on the young man, Josh reached for the receipt he'd thrown on the side table.

"So I should keep the receipt, huh? Look it over and make sure it matches what I ordered?"

His face relaxing in a smile, the kid nodded enthusiastically. "Yeah, you should. Have a good night."

Closing the door behind him, Josh flipped the lock and then looked out of the side window for any movement. Finding none except the young man who peeled out of the driveway as if he was being chased, he turned his attention to the receipt that had received so much attention and emphasis.

The front was a list of what they'd ordered, printed out as normal by the cash register. It was the back that was much more interesting. Handwriting.

Someone had written a note on the back of the receipt.

Willow, I saw that I was being followed so I double-backed and eventually lost him. I didn't think it was safe to go to Roy's or to come to your home. Instead, I raced as fast as I could and left the package in a place a winner like you could find easily. They're definitely watching both of us so I'm going into hiding and I suggest you keep as low a profile as possible. You should leave Midnight Blue Beach. They own everyone here, including the cops. Once you get the package, don't try and do anything with it yourself. I'll be back at the right time and we'll do it together. I'm sorry I didn't get to say goodbye but I'll see you soon. Stay safe, Grant.

Grant was alive and Willow was going to be thrilled and relieved. The evidence was out there but what did he mean by a place that he knew she could find? It didn't make any sense. If she could find it, then couldn't someone else?

Or maybe this note was a ruse. To lure them into a trap.

It was going to be a long night.

WILLOW LOADED THE last of the dishes into the dishwasher while Josh took Scout and Brodie out one last time before the furry duo went to bed. She didn't fool herself into thinking she would sleep, not after Josh had shown her the note from Grant. No, she and Josh would be up most of the night trying to figure out what Grant was talking about. He'd used the most vague wording and it left the field open wide. There were a million places she could find, but what did that mean exactly? Why did he call her a winner?

"Grant, you could have been a hell of a lot clearer," she muttered, wiping her hands on a dishtowel. "I've never been good at puzzles."

The door to the backyard opened and the two canines barreled in, wanting treats and kisses. Mostly treats. Josh followed and retrieved two bottles of water from the refrigerator. Chase, Bailey, Peyton and Ellis had gone home to try and get what little rest they could. They'd need their energy tomorrow as Ellis was pressing for all of them to leave town after what Grant wrote in his note.

"I can practically hear the wheels turning in your head, honey. Any thoughts on what he said?"

"Just that I wish he'd given us a better clue, although I suppose if I can't find it no one else can either. So wherever it is, it's safe until I get there."

The dogs settled onto their beds in the living room and Willow and Josh did the same on the couch, cuddled close so her head was resting on his shoulder.

"He had to keep it generic like that in case the note fell into the wrong hands," Josh pointed out. "Assuming Grant actually wrote the note, of course. So what have we ruled out? Where can it not be?"

Willow ticked them off on her fingers. "The house. He said it wasn't safe to come here. We also know it's not at Roy's."

"Is that it? It doesn't cut the list down much."

She sighed and burrowed closer, her fingers playing with the hem of his t-shirt. His arms tightened around her as images of the burning bar filled her head. Once they found the evidence – and she believed the note was indeed written by Grant – they needed to get the hell out of Midnight Blue Beach. She and Josh had discussed it, and they could pack up Scout and Brodie and head back to Williamsburg. Those two along with his six dogs would make a hell of a burglar alarm. According to Josh, Ramsey, the former police dog, would make sure no one got near Willow. Picking up the note, she read it over and over, looking for some clue.

Did all the capital letters make a word? No.

He'd said he double-backed. Were there any roads with the words "double" or "backed?"

No.

Had she ever won anything and if so, where? No.

They weren't getting far and she wasn't sure which direction to head next. Everyone had read the note and no one had come up with anything concrete.

Abruptly, she sat up, slapping her forehead. "Wait, I did win something once. I won a silent auction at a charity event a few years ago. I won a barrel full of fine chocolates. I lived on that for days."

Immediately, Josh looked wide awake. "Okay, but how would Grant have known something like that?"

"He said he kept an eye on me and I bet we have many of

the same friends. It has to be it because it was held at the civic center." Smiling, she grabbed Josh's arm excitedly. "That's where I met Bailey and Peyton. It's a sign, Josh. It's a sign. It has to be at the civic center."

"Then that's where we'll go."

THE CIVIC CENTER was a huge building on an even larger piece of property. This wasn't going to be a simple search by any stretch of the imagination. There were literally dozens of places that the evidence could be hidden and it complicated matters that they didn't know what form it took. Paper? A thumb drive?

Basically, it boiled down to this. They didn't know where to look for the thing they couldn't identify. Josh was operating on the principle that if they saw it they'd know it. He just hoped they'd see it.

"So should we go on one of those grid searches I've seen on television?" Josh asked.

Willow turned one direction and then made a one-eighty to look in the other. There wasn't a soul around, although if any cops were to drive by they might find two people walking around with flashlights pretty suspicious.

"Maybe we should split up," Willow suggested. "One of us do the parking lot and the other walk around the building."

She didn't have to finish her sentence before Josh shook his head. "No way. We stay together. Until the others get here, it's just the two of us."

The two couples had been asleep so it was going to take

them a little longer to show up, which was fine. Josh and Willow could handle the search until they arrived. He was sure they hadn't been followed but he wasn't as sure that there wouldn't be some sort of welcoming committee waiting for them. It was a relief that they were alone.

"Then I guess we start right here in the parking lot. Lead on."

He'd seen this done on forensic shows. People walked a grid, shoulder to shoulder, looking for clues. It seemed a reasonable method for searching the parking lot.

Reasonable but tedious. They weren't a quarter of the way through and they both were grumbling under their breath.

"I don't think Grant would have thrown the evidence down in a parking lot," Willow pointed out. "Anything could happen to it out in the open. We may be wasting our time out here. Maybe we should check around the building."

Rubbing his chin, Josh's gaze ran over the large, empty expanse. It would have been empty as well when Grant was here and it did seem farfetched that he would toss the evidence out of his car and onto the concrete before driving away. On the other hand, nothing about this investigation had been remotely normal.

"I think looking through your husband's vintage car collection was easier," Josh laughed. "At least that building was air-conditioned and didn't have any mosquitos. I'm getting eaten alive out here."

Willow grabbed his arm, her nails digging painfully into the sweaty skin. "What did you say?"

"I said—"

She waved him off and raised her hands to her face, pressing on her cheeks. "It was a figure of speech. I know what you said." She took several shallow breaths as she pivoted on her foot, taking two paces away, then turning again and taking two paces back. "Alex has a race car in his collection. It won some race but I don't know which one. It could have been the Daytona 500 for all I know but it won something. Grant said he *raced* to the place where a *winner* like me could easily find it. Jesus, what if he left it at the warehouse?"

His heart speeding up with excitement, Josh mentally ran through Grant's note again.

"I have to admit it would make more sense than this. Leaving it out in public is risky but leaving it in a place that you have control of is much safer. Plus, that warehouse is on a road that leads out of town. He could have dropped it there and then headed for a private airstrip or kept driving for the state line. Just one question here, would he know about the warehouse and how would he get in?"

"Alex took his friends there to show off the cars. It's feasible that he did that with Grant. Maybe he even saw the key code to get in. Alex wouldn't have tried to hide it. Not from his close friends. They weren't going to steal anything."

Josh had forgotten that Willow hadn't used a traditional key to unlock the door.

"A reasonable explanation. So it's your call, honey. Do we stay here or do we head to the warehouse?"

Her lips firmed and she whirled around and strode toward the car. "To the warehouse. It has to be there."

Chapter Twenty-Eight

T HE DRIVE TO the warehouse seemed to take forever. Willow kept pushing the imaginary accelerator on the passenger side of the car but the vehicle didn't go any faster, which was probably a good thing. Josh was already exceeding the speed limit on the winding, deserted roads. The warehouse was in the middle of nowhere, which meant that there was no quick route to get there. They had called the others and Chase, Bailey, Peyton, and Ellis would join Willow and Josh at the warehouse instead of the civic center.

As he pulled up, he parked behind the building so the vehicle couldn't be seen from the road. Willow moved to get out of the car but Josh stayed her movements with a hand on her arm. "Let me take a look around first. We need to be extra careful until the others get here."

Knowing that arguing would simply slow them down, she waited in the car while he walked around the area, gun in hand, looking for anyone that might be hiding in the shadows. The moment was so full of subterfuge it was almost comical. She'd crossed over into some spy world and she had no idea how she'd landed here. All she'd wanted that first night when she met the girls was a drink.

Coming around to her side of the car, he opened her door. "The area looks clear. I did see some tire tracks on the concrete as we drove in. That could have been Grant's vehicle."

It had rained earlier, as it did almost every day around four o'clock this time of year, and there was a puddle of water on the driveway near the road. If Grant had driven through it after dark there was a decent chance the tracks would still be visible.

She quickly entered the pass code – her birthday and their wedding anniversary – into the keypad and the lock clicked open. Anyone who knew much about them could figure out the code. She made a mental note to change it to something less obvious.

Josh insisted on going in first but she stuck right behind him, practically glued to his back. He wanted to protect her but she was in this too, and she'd never forgive herself if anything happened to him. He flicked the row of lights on and the place lit up so brightly she had to shield her eyes for a moment.

"Which car is it?"

Stepping farther into the expansive room, she ran her gaze from left to right, landing on the bright red car in the front row. It had been one of Alex's last acquisitions before he passed away.

"That one." She pointed to the low slung, bullet-shaped vehicle with oversized tires. "It's that one."

They almost fell over each other getting to the car. Josh checked the outside of the racer while she checked the tiny interior. Running her hands around the steering wheel, she scrutinized the gear shift, along the dashboard display, and around the seat. She had almost given up when she felt a small bump with her fingertips. She had to almost fold herself in half to reach it more easily, but there was a small slit in the leather. Digging into the hole, she pulled out a cell phone.

Her breathing had sped up along with her heart rate. This could be what the three of them had been looking for. This could have the answers they needed.

"Found it."

Hopping up from the front of the car, Josh peered over her shoulder. "A phone? Is it locked?"

Pressing a button, the phone came to life. "No, do you think it's in the texts? Or maybe the voicemails?"

Josh picked up the handgun where he'd set it on the floor while searching the race car.

"I'm not planning to hang around here and find out. Let's get this back to the house where we can take a good look at it."

Tucking the phone into her purse, she and Josh turned off the lights and exited the warehouse. They walked around the back of the building and froze in their tracks. They'd become sloppy.

Archer Caldwell was leaning on their car.

Holding a gun pointed at their hearts.

Shit and double shit.

Where was that grumpy cop Ellis when you needed him?

ARCHER STRAIGHTENED UP and smiled. "Did you find it? I hope so. I'm tired of keeping an eye on you. Frankly, I have better things to do, Willow. For a former stripper, you lead a boring as hell life."

Josh's stomach twisted in his abdomen as nervous sweat trickled down his back in the humid night air. He held up his own gun and pointed it at Archer but his first responsibility was to protect Willow. On the other hand, Archer had a gun and nothing to lose.

This wasn't a fair fight.

"That was a long time ago, Archer," Willow replied, her voice crisp even though Josh could feel her trembling slightly next to him where their arms touched. "But sadly, no. We didn't find it. I was wrong—there's nothing here. How did you find us anyway?"

"Simple. I placed a GPS tracking device on your car at the farmer's market. Not exactly rocket science. That way I was able to stay far enough behind you so you wouldn't see that you were being followed."

Josh was a fucking idiot. GPS. That hadn't even occurred to him. He really was a vet and not some kind of spy.

Archer clicked his tongue. "Now, Josh. You aren't going to need that gun so go ahead and throw it down. A man like you isn't prepared to take a life but me? It's something I was born for."

"I think I'll hold onto it if you don't mind."

Archer shrugged. "Suit yourself. It's not going to make any difference. You're no cold-blooded killer. Jesus, you rescue dogs and cats. You aren't going to shoot me or anyone else. Now let's go back to the subject at hand. You say you didn't find it?"

"Too bad you came up empty," Josh said, trying to slowly

insinuate himself between Willow and the gun. At the very least, make her a smaller target. "Better luck next time. I'm going to go out on a limb and say that you're quite interested in whatever we were going to find though."

Archer took a few steps back, still smiling in that smarmy way he had. "Luck is a funny thing, Dr. Coleman. For example, Grant's luck is running out. I know what he's doing and I'm going to stop him. Your luck has also run out, not that you had much to begin with. I've known what you've been up to even before you spent the weekend at The Retreat. I also know that you broke into The Clubhouse."

Shit. He'd known someone had seen him.

But Willow was shaking her head. "You were with me at the ball."

Chuckling, Archer waved the gun around, causing Josh's breath to hitch in his chest. That barrel was way too close to Willow. "Cameras. You see, Josh thought about the cameras at The Clubhouse and he did a great job staying away from them. Kudos to you. What he didn't realize is that there are cameras all over those wooded areas. Motion-sensor cameras that recorded your arrival and your departure. Did you find whatever you were looking for? You should have just asked me, Willow. A woman like you? I would have given you anything you asked for. For the right price, of course."

Now Josh wanted to puke. The thought of Archer's hands anywhere near Willow made him sick. "You were the one that gave her those phony files to send her off on a wild goose chase."

"Most of those files were the God's honest truth. Alex wasn't a good person, Josh. He never treated Willow the way he should have and keeping Grant a secret was just a small part of that. And Greg Nelson? He had an entire secret life tucked away in London. That's not a nice thing to do to your wife. Personally, I think Evandria and the world are better for their deaths. It might be painful for a while but in the long run it's kinder."

Willow's hands were in tight fists, the knuckles white. "Is that why you killed them? Because you didn't like how they treated their wives?"

"Are we sharing our feelings? How touching." Archer grinned, eyeing Willow up and down. "I'll tell you what. You tell me the truth about your marriage and I'll answer your question. Is that a deal?"

Josh wanted to tell Willow to say no but she was already nodding her head. This was going to get brutal and he couldn't help but admire her courage in the face of what was bound to be ugly.

"So here's my question. Why did you stay with the asshole? Was it the money? Was it the sex? Did you actually think the bastard was going to change or something pathetic like that? Tell me the truth, Willow. Why did you stay? That was something that I never could figure out."

SWALLOWING THE LUMP that was lodged in her throat, Willow answered. "Because I didn't think anyone else – anyone decent – would ever want me. And yes, there was a part of me that hoped he would eventually get the help he needed. But then I didn't know that he was in Arsenal and he was simply waiting to die."

"He was weak," Archer spat, his lip curled in disgust. "He couldn't take the pressure of playing both sides. Frank talked Alex and Greg into volunteering for Arsenal but they didn't have the guts, any of them. They were always afraid and it showed."

"You were in Arsenal."

"I was. It was a stepping stone to where I am now."

Willow steadied her breathing before continuing. "So answer my question. Why did you kill them? Because of the way they treated us?"

Archer laughed and shook his head. "Hell, no. That would be a stupid reason, wouldn't it? That was simply my opinion, although it made killing them much easier. No handwringing or soul searching about it. I slept like a baby after Alex ran off the road and into that concrete barrier."

Willow sucked in a breath at the heartless words but she was determined not to give him any reaction. "So why then?"

He shrugged. "It was business. I know you've spoken to Holmwood so you know that Evandria is split into two factions, both battling for power. Arsenal is the initiative that goes between those two worlds, keeping both in check. My side needed a distraction...something to take everyone's attention away from what we were really doing. Sort of like what a magician does on the stage. Get the audience to look over here while he's hiding the rabbit over there. Three operatives killed on Evandria's birthday was a big fucking deal inside the organization. It looked like an accident to you but everyone inside knew it wasn't and they scrambled to find out what was going on. Why were they killed and who did it. While they were busy doing that, my superiors were active elsewhere. And it worked.

We were able to consolidate more power while everyone else was running around like it was the end of the world that three less than stellar human beings died. You may be the only person that truly misses Alex, Willow. Isn't that a little sad?"

Tears pricked the back of her eyes and she had to blink rapidly to keep them from falling.

"Grant misses him."

"Grant is all but dead, and no one will care about him either."

Willow stood up straighter despite her trembling knees. "I will."

Archer's grin widened. "How sweet, although I'm not sure Grant deserves such devotion. He's no choir boy."

Josh had been slowly moving in front of her, one millimeter at a time until now he covered half of her body. The idiot was putting himself between her and Archer's gun. She tried to maneuver out from behind him but his left arm grabbed hers tightly, making her stay put.

It was gentlemanly but not very bright. Archer might not kill them as long as he thought she had a chance of finding the evidence.

"So you're in the rogue faction?" Josh asked. "What is the mission of that half of Evandria?"

"There is no rogue faction. Not really," Archer mocked with a laugh. "There are only two sides, each one wanting the same thing but going about it in different ways. If you think my side is evil and the other are saints, you are wrong, Josh. This is no black and white struggle, but the results are real. It would be easy for me to brand the other side as the devil but I can't do that.

This is war and like all wars through history each side believes in its just cause."

"There will be casualties," Josh observed, his fingers still gripping her arm. "Innocents will be hurt or die."

"Yes, but that always happens in times of great strife. Evandria was born out of bloodshed against a brother and it will be reborn in the same way."

Listening to this man speak...he was a true believer, and that was a terrifying thought. He was willing to do whatever he needed to do.

"You sound like a cult," she said. "Not a philanthropic organization."

"Evandria is no cult but those in the inner circle have to believe, Willow. I wish you had joined us. I was sincere in that offer. We could have used someone like yourself. Smart and hard working. You know how to get things done."

It was her turn to laugh even though she hardly felt merry. "I would never join you. I don't thirst for power. I don't want to rule the world."

"Even to make it a better place for all mankind?" Archer asked, taking another step closer and causing Josh's fingers to tighten like a steel band on her arm. "Let me ask you this, Willow. If you knew that your death or Josh's death would bring about peace and end hunger around the world, would you do it? Would you die to save your fellow man? Would you take this gun and shoot the man you love to save millions?"

"That's not a fair question. Taking a life is wrong."

"Even if it saves millions?" Archer pressed. "Come on, Willow. Don't wuss out on me now. Answer me."

He had to give her something in return. "If I do will you an-swer another question about their deaths?"

Shaking his head, he pointed the gun straight to her chest. "I like you, I really do. All right, it's a deal. Now answer mine first. Would you?"

"Yes, I would die if I knew that for certain it would make a difference."

He nodded toward Josh. "And would you kill him? Knowing you could bring about a nirvana for the survivors?"

Wiping her sweaty palm on her shirt, she tried to steady her voice. "No, I could never kill Josh. Taking my own life is different than taking another's."

"Love is such a beautiful thing. What about a stranger? If you could solve world hunger and homelessness with one act, would you do it? Would you kill a stranger to save millions? Be honest with me now. What if you knew they were a terrible person? They beat their kids and cheated on their wife. They didn't pay taxes and they'd hurt people just for fun. Would you kill them to feed starving children across the globe?"

She didn't like this game at all. "No. Every life has value. No one is completely evil."

Archer seemed to like her answer. He spread his arms wide and grinned.

"You believe you're above it but you're not. That, Willow, is the ultimate power. Who lives, who dies. That's what you can have in Evandria. Your life can have that great of a meaning, and you're lying to me and yourself right now. You only think you don't want power. You simply haven't admitted it to yourself yet."

She wasn't like him. She wasn't. Was that what Alex had wanted? God-like power? Had he taken life in some lame attempt at a better world?

"Now my question. You're one person. How did you kill all three men on three different continents on the same day?"

Chapter Twenty-Nine

A T THIS POINT, Archer was supremely confident and with any luck it would make him sloppy. Josh had managed to move Willow behind him about halfway without Caldwell noticing. If he could get her completely blocked he might think about pulling a Chase-move and rushing Archer, hitting him squarely in the gut. Honestly, the man didn't look any more comfortable with a gun than Josh was. He might even be a terrible shot.

"I had help," Caldwell admitted. "It wasn't difficult to find people who would do anything for the right price. Greg's death was the easiest of all. A chef with a gambling problem and lots of debt put a massive amount of peanut powder in the food. Done deal. Frank's was more complex. I'd originally planned to have him killed by a thief during a mugging, but when I found out he was going to the islands for some diving that made things easier. His diving companion that day was on my payroll. He was charged with befriending Frank in the bar and then convincing him to dive the caves, something he'd never done before. The man made sure to kick up a lot of silt, causing Frank to become disoriented inside the cave. It was all downhill for him from there."

This guy seemed a little too fucking proud of his handiwork.

"How many other people have you killed?" Josh asked, hoping his utter disgust was loud and clear.

"A few others but after they died I was promoted. I moved up the ladder of power quickly. My parents were very proud."

Willow had tears in her eyes from listening to Archer's story. "Did you kill Stephen Baxter?"

"That I did not do but I'm sure whomever did had a good reason."

They were afraid he might talk. Plain and simple.

"I'm not sure I believe you," Willow replied, her lips trembling with emotion.

"Why would I lie about it? Now, as much fun as this has been, I want the evidence that Grant left for you. Give it to me and things won't get ugly."

"We don't have it." Willow shook her head. "We didn't find anything. This must not be the right place."

"It's the right place." Caldwell waved the gun toward the building. "I put a GPS on Hollister's vehicle too. He came here instead of Roy's. So if you didn't find it, it's still in there. We can find it together. If you behave, I'll kill you painlessly. If you act up, then all bets are off and I'll find it myself. Josh, you can watch Willow go first, slowly."

Fuck you, asshole. Over my dead body.

Going inside might be better for them. There was an entire wall of heavy tools that Josh could use as weapons. But even better would be to find an opening to end this for good and get

Willow out of here. Sweat had pooled under his arms and at the back of his neck. His palms were slick but his fingers were secure around the cool metal of the handgun.

"We didn't find anything," she denied again. "There's nothing there. Maybe he knew you were following him."

Archer had apparently lost his patience. Stomping toward them a few feet, his lips turned down, he brandished his gun clearly trying to intimidate.

"Throw the gun away," Archer commanded, taking another few steps forward. They were only a few feet away from each other now, the barrels of their firearms inches apart. "I'm tired of these games."

Josh didn't move a muscle even as sweat poured down his back and chest. The gun was the only thing keeping Archer at bay but this standoff wasn't going to go on forever. Holding his ground was becoming increasingly difficult.

"This is bullshit. The dog and kitty doctor isn't going to do a goddamn thing. You better step away from her if you don't want her dead too."

He was lying. Archer didn't technically need either of them to look for the evidence. It might be easier with Willow helping but he had to know she wasn't going to lift a finger to assist him.

No, they were as good as dead in Caldwell's eyes. In the way and they knew too damn much. They were like Stephen Baxter, loose ends to be tidied up.

Josh's arm was getting tired, the gun like a lead weight pulling his sweaty hand down. Gritting his teeth, he had to concentrate to keep still, no matter how much his muscles screamed in pain and fatigue. This was no time to fail and give up. If his arm hurt, Archer's had to as well. Josh would stand here until his entire fucking hand fell off if he had to.

Bright headlights flashed into Archer's eyes, blinding him as a car pulled into the driveway. Knowing he only had a fraction of a moment, Josh shoved Willow to the ground and lifted his right arm, bringing it down on Caldwell's arm and knocking the gun away.

Archer let loose a roar that echoed in Josh's ears right before the other man tackled him to the grass. They both landed with a thud that knocked the breath out of Josh who was on the bottom, but he managed to get in a punch in to Caldwell's ribs that had the man struggling for oxygen. Grunting with effort, Josh took a nasty right hook to the jaw right before he gave Archer an uppercut to the solar plexus, feeling the air whoosh out of the other man's lungs.

"Hold it right there, asshole. Don't move a fucking muscle or you're dead."

Ellis. Finally. The vacationing cop was holding a gun to Caldwell's temple. Josh took the opportunity to slide away and then pushed himself to his feet. He automatically sought out Willow and he found her being helped by Bailey.

Josh's gaze raked the woman he loved head to toe but she was thankfully uninjured.

"Took you long enough."

Ellis gave him a sheepish grin. "We took a wrong turn about five miles back and didn't realize it for awhile. Sorry about that."

"We're good," Josh grunted because his friends had shown up in the nick of time. He and Willow were okay and now Caldwell was caught.

Unlike Archer's description, there was no rush, no feeling of power now that Josh had won the skirmish – with a little help from his friends. He had protected Willow and the greater good but there was no triumphant emotion coursing through veins. Willow was clinging to him, her arms around his waist as Chase came to his side and picked up the gun where Josh had dropped it on the ground when he'd been tackled. "He would have killed you, bro. No question. No one would have blamed you if you'd shot him. Once he got the evidence you were dead."

Josh was glad that it hadn't come to that. There was no question he could have killed to protect Willow but it wouldn't have been his first choice. But what were they going to do with Archer? Call the police? And tell them what? A secret society was out there killing people and running the world? They'd be laughed out of town.

Now that his hands were free, he wrapped his arms around Willow, running his fingers through her hair, trying to soothe her as much as himself. He needed to feel her, solid and real in his arms, against his body.

Ellis pulled Archer to his feet and slapped a pair of cuffs on him. He was like a Boy Scout, always prepared.

Peyton looked at Archer and then at Ellis. "Should we call the cops? Someone might have heard something."

Pulling slightly away from Josh, Willow shook her head. "There isn't another building anywhere close, but we probably should call the police."

"I don't want to pour cold water over that idea," Josh said, pulling a shaking Willow closer. "But what in the hell are we going to say?"

More headlights had them all turning to see a line of three dark SUVs pull in behind their own cars. Huddling together, Josh held his breath, his arm wrapped closely around Willow, once again placing her behind him. He didn't know who their new company was but after the night he'd had he wasn't taking any chances.

There was a collective breath from all of them when Nigel Holmwood stepped out of the middle vehicle and strode quickly toward them, several large men at his heels. Stopping about ten feet from Archer, the older man seemed to quickly assess the situation.

He didn't look all that surprised either.

"Uncle Nigel," Bailey breathed, launching herself forward and into the man's arms. He chuckled and gave her a hug, patting her on the back before guiding her back to Chase. "You're alive."

"I am indeed, my child. Once I saw Archer today I knew he was up to something. After years in Evandria, you develop a sixth sense about these sorts of things. I'm sorry I couldn't let you know right away that I was alive but I didn't want Caldwell to know." He glanced at the cuffed man who had yet to say a word. "What do you have to say for yourself, Archer?"

Glowering, the prisoner just stared vacantly into the distance. "I have nothing to say."

"You're welcome to that defense in front of the Council but they may want more details of your crimes."

Josh stepped forward even as Willow tried to hold him back. "He killed Alex, Frank, and Greg plus he was threatening our lives and also Grant's."

"I don't doubt it." Nigel's British accent sounded more clipped than usual. "Did he get his hands on the evidence?"

Josh shook his head. "No, he didn't."

Holmwood inclined his head. "Good. Now did you find what Grant planted?"

Willow answered before he had a chance. "No, we didn't. We looked everywhere too."

Not allowing himself to reveal his surprise, Josh didn't even turn toward her, simply nodding in agreement. They were the only two people who knew that the evidence was in their possession and it was probably best that it stay that way.

Trust no one.

Nigel nodded his head toward the warehouse. "Would you allow my men to search the building? They may find something you've overlooked?"

Willow looked reluctant, taking her time before giving her consent. When she did, Nigel sent in four burly men after Willow unlocked the door for them.

"Now as for this situation." He glanced at Caldwell. "Have you called the police yet?"

"We were just about to do that," Peyton spoke up. They'd all been rather silent as they tried to comprehend all that had happened today and tonight.

"No need," Nigel dismissed. "I'll take care of cleaning this up. The local police would have no idea what to do with him and he wouldn't stay in custody long. Wealthy people rarely do, especially as we have no evidence of his crimes. Not the kind that would convince a prosecutor anyway. He needs to face a jury of his peers, which is exactly what will happen in Evandria. If anyone asks, you weren't here tonight. You were at the symphony. Here are your ticket stubs."

He handed them to Bailey but Josh wasn't ready to relinquish all control over to some guy he'd only met a few times. What if he double-crossed them?

"You just happened to have six used ticket stubs to the symphony?" Ellis queried, his expression hard. "And I'm to just hand over a killer to you? How do I know that you aren't working with Caldwell?"

Bailey stepped forward, her brows pinched together. "He wouldn't do that. He's on our side, Ellis."

Josh had to admire Bailey's loyalty. He, on the other hand, wasn't feeling the love for the older man. So far skeptical seemed the way to go.

"No offense, but how do we truly know that?" Ellis asked. "There's no way to prove that we can trust him."

Nigel chuckled, a smile playing on his thin lips. "I think there may be a way."

Chase threw up his hands. "You can try."

Nigel stepped forward to where Willow was now stationed near the warehouse door, leaning down to whisper something in her ear that Josh couldn't hear. Her eyes widened for a moment but then she nodded, her gaze darting to where he stood.

"Give him Archer," she said softly but firmly. "He's going to take care of this for us."

For a minute it didn't look like Ellis was going to comply but then he sighed and handed the man over to Nigel, who nodded in thanks and smiled.

"You all need to get out of here. I have a team coming in to clean this area up. In less than twenty minutes it's going to look like no one was ever here, I promise you."

Grabbing Josh's hand, Willow led him back to the car. They drove back to the house in silence, not saying a word. The entire evening had been beyond surreal and he had to keep reminding himself that it had really happened. They'd found the cell phone and they'd caught the murderer that had killed Willow's husband.

Josh had a myriad of questions – mostly about why Willow trusted Nigel – but there was no point asking them when the others weren't there. He could wait but only that long. By some unspoken agreement they all ended up at Willow's house, sitting in the kitchen. The dogs had been roused by the noise of their arrivals and he and Willow each had a canine on their lap, getting a belly rub.

"Talk," Ellis commanded, pacing back and forth, lips a hard line. "What the hell happened tonight? You didn't get the evidence? Because we didn't find anything at the civic center. I knew it was a bad idea to let you go to the warehouse alone. I blame myself for this. It should have been me in a showdown with Caldwell."

"I blame you too," Peyton sighed with a smirk. "Frankly, this is all your fault."

Halting, Ellis gazed at Peyton open-mouthed. "How is this my fault?"

She shrugged. "I don't know, I was just agreeing with you. There's no making you happy, is there? I argue and you get huffy. I agree and you're all pissy. Make up your mind."

Josh held up his hand. He'd had enough. "It's not your fault.

It was our decision to go to the warehouse alone. We've been all over by ourselves and I thought we'd be okay there too. I was wrong."

"So what did happen?" Bailey asked, settling next to Chase on the loveseat.

In fits and starts between them, he and Willow were able to explain what had happened before they arrived. When they got to the part about finding the cell phone, Bailey slapped her thigh and looked livid.

"You lied to us and Nigel. You did find the evidence. What does it say?"

Willow sighed and rubbed at her temple. "We haven't looked at the evidence yet. And I don't think your uncle cared about the evidence as long as it didn't fall into the wrong hands. Personally, I think he already knows what's in it."

That was news to Josh. "What do you mean, he knew? Is that what he was saying to you?"

She nodded, her hands wrung together. "Kind of. First, he told me that Archer was only following orders when he killed our husbands, which goes along with what he himself told us. That people higher up are the ones in true control. Nigel then said he was going to go one further and tell us something we might not have known. He said that he believes the same person who killed Stephen Baxter planted that package bomb that injured Peyton. He also said that he believes the gunshot when we were horseback riding was that same person. The rogue faction of Evandria thinks we're getting too close. He said that none of us are safe and that we should leave Midnight Blue Beach immediately. Once members realize that Caldwell is in Evandria custody, things are really going to hit the fan. It will be chaos within the organization."

Ellis's face was red. "I bet the old fart knows a hell of a lot more. He's known all along that Baxter killed Gwen but he said nothing. He's known all along who tried to kill Peyton. Still silence. Sorry, Bailey, but I'm not sure that your uncle isn't playing some deadly games of his own."

Bailey's expression was conflicted and she clung to Chase, shaking her head. "I can't believe he would place us in danger but I agree his actions are suspect. What are we going to do?"

Ellis's jaw snapped together and his eyes narrowed. "I don't know about you all but I'm going after the sons of bitches that tried to kill Peyton. We've done pretty well so far without Holmwood's help."

Josh had the exact same thoughts. "I agree. We've disrupted the organization. If we back off they might not kill us but they'll always be watching. If we don't bring them down, we'll always have them hanging over our heads."

Willow's lips were pursed and her color was high. "Sometimes I want to kick Alex right in the balls."

"Ditto," Bailey echoed. "If Frank were here, I'd kick him hard."

"And Greg," Peyton added. "He deserves a good swift knee to the 'nads. He has another damn family so make that two knees to the groin."

Although their late husbands absolutely deserved the assault, Josh couldn't stop himself from crossing his legs in sympathy. These women were pissed.

Peyton crossed her arms over her chest. "It's just like Greg too. Get himself into a bad situation and then drag me along with him. I was always bailing him out of scrapes."

Ellis stopped pacing and looked around the room. "Are we saying what I think we're saying? Because if we are then we need some sort of plan—after we get the hell out of this town, that is."

Josh held up the cell phone. "First things first. Let's find out what the evidence is."

Willow placed her hand on his. "Actually, the very first thing should be to get the jet gassed up and head for Williamsburg. We can look for the evidence once we pack and get out of here."

After Willow called the pilot and told him to get the plane ready, she met Josh upstairs. He'd thrown the few clothes and toiletries that he'd brought into his bag and now he was scrolling through the phone trying to find whatever message Grant had left them. So far, he'd come up empty.

"How long did it take you to pack?" She dragged a large suitcase from the closet. "It's not fair. Women need more stuff than men. Did you find anything?"

"Not yet." Josh closed one app and set the phone on the bed before standing and joining her in the closet. He pulled her into his arms and inhaled the fresh vanilla scent of her hair. After the night they'd had, he needed this. Just holding her made everything better. "Are you okay, honey? We had a close call tonight."

She looked up at him and he couldn't stop himself from kissing her, her hands cupping his jaw where it was bruised. "I'm good. You were kind of a super hero, getting that gun out of his hand and throwing some punches. My protector."

"I'd die for you. I love you."

He didn't even hesitate to say it. It was true. He would have jumped in front of that bullet without a second thought to save her life.

"I'm glad it didn't come to that. I love you too. So very much, Josh."

He could hear the love and passion in her voice but even if he hadn't, he could see it in her eyes, soft and golden as she gazed up at him. He could feel it in her touch but mostly he could feel and hear her heart beating in time with his own.

"You've found Alex's killer. Can you…you know…move on now? With me?"

Her fingers threaded through his hair and she smiled an achingly tender smile that he hoped to see every day for the rest of his life. "I can and I will. We're going to have that future together. You, me, and about a dozen rescue dogs. Think you can handle it?"

He pressed his forehead to hers and smiled.

"Honey, it will be my great pleasure to try."

Chapter Thirty

T HE CAPTAIN ANNOUNCED that they could unfasten their seatbelts and move freely around the cabin. Willow popped hers open and went straight to the small refrigerator, pulling out two bottles of water, one for her and one for the two dogs who were in their kennels in the last row. She opened the wire mesh doors and filled their bowls, hoping they wouldn't hit much turbulence. Scout was a good flyer but Brodie got motion sick. Ruffling their fur, she scratched them behind the ears, taking comfort in their soothing presence.

She'd put up a good front for Josh but inside she was still reeling from the earlier events at the warehouse. She'd been terrified Archer was going to shoot them and then she'd been even more frightened that he was going to kill Josh. It had been a shock when he'd shoved her to the ground and knocked the gun out of Archer's hand. She was angry and relieved in equal measure – angry that he'd taken such a huge risk with his life and relieved that Archer Caldwell was now in custody.

Albeit Evandria's custody.

Although she'd decided to trust Nigel Holmwood with

Archer's justice, she wasn't as convinced they could trust the older man when it came to bringing down the people that wanted her and her friends dead. He seemed to know quite a bit of important information, and he wasn't sharing it generously but doling it out in dribs and drabs.

But still they'd now managed to find Gwen Baxter's killer and also Alex, Frank, and Greg's killer. That had to count for something. The fact that they'd angered Evandria and were now stuck in the middle of an inner-organizational war was a nasty consequence. If they ever wanted to sleep peacefully again, they had to find a way to neutralize the people that threatened their lives.

The question was... Was it the rogue or the so-called good faction? How much overlap was there? And how "good" were they really? She didn't think they were going to be able to avoid taking sides and that was never a positive thing.

"I've got it."

Everyone's attention turned to Josh who had a grin on his face. He'd been playing with that damn cell phone for over an hour.

Ellis unclipped his own seat belt and sat next to Josh. "Is it a file? Pictures?"

Josh pulled out his ear bud. "It's a recording. A phone conversation between Archer Caldwell and some guy who isn't named. They're talking about the plans to kill the men and the backup plans if they somehow survive. They did mention someone else though. They said the name Jensen."

Peyton's sucked-in breath was audible to the entire group. Her already fair skin had paled and she'd grabbed the armrests on the seat. "What did you say that name was?"

"Jensen," Josh replied. "No last name though."

"Let me hear it," she said quietly. Willow had a gut feeling that Peyton knew this Jensen person. It would be a plus when it came time to talk to him.

Josh cued up the recording and held out the cell phone so everyone could hear. The first voice was easily recognizable as Archer's.

Did you talk to him? Is everything set?

An unknown man's voice came next.

Yeah, everything is a go. Greg and I are having lunch together. The chef has been paid half up front with half when he finishes the job.

Archer: *If this doesn't work...*

Unknown male: *It'll work. He's incredibly allergic. He won't make it to the emergency room with the amount the chef is going to put in the food. It's a done deal.*

Archer: *It has to be finished on that day. If it doesn't work, you'll need to step in at the hospital. Make it look like an accident though. Maybe suffocation.*

Unknown male: *I've got this. Greg won't survive.*

Archer: *What about his wife? What if she wants to come along with you to the restaurant?*

Unknown male <laughing>: *We'll get Jensen to handle Peyton. She'll stay home, don't worry.*

Archer: *Call me when it's done. Greg will be the first because of the time difference, then Frank, and Alex last. His car accident is tonight, the stupid drunk bastard.*

Unknown male: *I'll call you. Is there anything else you need?*

Archer: *Yes, don't fuck up.*

<Call ended>

Willow shuddered in revulsion, listening to these two men talk about murder as if they were planning a golf outing. Alex had been a drunk and drug addict but he hadn't deserved to be murdered. No one deserved that.

Ellis had moved back next to Peyton, his arm around her shoulders. "Do you know that voice? Do you know Jensen?"

Sniffling, a tear carved a path down her cheek. "I don't know the other voice but I have a brother named Jensen. God, he was in on Greg's death."

Willow reached across the aisle and placed her hand on Peyton's arm, although Ellis had a hold of the woman who was visibly shaken, her blue eyes huge in her wan face.

"Not necessarily," Willow replied firmly, wanting desperately to do something, anything, to make her friend feel better. She'd been through so much in the past several weeks. "These guys just say that they'll get Jensen to handle you if you want to go to lunch. That doesn't mean he's in on the plot. It only means that he might be friends with these assholes. Don't go there until you have proof. Don't do that to yourself."

Swiping at her wet cheeks, Peyton took a deep breath. "He's in London, which is quite convenient because that's also where Greg's other family lives. I think Ellis and I should take a trip there and talk to them. See what they know."

Josh nodded. "That's a good idea. We'll all go."

Ellis was already shaking his head no. "Someone has to stay in the states and keep an eye on Holmwood and Evandria. With Caldwell out as president, there's going to be a huge struggle for control of the organization. We need you guys to monitor the situation, plus you might want to look for the other person in that recording. He had an American accent so he's probably from here, maybe even Midnight Blue Beach."

"Which we just left," Chase added. "Because it's not safe, supposedly."

Ellis grinned. "I didn't say it would be easy."

Josh tucked the cell phone into the pocket of his carryon. "Let's get to Williamsburg and get settled, then we can figure out what to do from there. Maybe we can make a visit to that senator friend of yours, Chase. He might know who's vying for control."

"If he'll talk," Chase warned. "He's loyal to the *mission* and he owes his entire career to them. He won't turn easily."

"Then we all have our assignments." Ellis finished pouring a ginger ale for Peyton. "We'll go to London and get back as quickly as we can. You guys will keep track of the status of Evandria and at the same time stay safe. That's enough for all of us to do."

Stay alive. Catch more killers. Willow wanted a future with Josh and if this was the only way to get it then so be it. It was time to end the war in Evandria.

Thank you for reading
Midnight Blue Beach –
Midnight of No Return

Sign up to be notified of Olivia's new releases:

oliviajaymesoptin.instapage.com

About the Author

Olivia Jaymes is a wife, mother, lover of sexy romance, and caffeine addict. She lives with her husband and son in central Florida and spends her days with handsome alpha males and spunky heroines.

Look for Olivia's new Contemporary Romance series *The Hollywood Showmance Chronicles* in the spring of 2017.

Visit Olivia Jaymes at

www.OliviaJaymes.com

Danger Incorporated
Damsel In Danger
Hiding From Danger
Discarded Heart Novella
Indecent Danger
Embracing Danger
Danger In The Night

Cowboy Justice Association
Cowboy Command
Justice Healed
Cowboy Truth
Cowboy Famous
Cowboy Cool
Imperfect Justice
The Deputies
Justice Inked
Justice Reborn

Military Moguls
Champagne and Bullets
Diamonds and Revolvers
Caviar and Covert Ops
Emeralds, Rubies, and Camouflage

www.ingramcontent.com/pod-product-compliance
Lightning Source LLC
Chambersburg PA
CBHW020259200626
46816CB00001BA/370